THE DEATH CABIN

NICOLE GARDNER

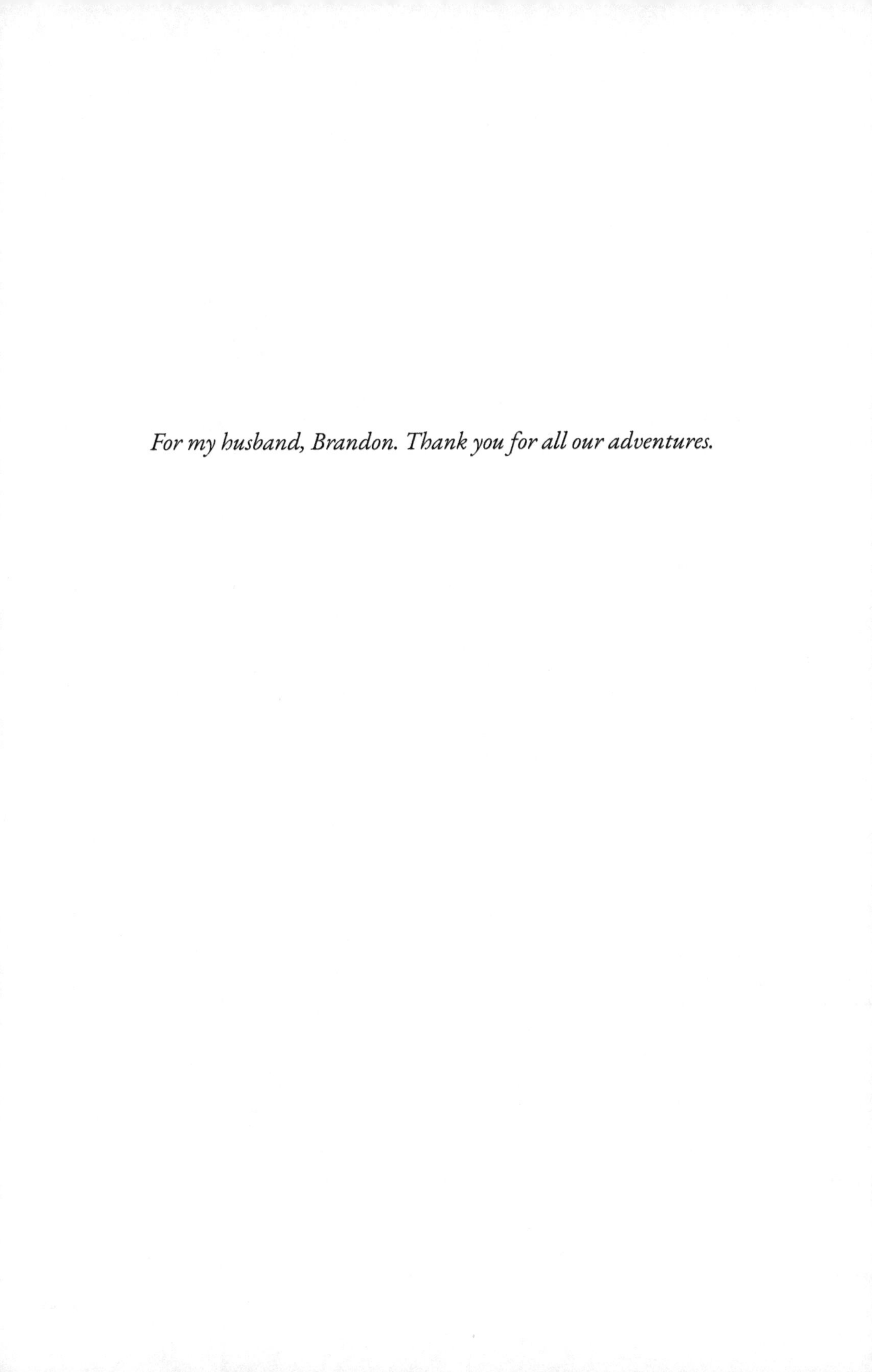

Chapter One

Olivia

A tight knot formed in my stomach as my mind rehearsed the countless things that could go wrong if my car gave up the ghost out here in the boondocks. Thirty minutes of bone-rattling roads, with my hands gripping the steering wheel, and I didn't seem to be any closer to my destination. I double-checked my GPS, frowning. The gravel ahead of me seemed endless.

When I'd booked this cabin, I hadn't realized how remote it was. The location boded well for the work I needed to do, but the drive was miserable. I could barely even see when the pickup trucks—driven by people who apparently knew the area—flew by me, sending up thick clouds of dust. The car rattled so hard I irrationally worried it would simply fly apart, leaving me stranded out here.

What on earth had I been thinking?

I knew exactly what I'd thought: that I couldn't stay in my father's home for even one more night. Between the press camped outside, clamoring for a photograph, and my parents' endless bickering, the place that was supposed to feel like a haven had turned into a nightmare—and that wasn't even counting the added security and constant reminders that everything had changed.

I needed to breathe. Needed space to process what was happening without being told what to think. I was going to lose my mind if I didn't get away from it all. A work retreat was the perfect excuse to do it without being accused of abandoning the family in their time of need.

I'd picked the tiniest, most remote place on the map within a day's drive, hoping it would give me the peace I needed. Admittedly, I had never planned on being quite so alone in the middle of nowhere. But then again, bad ideas rarely came with a warning.

This was taking forever. When I had turned off the highway onto the first gravel road, I had assumed I was close to the cabin.

Obviously not.

For the first half hour, houses had been scattered along the sides of the road. The farther I got from anything that could be called a town, the more I wondered about the people who would choose to live out here.

It was beautiful, sure—especially this time of year. The northern forests of Wisconsin were alive with color. Flaming red sugar maples and fiery orange oaks contrasted with the deep greens and blues of the ever-green trees, and the sky had taken on that particular softness that only seemed to come in the fall. Living out here had to be peaceful, without city traffic or noise pollution, but I couldn't imagine making this long trek anytime I needed to pick up groceries. It was a completely different life than I was used to.

Although, the worse things got at home, the more I fantasized about disappearing altogether. Moving somewhere nobody would know me, where I could start fresh and keep my life simple. Maybe the people out here felt similarly. Maybe a peaceful life was worth the inconvenience of being in the middle of nowhere.

The farther I drove, the fewer houses I saw, as the land became more and more isolated. It sent a thrill up my spine to think I would be staying out here by myself for nearly a week. Sure, I'd be set up in a cabin with modern amenities—everything except high-speed internet, as the advertisement had made clear. But I'd have a bed, a hot tub, and a full kitchen. It didn't exactly count as roughing it. Still, it was an adventure, and more importantly, it was a break from the rest of the world.

Assuming the cabin even existed. I was starting to wonder if I'd been scammed out of my deposit.

When I was almost ready to give up and turn around, I saw a little wooden sign tucked into the trees, barely visible on the side of the road: Hidden Gem Resort.

The owner must have had a sense of irony.

"Oh yay. More gravel," I said as I turned onto the private drive. The one-lane road was nearly overgrown with trees that desperately needed to be cut back. The internet advertisement had mentioned a hundred acres of hiking trails. I hoped they were kept in better condition than this.

But after another couple of minutes, the lane widened and finally opened up to the image that had made me instantly book my reservation: gorgeous Hidden Gem Lake.

The surrounding forest was glowing with the most glorious hues. Near the water, the colors of the oaks and maples seemed even more vibrant than they had on my drive. One side of the lake had a thick strip of birch trees, with golden leaves and stark-white trunks. Pine and spruce provided dark green for contrast, and all of that incredible color was reflected on the surface of the pristine lake. Low-hanging golden-toned clouds added interest to the sky and cast hazy reflections on the sparkling water.

It was the perfect place to paint.

Another small sign was stuck on a pole beside the road. It read *stop here* with an arrow pointing toward a tiny house tucked into an alcove in the woods. I turned down the long driveway, parked, then grabbed my purse and stepped out of my car, grateful to finally stretch my aching legs.

The weathered yellow home had a sign out front, hand-painted with the words *Caretaker's Cottage.* The house was quaint but a bit run-down. I gripped the rough handrail, the old wooden steps sagging underneath my feet as I stepped up to their front door. There was no doorbell—just an old-fashioned metal knocker. I wrapped my hand around the cold metal and knocked, feeling like I'd stepped back in time at least a hundred years.

"I'm coming! Hold your horses," called a cranky voice from inside the house.

Slow footsteps thudded toward the doorway before the door creaked open just three inches, barely giving me a peek inside.

"Can I help you?" The woman speaking had short, thin hair, a deeply lined face, and a scowl that suggested she didn't want to help me at all.

"Hi," I said, offering her a smile. "I'm Olivia Mitchell. I have a reservation for cabin number seven."

A large, leathered hand gripped the door, yanking it open and pushing the woman back in the process. A tall, older man appeared. He was bald but had a thick white beard and piercing eyes that made me squirm. He wore a red flannel shirt tucked into high-waisted black pants held up by old-fashioned suspenders. Truly a relic from another age, just like this house.

"Well, well, well. What do we have here?" he asked, chuckling. He looked down at the woman, who just scowled back at him. "Another one."

She rolled her eyes and turned back to me. "You filled out the paperwork, right?"

"Yes," I said, nodding.

"So you know the rules?"

"Rules?" I asked before I could hide my surprise. I didn't remember any rules. To be honest, I hadn't paid much attention to the rental agreement. But I figured it had to be pretty basic—no loud parties, pay for damages, no smoking. So I smiled and tried to cover my confusion. "I mean, yes, of course. Sorry."

She gave me a keen look. "I'll get your key."

"Wait," the man said, putting his heavy hand on her shoulder. "Give her cabin thirteen."

"But she booked number seven," the woman said, glaring at him.

He shook his head and gave her a warning look.

She huffed but then looked back at me with a faint smile. "Sorry.

He's right. We need to move you to number thirteen. Had a problem with cabin seven earlier."

"Okay..." My unease grew.

She shuffled away.

But he stayed put, leaning against the doorway with a twisted smile on his face. "What brings you to Hidden Gem?"

"I need to get some work done," I said, trying to be polite but also shut down conversation.

"What kind of work do you do?"

I opened my mouth to answer but sighed in relief when the woman came back and shoved a key into my hand, acting as eager to get me out of there as I was to leave.

"Here," she said before scowling up at the man. "Number thirteen. Just get back on the road and drive down to the lake. Thirteen's the last cabin, all the way at the end. Has a nice view of the sunset. I'm Deb, and this here is Felix. We're the caretakers. I can't imagine you'll need anything"—she gave me a look that seemed to indicate I shouldn't mention it if I did—"but you know where to find us if you do."

"Thank you," I said, giving them an awkward wave as I backed down their walkway.

They both stared at me as I got into my car. They were still in my rearview mirror, watching, as I drove away.

CHAPTER TWO

Sawyer

I COULDN'T STOP MY GRIN AS I TURNED ONTO THE GRAVEL road marked with the Hidden Gem Resort sign. It was always this way on a hunt. No matter how sad the details surrounding the case were, I couldn't help but get excited about having a puzzle to solve—or feeling that familiar surge of adrenaline as I knew I was getting close.

I wasn't sure what that said about me.

Then again, I tried not to look too hard into my psyche. Navel-gazing wasn't for me. I was only interested in action.

I pulled up to the building marked *Caretaker's Cottage* just as another car was pulling out and heading toward the cabins. It caught me off guard. Part of me had hoped I'd be the only one here this weekend, but that was unrealistic. The resort wouldn't stay in business long if it only had one traveler at a time.

Though, based on what I knew so far, I was surprised it was still in business anyway. Most people didn't want to spend their vacations at a place with a long history of odd accidental deaths.

Most sane people, anyway.

The apparent caretakers were standing in their doorway. They both watched the sporty red car pull out before simultaneously turning their eyes to my SUV. When Jim had asked me to come here, he had told me that Grace said they were as creepy as hell. I'd assumed she'd been exaggerating, but after seeing them, I decided she'd given it to him straight.

I swung out of my SUV and pulled my sunglasses off, heading up toward them. They stared, silent. The lady had her arms crossed over her old-fashioned house dress, a faded floral muumuu that looked entirely too thin for this chilly weather. The man gave me a once-over, then grabbed his suspenders with both hands, sticking his chest out in what appeared to be a show of bravado.

Interesting.

"Hello," I said, giving them a friendly smile as I stuck my hand out.

The old man took it, shaking mine with a strong grip that surprised me. "What can we do for you?" His voice was clear and sharp, despite his age.

"Name's Sawyer Reed. I have a reservation. Cabin thirteen."

The woman glared at the man and walked away without a word.

The man turned his head and watched her disappear into the back room. "We had to make a change," he said before spitting on the grass beside my feet. "You're in number eleven now."

That wouldn't do at all. "I specifically requested number thirteen," I said firmly. "It's on my reservation."

He shrugged. "And per the rules of the rental agreement you signed, your cabin may change and isn't final until arrival."

I pulled out my wallet, fishing out a crisp one hundred dollar bill. "Perhaps we can change it back."

He didn't even react. Just shook his head. "Can't. It's already occupied."

The woman came back and shoved a key into my hand. "I'm Deb and this is Felix," she said, rattling it off in a monotone voice that suggested she gave the exact same spiel to everyone. "We're the caretakers. I can't imagine you'll need anything, but you know where to find us if you do."

I gave them a tight smile and turned to head back to my vehicle.

This was an unwelcome turn of events. It was crucial that I got inside cabin thirteen. I'd just have to get to know whoever had stolen it from me and see if I could take a look around in there.

I drove down the lane and pulled up to cabin eleven, noting that the red car from before was the one who'd been moved to the cabin I wanted. I wondered why the caretakers had changed it. Had this person specifically requested it, maybe greased their palms to steal my reservation? Was someone here looking for a scoop? If so, that could complicate things.

But then the woman climbed out of her car, stopping my thoughts in their tracks as she took a moment to stretch before popping her trunk. She was young. Early twenties, by the look of it. Honey-blonde hair fell in soft waves around her face. Petite, with a dancer's body. She looked like she'd stepped out of a magazine from another era, wearing dark skin-tight jeans and a tan leather jacket, with matching leather gloves and a vintage scarf wrapped loosely around her neck. The look was topped off with a jaunty red beret.

She was absolutely stunning. But that wasn't why I couldn't stop staring at her.

The style was all different. But the hair? That body? She could have easily been Grace's sister. From a distance at least, they could almost be twins. Same height, same coloring, same age range.

Grace, Jim's fiancé, was the whole reason I was here. She'd died at Hidden Gem Lake last October.

Jim was convinced she'd been murdered.

Chapter Three

I PULLED MY CAR OVER IN FRONT OF CABIN THIRTEEN, GIVING it a close look. It was a small hand-hewn log cabin, the oldest out here by all appearances. But it seemed to have been well-kept and modernized with a green metal roof and a nice front porch.

All things considered, the cabin change might have been a move in my favor.

I'd chosen number seven on the website because the photograph showed a beautiful view of the lake from the front windows. But this one was on the very end, with more privacy than the others. It had a porch swing that faced out toward the woods, offering a spot for my morning coffee where I might actually be able to pretend I was completely alone out here. The landscaping was rustic but pretty, with a little picket fence and a stone walkway separating the yard from the road. And despite being off to the side a bit, the spot still had a nice view of the lake.

I liked it immediately.

I got out of my car and stretched, taking an automatic look around. A man got out of his SUV a couple of doors down and immediately caught my eye—partly because he was staring right at me.

He was wearing a fitted flannel shirt that looked to be brand new. I got the feeling he'd bought it just for the trip and it wasn't the kind of thing he normally wore. Faded hiking pants and scuffed leather boots—those, at least, had gotten some use. He had thick chestnut-brown hair with a hint of red, like the handful of trees whose leaves were beginning to fade, and an even thicker beard that hid most of his face.

He was powerful. I could feel it from here. Unlike the kind of power my father held through his influence and money, this man's power came from within. It was physical strength, clearly—the man was built like a Norse god—but also something more than that. Something I couldn't quite put my finger on but recognized just the same.

He gave me a cool nod before pulling a well-worn bag from his SUV, slinging it over his shoulder as if it weighed nothing, and striding up to the front door of his cabin. Butterflies danced in my stomach.

He was the kind of man I'd like to paint. To try somehow to capture that sense of calm control and precision even as I tried to capture the way the sunlight brought out the warm tones in his hair.

I had no interest in him beyond my art. Powerful men weren't easy to live with—life at home had taught me that. Besides, I was quite happy staying free from romantic entanglements. Freedom was something I'd never really experienced, and I was only beginning to get glimpses of what it felt like to make my own decisions. I had no intention of complicating my life with a man who'd expect me to fall in line and support his dreams instead of my own.

Even so, I found myself thinking about him as I unloaded my bags, and I knew he was the first thing I'd sketch when I got my supplies unpacked.

I lifted my suitcase from the trunk of my car and began pulling it awkwardly over the stone pebbles that made up the pathway to the front of the cabin. The landscaping had clearly not been planned with rolling luggage in mind. Traveling with a shoulder bag almost would have been easier, but I needed the extra space for my gear.

The man came back out of his cabin, throwing me another one of those cool nods. "Need some help?" he called, gesturing toward my bag.

I hesitated. Although I didn't want to get too friendly and give him any wrong ideas about the upcoming weekend, I really wouldn't mind the help—or a closer look at his facial structure.

So I gave him a faint smile and nodded. "Thank you," I called back. "I would appreciate that."

He crossed the distance separating us in long, quick strides, then grabbed my bag, lifting it easily with one hand. His eyebrows immediately shot up. "How long are you planning to stay here?"

I shrugged. "Not sure." I had no intention of telling a complete stranger my travel plans. That was just asking for trouble.

He gave me a knowing look, then gestured for me to lead the way. I did, heading up to the door to unlock it before he got there.

"Careful," I said as he began to set the case down. "It's fragile."

His eyes shone with curiosity. "Fragile? Interesting. You're telling me it's not just a hundred pounds of clothes, shoes, and makeup?"

This one was bold. Heaven help me, I kind of liked it. My mouth twisted in a smile before I could stop it. "Maybe twenty pounds of clothes and shoes. The rest is...supplies."

"Supplies?" He cocked his head, his lips turning up in a grin of his own. "What kind of supplies?"

I shrugged again. "Mine. Thank you for the help." I reached out and put my hand on the suitcase, gently tugging it out of his grip.

He threw his head back and roared in laughter. "'Mine.' That's hilarious. Sounds exactly like something I'd say. You're really not going to tell me what you've got in there after I went to the trouble of hauling it up here for you? That heavy case was no joke."

I smiled, enjoying the banter, before letting my eyes land pointedly on his impressive biceps. "It didn't appear to be any trouble at all."

His grin let me know I was right about that one—and that he appreciated the compliment. "What if I guess? Will you tell me then?"

I moved my head back and forth, contemplating. "Okay. You can have three guesses. If you guess correctly, I'll tell you. If you don't, I suppose you'll just always have to wonder."

"Give me a second," he said, looking me over as he brought a hand to his chin, thinking. "You obviously have an interest in fashion. Maybe you work in the industry and you're here to finish up some projects. You have a sewing machine in there?"

I shook my head, fighting a smile. "I'm afraid not."

"Hmmm... You're witty and evasive." His eyes twinkled. "CIA operative on the run? Got a case full of cash, weapons, and disguises?"

I couldn't help but laugh this time. "No. That's wrong twice. You have one guess left."

His smile dropped and his eyes narrowed. "You're not a writer, are you? Please tell me you're not a writer."

I frowned. "What do you have against writers?"

He sighed. "I knew it. You're a writer, here to get your big scoop, huh? Let's have it. Journalist? Blogger?"

His reaction confused me—and, in some ways, hit too close to the truth. "No. I'm not a writer. And that was your last guess. Thank you again for carrying my case over the rocks. Now, if you'll excuse me." I cracked the door open and moved to go inside.

"Wait," he said, putting a hand on my door.

I raised my eyebrows, looking first at his hand and then at him, saying nothing.

"Sorry," he said, immediately dropping it. "I'm Sawyer. Sawyer Reed. I didn't catch your name."

"You didn't catch it because I didn't give it."

"Can't you at least give me that?" he asked, his eyes twinkling again. "After all, I'm going to be awake all night wondering what's in that damn suitcase."

"It's Olivia," I said, deliberately leaving off my last name. "Nice to meet you, Sawyer. See you around." I pushed the door open and walked inside, closing and latching it behind me. Then I leaned against it and smiled.

I still wasn't interested in anything except my work. But Sawyer was interesting. Likable. Charming, even.

Not that it mattered. My father had warned me that this wasn't the time to let anyone new into my life. *Keep a low profile*, he'd insisted. *You never know who'll be looking for a story. Don't trust anyone.*

The last few weeks had proven he was right.

CHAPTER FOUR

Sawyer

I HAD TO SHAKE MYSELF WHEN OLIVIA CLOSED THE DOOR and locked it—loudly—letting me know our conversation was finished.

Damn. She was fascinating.

With that vintage style, she looked completely different than most women I knew. She acted different too. Aloof, but not rude. She had the air of a princess. Gracious and polite, but kept her walls up. Had no trouble setting clear boundaries. Wasn't interested in attention and didn't seem to have a need to share her story with the world.

She was a woman with secrets. And there was nothing I enjoyed more than sniffing out secrets.

I stuck my hands into my pockets and whistled as I walked away from her cabin, reminding myself that I already had a mystery to solve this weekend. One that didn't involve the evasive Olivia.

Unless it did.

I frowned. There was something incredibly familiar about her. But now that I'd gotten a closer look, it was clear she didn't resemble Jim's fiancé as much I'd thought.

Grace had been drop-dead gorgeous in an American-prom-queen kind of way. Olivia's pale freckled skin, naturally pink lips, and bright blue eyes reminded me of some of the women I'd known in Europe. It'd be easier to imagine her collecting roses in the English countryside or sipping ale from a beer stein in Germany than it would be to imagine her cheerleading at a college football game.

Two very different women up close. But from a distance, they were similar. Close enough to be the "type" of a serial killer.

Grace's death had been ruled an accident. It had been suspicious enough to get me out here, considering the circumstances, but there was absolutely no reason to believe that a serial killer was involved. Nor would that account for the other deaths I'd found linked to this place, most of whom were older people who didn't fit that type at all.

Still. There were a couple others who did. Young blonde women who'd tragically lost their lives here. Always an accident. Always with a logical explanation. But it was something to keep in mind, especially with the odd change of cabins.

After all, Grace had also been moved to cabin thirteen before she died.

I quickly unpacked my things, keeping an eye out my windows as I did. A few more vehicles arrived, and other visitors began unloading their bags and checking into their cabins. I doubted the place would fill up completely, but there were more people staying than I'd expected.

It was something to keep in mind. Multiple deaths at a particular vacation resort was odd, but if this place was consistently full, the pure volume of people coming through here made a handful of deaths over the course of decades less suspicious. After all, accidents happened on vacations. People got drunk and cocky, took chances they wouldn't ordinarily take.

Not Grace though. She'd had her head on her shoulders, which was why the story of her death just didn't sit right with me or Jim. I hadn't known her as well as he had, obviously, but I'd known her well enough. Despite her prom queen looks, she'd been a serious, stable, good-hearted woman. She'd saved Jim's life, given him something real to hold on to.

That gave me a reason to owe Grace, too.

I pulled out my binoculars, scanning the area and taking a closer look at the people arriving. Some of them were easy to peg—like the family in cabin five with the teenage daughter.

They were obviously attempting some kind of family bonding trip. There was tension there between the parents, but they both appeared to be making an effort with false smiles. The mom—a classy, suburban wife type with highlighted hair and the kind of expensive outfit you'd see the royals wearing on a staged hike—kept throwing worried glances toward the daughter, making me wonder what the story was there. The daughter wore baggy jeans and a faded sweatshirt—a clear statement that she had no desire to be like her mother—and walked around with her arms crossed. The father appeared dressed for an office instead of a cabin vacation, in slacks and a sweater. He seemed to be ignoring the tension between his wife and his daughter, more interested in checking out the scenery and watching the other guests.

The family in cabin eight had a visibly angry teenage son—both the son and the wife seemed miserable, while the overly enthusiastic dad ignored their resentment and tried to stir up excitement. The dad had brought more fishing gear than he could possibly need, and by the looks of it, I doubted he knew how to use any of it. He wore what appeared to be a brand-new fishing vest and hat, and he kept gesturing toward the lake, trying to get the teenager interested. The boy—a gangly teen in baggy jeans with a baseball cap shoved down over his curly brown hair—rolled his eyes and argued before taking notice of the teen girl from the cabin three doors down. He watched her for a bit, then stormed off by himself. The dad was momentarily deflated, but then he shrugged and started trying to get the wife excited instead. She pushed him away and headed inside, leaving him on his own.

Two doors down from me was a young couple that was all over each other. Nothing about them suggested that they were here for the scenery or to connect with nature. The girl wore black shredded jeans, combat boots, and a black long-sleeved -shirt...to match her jet-black, waist-length shiny hair. The guy was clearly on the same style train, in dark jeans and a matching hoodie. Together, they hauled nearly a dozen black duffel bags out of their vehicle. Unloading took them forever, as they couldn't seem to manage more than a few steps without stopping to make out. Then the girl held out her left hand, wiggling her ring finger to watch her ring sparkle in the sunlight. I cracked a grin, doubting we'd see much of them this weekend.

An old beater car was parked in front of the very first cabin. My guess, based on the grass that had grown up around the tires, was that it belonged to a semi-permanent resident of the campground. I'd have to do a little digging and see if I could find out who.

Six cabins occupied, counting mine and Olivia's. Not a full house, but still more people than I'd wanted here. Ten guests, plus whoever was in cabin one and the caretakers in their cottage.

There was also the large house on the hill. I knew from my research that it belonged to Richard Moore, the current owner of Hidden Gem lake and all the cabins on it.

I swung the binoculars toward his house, then dropped them when I saw he was doing the exact same thing: watching all the campers below with binoculars of his own.

Chapter Five

Olivia

After carrying in the groceries I'd brought for the weekend, I pulled my suitcase to the bedroom in the back of the cabin and unzipped it, grabbing my sketchbook and a few charcoal pencils. I wanted to get Sawyer's features down on paper before I lost any of the inspiration. Not that I was in danger of forgetting him anytime soon. I'd studied his face—and his body—with an artist's eye during our brief interaction, committing the details to memory.

Broad shoulders. Impossibly large biceps. A thick but well-trimmed full beard obscuring what I imagined was a sharp jawline. The slightly crooked nose, suggesting it had been broken a time or two. A deep tan, the type that told a story of days spent in the kind of sunshine we didn't have here in Wisconsin. Lines etched into his skin that spoke of contradictions—the worried furrow in between his brow and the gentler laugh lines. A small scar above his right eyebrow.

That twinkle in his eyes when he teased me.

His body told a story of power, strength, and battle. Yet his expressions suggested a sense of humor, a playfulness about life, and marked intelligence. His eyes twinkled, but they were also sharp. Aware. Vigilant.

And somehow...kind. There was a depth to him. Empathy. Something...unexpected.

I chewed the end of my pencil, looking at my work. It was good. But it wasn't quite right. I hadn't managed to fully capture everything I'd seen in him.

My mouth turned up in a little smile. Maybe I'd have to spend more time with him after all. Now that was an interesting—and dangerous—idea.

A noise startled me, pulling me out of my thoughts. I froze as my heart thudded in my chest.

Someone was in the cabin with me.

My breath came in shaky gasps as I fought to control my heart rate. I couldn't panic. Not now. I squeezed my eyes shut and forced my breathing to slow. With a trembling hand, I reached for my purse, removing the pistol I kept there. I tucked the gun into my jacket pocket to conceal it. Then I slowly stood and moved toward the bedroom door.

More noises. Whoever it was wasn't even bothering to hide the fact that they were here.

This could not be happening again.

I took another shaky breath, then forced myself to walk down the hallway toward the kitchen, trying to keep my hand steady on the weapon in my pocket. It was something I never wanted to use. But I would—if I had to. I'd bought it as a promise to myself that I'd never feel completely defenseless again.

I turned the corner. The kitchen was empty. But the noises were coming from behind a sliding barn door off to the side.

"Hello?" I called out, moving slowly toward the sounds. "Who's there?"

No answer.

I kept my right hand on my gun and used my left to push the barn door open, revealing a woman with dark, stringy hair. She jumped, clutching her chest and letting out a scream like she'd seen a ghost. She stared at me for a moment, mouth open, then shook herself and pulled the earpods out of her ears.

"I'm so sorry!" she said. "I didn't know you were here! I thought this cabin was empty this weekend. The caretakers don't rent it out unless we're full."

"Can I help you?" I slipped my hand out of my pocket and let my jacket fall into place, hoping she hadn't noticed the weapon inside.

She gestured toward the washer and dryer in front of her. "I'm Penny, the housekeeper. The dryer went out in one of the other cabins. I had to bring their linens over here to finish up. I'm so sorry. They don't want me in the cabins when guests are here. I'm supposed to be done with everything by check-in time. Please don't tell them!"

I frowned. The woman was scared out of her mind. "It's fine. I won't tell anyone."

Relief flashed across her face. "Thank you. I appreciate that so much. I can't get in trouble again."

"Why would you get in trouble for a dryer going out? That's not your fault."

She twisted her hands and bit her lip, obviously not wanting to answer. "I'll just keep that door closed. You won't even know I'm here. I'll go in and out this back door"—she gestured behind herself to a small screen door I hadn't even noticed—"when I need to change things out. I, um, have a couple more loads to do. They used a lot of towels."

"Okay," I said, fighting a sigh. Equipment malfunctions certainly weren't her fault, and I didn't want her to get in trouble. If she needed to use the cabin to finish her work, that was fine.

But I had to admit I didn't feel entirely comfortable with her having access to the cabin while I was staying there. That was silly, I told myself. She was probably perfectly nice, and you couldn't stay on someone else's property without housekeepers and maintenance crews coming in. It was just part of it.

It had never bothered me until...well, until recently.

I was just shaken up, I tried to tell myself. Thrown off by hearing someone in the cabin and not knowing who it was. After everything that had happened, it was no wonder I was a little on edge.

"I'll leave you to your work," I said, forcing myself to give her a smile.

"Thank you. And thank you again for not saying anything. If there's anything I can do for you this weekend, you just let me know, okay?" She nodded eagerly, obviously grateful. "Extra toiletries or kitchen supplies. Whatever you need."

"Thanks. I'm sure I'll be fine."

I closed the door to the laundry room and decided I would pack up my gear and head outside to do a little *plein air* painting while Penny finished up.

Because regardless of how nice she was, I did not feel comfortable staying in this cabin alone with her.

Chapter Six

Sawyer

I PICKED MY BINOCULARS BACK UP AND LOOKED AGAIN AT the man standing on the deck of the big house on the hill. He was still scanning the area, watching. But he wouldn't be able to see me. I knew how to position myself so I wouldn't be noticed, and I took those precautions automatically, even here where it wouldn't matter anyway. Lots of people brought binoculars to the woods for birdwatching. I could always write it off as that.

Hell, that could even be the reason he was using his. Though I was pretty damn certain he'd been watching the young couple unload.

I looked again. He swung his binoculars slowly over toward his right—toward cabin thirteen.

I stepped out onto my porch, pretending to stretch and look at the lake so that I could see what had caught his attention.

Olivia was standing in the front yard of her cabin, with a small canvas backpack slung over her shoulder. She looked around like she was searching for something. After a minute or two, she made her way down the pebbled pathway and turned left, heading away from the lake toward the woods.

I didn't like it. Not here, not now. Not with that guy watching her. Walking alone in the woods was just asking for trouble. And based on my initial impressions of her, I was pretty sure that, if trouble came knocking, she wouldn't have a clue how to handle it. Not because she was a woman. I knew many women who were more than capable of taking care of themselves. But Olivia seemed different. She wasn't at all like my sister—a force of nature even I wouldn't want to go up against. No, Olivia was entirely too soft, too guarded.

She didn't need to be in the woods alone. Not until I knew for sure what was going on out here. I grabbed my own pack and headed out to follow her.

Olivia walked slowly, her head moving constantly as she looked around. She seemed to be taking in everything, acutely aware of her surroundings.

Which meant it wouldn't be easy to fake an accidental run-in. Annoying, but I felt oddly proud of her for at least staying aware. Made me a little less worried about her being out here by herself.

So I went for the direct approach instead. "Hey, Olivia," I called, jogging toward her.

She turned and gazed at me warily as I approached. "Yes?"

"Going for a hike?"

"Something like that." She studied me, still unwilling to let me in on her plans.

I blinked a couple of times, thrown off by her non-answer. Though I shouldn't have been. It's all she'd been giving me since we'd met; I didn't know why I would expect anything else. So, again, I tried the direct—if not completely honest—approach. "I was hoping to get some exercise myself. Can I come with you?"

She backed up a step. "I'd rather you didn't."

"Look," I said before blowing out a breath as I grabbed the straps of my pack. "I know you didn't ask me for advice. But I don't really think it's a good idea for you to hike out here alone."

She was clearly annoyed. "I can take care of myself."

I gave her a level look, then decided to lay some cards out on the table. "Why do you think that? Because you've got a pistol shoved in your pocket?"

That hit a nerve. She jumped, looking guilty. "How do you—"

"You're printing," I said, gesturing to it. "You need to get a holster. Not a bad idea to let people know you're armed, but shoving a gun in your pocket is a bad move. Ups the chance of an accidental discharge, and makes it too hard to draw quick and clean. You think that pistol's going to do you any good if you can't get to it?"

"What on earth makes you think I wouldn't be able to get to it?"

This time, I was the one who was annoyed. I rolled my eyes, then reached out and grabbed her, quickly spinning and pinning her to my chest with her arms behind her back. I slipped my free hand into her jacket pocket, disarming her. She tensed and tried to pull away but couldn't. I dropped her wrists and let her go, holding the gun out for her to take back.

"How dare you." She snatched the pistol out of my hand and shoved it back into her pocket, rage flaring in her eyes. "Why the hell would you do something like that? Who do you think you are?"

"Someone who just proved my point. You couldn't get to your weapon and didn't know how to get out of the hold. One split second and you were disarmed—and I had a weapon I could have used against you."

"I wasn't expecting to need to defend myself." She practically spat the words.

"That's sort of the point. You never know."

"Got it. I'll take your advice and stay away from dangerous men— like you." She nodded, turning on her heel.

I reached out, stopping her. "I'm not here to hurt you."

"Then why are you here?" she demanded. "Because it's starting to look like that's exactly why you're following me."

"No." I shook my head and ran a hand through my hair. "Look. My buddy... His fiancée died last year. She was vacationing alone. Some-place a lot like this. I just... I just don't want anything to happen to you."

I wasn't ready to tell her Grace had died *here*. Or that they looked a hell of a lot alike. Or that Grace had been staying in cabin thirteen at the time.

Olivia's eyes softened. "I'm sorry about your friend, but I'm fine. And regardless of your concerns, you shouldn't go grabbing people like that."

"You're right. I just had a feeling you didn't have any moves to back up that firepower, and I wanted to show you that things can still go bad. Don't let a weapon give you a false sense of security. It's safer to hike with a buddy. That's all I'm offering." I felt lame even as I said it. I'd clearly screwed things up, which was odd—I was normally a hell of a lot smoother than this.

Something about Olivia had thrown me off my game.

She glared at me. "I'm well aware of how badly things can go. But in case you haven't noticed, I'm alone out here except for you. So tell me again how I should let you walk into the woods to 'protect' me."

I clenched my jaw. "Fine. I'll leave you alone. Just...please be careful, okay?" I automatically glanced up at the house on the hill.

She followed my gaze, frowning. "Okay."

I held my hands up in surrender and started to leave, then turned around. "Can I ask you one question?"

"What?" Her guard immediately went back up.

"Why are you in cabin thirteen? Did you request it?"

She frowned again. "No. I booked number seven. When I got here, the caretakers told me a change had to be made, and they moved me to that one. Why?"

It was the most information she'd given me thus far, and I could tell it was the truth. "Just wondering," I said, shaking my head. "I'd asked to stay in thirteen myself."

"Why?"

Because she'd been honest with me, I contemplated telling her the truth. But I didn't want to scare her any more than I already had—unless I had to, in order to keep her safe. "Privacy," I lied. "It's off on its own."

"Not so private," she said, giving me a rueful smile.

"What do you mean?"

"Nothing." She closed off, apparently deciding not to tell me after all.

"Okay. Enjoy your hike." I attempted a smile.

"I will."

I noticed she stayed still, watching me walk all the way back to my cabin before she headed down the trail again.

CHAPTER SEVEN

Olivia

A MIX OF EMOTIONS SWIRLED THROUGH ME AS I WATCHED Sawyer walk away.

The man was infuriating.

He was cocky, rude, and annoying. Acted as if he was used to being in charge and expected me to simply fall in line. It didn't help that, with his size and obvious strength, most people probably did simply defer to him.

But I was tired of deferring to other people. Tired of being told to shut up and color, to let the adults handle everything. Tired of being "protected."

Especially considering where that had gotten me.

I sighed in relief when Sawyer climbed the steps to his cabin and turned. Then he gave me one more long look before going inside.

He was infuriating, yes. But I had to admit there was something else there too. Cocky or not, he'd shown some legitimate anxiety about me being here alone. And without meaning to, he'd revealed that it had to do with that big house on the hill, the one he couldn't stop himself from looking at when he'd told me to be careful.

It was interesting—and annoying, as he'd ruined my plans for the afternoon. I'd already felt nervous hiking by myself. Despite what he thought, I did understand the dangers facing women who traveled alone. Not that I'd ever once had a problem.

No, the only real danger I'd ever been in had been in my hometown, thanks to the people who hated my father. Traveling offered me an anonymity that equaled safety. Under normal circumstances, I'd feel a thousand times safer walking alone in the woods here than I would just going out to eat back home right now. But Sawyer's anxiety, coupled with the oddness of the place, had me feeling out of sorts.

I didn't want to go back to my cabin though. Not with Penny still doing laundry there. So I sighed, resigning myself to the fact that he'd ruined the bravery I'd worked up to hike alone, and decided to walk down to the lake instead. There was an added element of safety to staying out in the open, in view of all the other cabins. And a good portion of my work would involve the lake anyway.

So I walked down to the water's edge, picked a spot, and set up my watercolors.

I WAS DEEPLY ENGROSSED IN MY WORK WHEN A TEENAGE GIRL walked up and looked over my shoulder.

"Wow," she said, obviously impressed. "You're good."

I glanced up and smiled at her. "Do you like art?"

"Yeah." She plopped down beside me. "I'm not as good as you though."

"We all start somewhere. I bet you're better than you think." I gave her a close look.

Mousy brown hair, delicate features. She had a sweetness about her, but more than that, I could see sadness. Like her heart was so full of pain that it overflowed and colored over all of her other features.

I felt an immediate kinship with her. I knew what that kind of sadness felt like, and I understood how brutal the teenage years could be.

"I'm Olivia," I said, giving her a quick smile before turning my focus back to my work. If she was interested in art, the best way to draw her into conversation would be to continue what I had been doing.

"I'm Sadie," she said a little shyly.

"Did you bring your supplies?"

She nodded. "Nothing as sweet as your kit. But I have a sketchbook and pencils."

I gave her a look of encouragement. "I'll be painting a lot while I'm here. You're welcome to join me anytime. I'd love to see your sketches."

"Oh." She blushed. "Mine aren't really worth seeing."

I shrugged. "You might be surprised. But I'm also happy to offer you any tips if you want to improve."

"Are you, like, a professional artist or something?"

I smiled, feeling the little flutter of pride that came when I thought of what I was creating for myself. "Yeah, I guess I am. I illustrate children's books."

Her whole face lit up. "That's really cool. What are you working on now?"

"An adorable little story about a family of river otters that live on a lake like this one. The author wanted it done in watercolor, which is my specialty. I thought a weekend at a lake would give me the inspiration I needed for the scenes."

"That's so cool," the girl repeated, obviously in awe. "I would love a job like that someday."

"It's pretty great," I agreed. "So, what are you here for?"

She rolled her eyes. "Mandatory family fun."

"You sound thrilled."

She hugged her knees into her chest, rocking back and forth as she glanced toward one of the cabins. "My mom thinks, if we just get away for a weekend, everything will go back to the way it used to be."

"What way is that?" I asked the question casually as I mixed up some green tones to add foliage around my lake scene. I could never use greens straight from the tube—I liked for mine to have their own character, mixing in yellows, blues, and even a little bit of red to create more realistic earth-toned hues.

"Doesn't matter." She shut the conversation down and stood up, brushing the dirt from her jeans. "I'm going to walk around, see if I can get reception anywhere before they call me back for dinner. I'm dying to talk to my friends, but this stupid phone barely works up here."

I winced. "That's rough. I'm sorry. Well, if you need a break from the mandatory family fun, the offer stands—you can bring your supplies and sketch with me whenever you want."

"Thanks, Olivia." She gave me a shy smile, then headed off toward a hill, cell phone in hand.

I got lost in my work again until the sun began to set behind the trees. The whole world felt aglow as the treeline across the water became nothing more than a dark silhouette against the golden sunlight. Heavy clouds cast dark shadows across the surface of the lake, and the trees around me began to rustle as the breeze picked up. It was so beautiful that for once I didn't even bother trying to paint it. I just sat and soaked it in—until footsteps approached, raising my guard again.

I looked up and saw Sawyer staring down at me, his hands tucked into his pockets and a sheepish look on his face.

"I'd like to apologize for scaring you earlier," he said after clearing his throat.

Gone was the cocky attitude. In its place was something different—a vulnerability. It was honest, and it made me want to forgive him.

"It's fine," I said, starting to pack away my brushes.

He sat down and put a hand on mine, startling me. I stared at it for a second. He wasn't grabbing me, holding tight this time—it was a soft touch, almost tender.

A touch like that felt even more dangerous.

"I wasn't totally honest with you," he said. "I'd like to explain."

"Alright," I said, staring at him. The man seemed to have a million moods and I was having trouble pinning him down.

"I told you I had a buddy whose fiancée died on a trip."

"Right. At a place like this."

He shook his head. "No. That's where I wasn't honest. It wasn't just at a place like this. She was here."

"*Here*?" I felt the color drain from my face.

"Yeah."

"What happened?"

He stared out at the lake like he was reliving some kind of nightmare. "She drowned. It was ruled an accident."

I breathed a sigh of relief. "Well, I can understand why that would have you shaken up, but that doesn't have anything to do with me hiking alone. Accidents happen."

He turned and gave me a piercing look. "What if it wasn't an accident?"

My heart stilled. "What do you mean?"

He looked away, studying the dirt in front of him. "This is going to sound crazy."

"Tell me anyway."

"Last year, she came up here by herself. She and Jim had plans to come together, but he had a work thing come up—emergency. So she came alone. Texted Jim that night, laughing about how creepy it was and how, when she got here, the caretakers changed her reservation and put her in cabin thirteen."

My jaw dropped. "Are you serious?"

He nodded, then glanced up at the house on the hill. "Texted him again the next day. Said some weird things had happened. Jim said she was real spooked. Then the next morning, she texted that she'd met the owner—Richard—and that he gave her the creeps. Bad. Told Jim she was going to pack up and come home early."

"But she never made it," I whispered, knowing already how the story must end.

He picked up a rock and threw it into the water. "Jim got a call the next day that there'd been an accident. They found her here on the shore. Local sheriff investigated. Took forever to get answers. Eventually, Jim was told that she had drugs in her system. Had gotten high and went for a late-night swim. Autopsy confirmed drowning as the cause of death. Everyone said she must have made a bad choice and got in the water when she wasn't fully cognizant. Passed out or something."

"I am so sorry. I don't know what to say."

He looked back at me. "Grace didn't do drugs."

I reached out and put a hand on his forearm this time. "Sometimes people do things that are out of character. You never know."

He shook his head. "I know she didn't do that. Look, maybe it was an accident. But it doesn't add up. What happens if you drown in a lake while you're swimming?"

I frowned. "What do you mean?"

"You sink," he said, staring at me like it was the most obvious thing in the world. "When you drown, you sink. Fast, when you're talking freshwater like this. There's mathematical formulas for it, believe it or not. Someone like Grace... You've got seconds before she's eight feet below the surface. Not much longer before she's on the bottom." He gestured at the water in front of him. "It takes three to five days for a body to float back to the surface. Besides, this is a small lake. No tide. How could she have washed up on shore the next morning?"

"That's...that's a very good point. But if she really was high, she may not have been swimming," I pointed out. "Maybe she just came down here to put her feet into the water and fell or something. Passed out with her head under. They say you can drown in two inches of water."

He nodded. "Yeah. That's what they said, that it could have been something like that. There was a small cut on her head, where they thought she might have hit it. The report said her hair and her bathing suit were wet though. Like she'd been fully submerged. But Grace was a hell of a swimmer. And like I said, she didn't do drugs."

A chill went through me. "I'm sorry," I said, not knowing what else I could possibly say.

"There's also this." He took his phone out and pulled up a photograph, then handed it to me.

The picture was taken from a distance, but even so, it was clear there were a lot of similarities between me and her. She was grinning at the camera, her arms thrown up in the air. She looked so happy.

"Is this Grace?" I asked in a whisper, feeling sick just looking at it, knowing that her life had been cut so short. It was awful.

Sawyer took the phone back, shoving it into his pocket. "Yeah. It is. Jim is convinced that the owner killed her. Asked me to come look into things. I wasn't planning on telling a soul why I was here unless I found something. But then I got here and saw you—moving into cabin thirteen of all places, the cabin I'd specifically requested—and kind of lost my mind for a minute."

I swallowed hard. "I understand now why you felt the need to stop me from hiking."

"When you left your cabin, the owner was watching you through binoculars. I didn't want you out there alone with him knowing."

My jaw dropped. "What do you mean he was watching me? How do you know that?"

"Because I was watching him. Saw him turn his binoculars toward the direction of your cabin. Took a look and saw you were heading out on your own."

"What would you have done if I had kept going?"

He smirked. "I'd have given you a head start, then followed you at a distance and kept an eye on you."

"And I could have noticed, freaked out, and shot you."

His smirk widened to a full grin. "Honey, you'd have never known I was there. But even if you did, it wouldn't be the first time I've been shot at."

"Hmm." I gave him the side-eye. "Are you a detective or something?"

"Something like that."

I arched an eyebrow. "Not going to tell me?"

"Maybe once you tell me your secrets, I'll tell you mine."

"I don't have secrets."

He gave me a pointed look. "You wouldn't tell me your last name. Wouldn't even tell me what you do for a living or what was in your suitcase, though I'm realizing now it was likely art supplies." He gestured to my painting. "Nice work by the way."

"Thank you."

"You're aloof. Quiet. And you're still carrying that damn gun in your pocket. I'd say you've got secrets galore, Olivia."

I rolled my eyes. "Not wanting to tell a complete stranger my life story isn't the same as having secrets."

"Whatever you say."

"So, what are you going to do now?" I asked, changing the subject away from myself. Sawyer was perceptive, and I didn't want to talk about my life to someone like him.

"Well, for one thing, I'd like to check out cabin thirteen, see if there's anything the sheriff missed."

"Didn't you say it's been a year?"

He nodded. "Yeah."

"Why are you just now getting out here?"

He shuffled his feet a bit and looked away. "Well, at first, I was giving the sheriff time to do things his way. Didn't want to step on his toes. They have a small operation here, with limited resources, and investigations take time. But then I got busy with a"—he paused, clearing his throat—"project. Just now found the time to get away."

"Hmmm. That's a long time. It's been cleaned countless times since then," I said, shaking my head. "I doubt any evidence would be left behind."

"You'd be surprised what gets overlooked. Are you going to let me look around or what?"

I paused, debating. "Is this just a ploy to get me alone in there?"

He grinned again, that cocky attitude of his making its return. "If that's what I was after, I've got better ways of convincing you to let me take you to bed."

"Doubtful," I smirked. "Show me the article."

"What article?"

"Something written publicly about Grace's death. An article or obituary. I want to see if you're telling me the truth before I let you into my cabin."

Something like admiration shown in his eyes. "Okay." He tapped a few words into the search feature on his phone. It was slow to load, but when it did, he handed it to me.

I quickly scanned the news article, confirming his story. Accidental death, drowning, the victim's name, the location—it was all there. He was telling the truth. About this, at least.

"Fine. You can come take a look around. But when you're finished, you'll need to leave. I still have work to do tonight."

"Same," he said, standing. "It's a deal."

Chapter Eight

Sawyer

Olivia insisted on carrying her own bag even though I offered to carry it for her, so I shoved my hands into my pockets as we walked toward the cabin. I was fighting an odd urge to take her hand or put an arm around her like she was mine. But I'd crossed a line earlier by grabbing her, and I regretted it. So much that I'd even apologized, which was a new thing for me.

I rarely felt like I had anything to apologize for.

When I'd set out to make things right, I hadn't actually planned on telling her the truth about Grace. But in the moment, it felt like the right thing to do. Plus, it eliminated the need to come up with an excuse to get into her cabin.

Because I didn't want to lie to her.

That, too, was an odd thing for me. Lying was practically part of my job description. We called it "pretexting," a word that made it sound prettier. More innocent. But it was lying all the same. I conned people into giving me the information I needed. And I'd never once felt guilty for it.

But when I'd lied to Olivia the first time, about Grace dying somewhere "like this," it had felt...wrong. Like a grain of sand caught in my eye, irritating me and hurting way the hell more than you'd think a tiny piece of sand ever could. I didn't like it. And I didn't want to do it again.

Which was another thing I didn't want to spend too much time thinking about.

Truth be told, this woman was taking up far too much of my headspace—headspace I needed in order to do my job this weekend. I didn't have time to get distracted by a beautiful face who had no business being out here on her own. But something about Olivia was incredibly intriguing. And it was only partly because I wanted to uncover all her secrets.

At this point, I was convinced she had about a million of them—which was another reason I wouldn't mind getting a look into her cabin.

But before we made it there, the young couple I'd seen earlier flagged us down. They were still decked out in head-to-toe black and couldn't keep their hands off each other.

"Hey!" the guy called, walking our way with his arm slung around his girlfriend's neck. His gait gave the impression that he'd had a drink or two already.

Olivia and I both stopped. I watched that guarded look come back over her face.

"What do you think?" I whispered, trying to lighten her mood. "Honeymooners?"

Her lips curled up in a tiny smile. "No. They're too young. Dating, I'd say."

"Engaged at least," I said.

She shook her head in disagreement.

The couple reached us and the man stuck his hand out. I attempted to shake it before realizing he was actually trying to fist-bump. I heard Olivia make an odd noise and looked down to see her stifling a laugh.

"Yo, I'm Adam," the guy said, gazing at his girl with a look of adoration before planting a big kiss on her mouth right in front of us. "And this beautiful girl right here is Eve."

Olivia blinked a few times. "Adam and Eve? Are you serious?"

"Yeah," Eve giggled, wrapping her arms around Adam's waist. "Those are our real names. It's how we knew we were meant to be together."

"Yeah," the guy said, drawing the word out. "Like in the garden, man."

Olivia and I exchanged looks. I decided that, in addition to the drink or two, the guy had been smoking something as well.

"Listen," the girl—who, unlike Adam, appeared to be sober—grabbed Olivia's arm. Olivia recoiled slightly, though to her credit, she kept a polite smile on her face. "We're having a bonfire tonight. It's at the big fire ring, the communal one back behind the cabins. You guys should totally come."

"Oh, ah," Olivia began to stammer, looking for an excuse.

"We'd love to," I said, answering for her.

She glared at me.

"Great!" Adam said with a dorky smile on his face. "We've got beer and s'mores, and we're inviting everyone. It's a celebration!"

"What are we celebrating?" Olivia asked tightly.

"Well..." Eve stuck out her left hand, showing off a tiny diamond ring.

"Congratulations." I winked at Olivia. "What time is the bonfire?"

"We're getting it started in about an hour," Adam said. "You know, when it's *really* dark."

"We'll see you there," I said before touching a hand to Olivia's arm and steering her back toward her cabin.

As soon as we were out of their earshot, she hissed at me. "Why did you say I would come?"

I didn't answer right away. The truth was that I felt responsible for Olivia while she was here. The questions surrounding Grace's death made me uncomfortable letting her out of my sight, especially after the way she'd been moved to cabin thirteen.

An infamous cabin she didn't seem to know anything about.

"I just want to make sure you're safe tonight," I finally said, giving her the truth—again—even though I felt funny admitting it.

"I don't know whether to say thank you or tell you that you're becoming seriously annoying," she grumbled.

"I'd prefer thank you," I said, flashing her a grin.

"I bet you would." That left eyebrow arched again. I had the strangest desire to kiss it.

We walked up the stairs of her porch. Olivia pulled the key out of her pocket and opened the cabin door, sticking her head inside like she was listening for something.

"What are you doing?" I asked, frowning.

She glanced back at me before opening the door and letting me in. "Nothing." She raised a hand, gesturing around. "Here you go. Do your thing."

"Thanks." I stepped forward and went into my zone.

At first glance, the front room appeared to be a cozy living space, with warm colors on the walls, the fresh shine of polished wood floors, and oversized furniture just made for getting comfortable.

But I knew that the devil was in the details.

"Someone really likes dead things," I said, shooting Olivia a glance as I pointed to the decor. Frozen faces stared down at us from every wall. It was far beyond the typical prized deer mount or two. These walls were covered with dead animals—raccoons, squirrels, rabbits, and even a red fox. I paused, studying what had once been a majestic deer with impressive antlers. My mind drifted as I imagined this beauty walking calmly through the forest before being struck down for a trophy.

"I think it's typical for cabins to be decorated like this," Olivia said, but I could hear the hesitation in her voice.

"I've seen hunting decor before. But you have to admit this is overkill," I said, pointing at the windowsills. Even they were covered in small antlers, the kind you'd normally buy at a pet store as a dog treat.

"It is a little much," she admitted, moving to my side.

"What'd you think when you first came in?" I asked, always interested in first impressions. Sometimes people gathered more information than they realized.

She blushed. "I didn't really look around. I headed straight for the bedroom and started working, then realized I was hearing noises."

"Noises?" I frowned. Had she already had an experience here? If so, that was all the more reason to get her to the bonfire tonight.

Not that I actually believed the ghost stories.

"Yeah. It was nothing." Her face shut down and I could see she didn't want to tell me anything more.

I started walking the room again, looking around, even though I wasn't exactly sure what I was looking for. Grace hadn't taken her last breath in this room, so even if she had been murdered, it was unlikely there would be signs of a struggle here. On the other hand, you just never knew. If something had happened in here, there might still be the smallest piece of evidence left behind. A blood stain that had escaped normal cleaning, or a bit of damage that told a story about what had happened. Sometimes the smallest detail was all I needed to figure out where to start.

I stopped in front of a bookshelf, studying the titles.

Olivia stared at them as well before giving me an uncertain look. "Thinking he hit her over the head with a book?"

I shook my head. "No. Just trying to get a sense of the owner. Look —it's almost all military history and obscure thrillers. Seems like a personal choice. If you were stocking a shelf for tourists, what would you put on it?"

"Hmmm," she mused. "Probably local history and a variety of best sellers. I'd try to cover the top-selling genres and have a little something for everyone. Maybe even picture books for young children, since families might stay here."

"Exactly." I picked up one of the thrillers and flipped through it. It appeared to have been well-loved, with dog-eared pages.

Olivia moved past me, apparently noticing something I hadn't gotten to. "Come look at this," she called.

I walked over, noting that her already large eyes had widened. She pointed at the photographs lined up on a shelf. From a distance, I hadn't noticed anything odd about them, but when I got closer, I realized they were obituaries. There were eight of them, carefully clipped and displayed in frames.

The one on the end was Grace's.

"That's...really weird." I frowned, unsure what to even make of it. As a personal choice in a home, it was strange. As decor in a vacation cabin rental? It was unthinkable.

"It is, isn't it?" Olivia shivered involuntarily, and before I knew what I was doing, I'd put an arm around her. To my surprise, she didn't tense up. If anything, she leaned into it for a moment before slowly pulling away.

"I don't like this at all," I said.

"I don't, either. Why would he have all those displayed like that? Do you think all these people died here?"

"I did a little research before I came," I said carefully, not wanting to reveal too much. "Grace's death wasn't the first. Some of these names ring a bell."

"Most of them are older people," she said, studying their images. "I'm glad it's not eight young blondes."

I looked at her, realizing she was genuinely scared—and that while the fear was valid, it was also my fault. If I hadn't told her what I was up to, she would still be oblivious.

Oblivion didn't equal safety though.

"There's definitely not a pattern like that," I agreed. Although an argument could be made that there was a different kind of pattern—one based on the ghost stories connected to this place. That was more than I wanted to get into though. "Still, if you're worried about it, you could leave. I saw you have Wisconsin plates. Pack up and hit the road. You can make it home tonight."

Something hard shuttered over her face. "I can't."

"Why not?"

"I just can't go back to the city tonight." Her hand trembled slightly before she tucked it into her pocket. "Bad night vision. Wouldn't be safe for me to drive."

She was lying. I could hear it in the way her voice had thinned slightly, could see it in the way she looked away.

But I recognized that it wasn't the time to push. "You could trade cabins with me," I suggested. "Then leave in the morning."

"I'll think about it."

I hoped she would. Because I knew Grace wouldn't have done drugs.

And the longer I was here, the more convinced I was becoming that something truly terrible had happened to her.

Chapter Nine

Olivia

I HUNG BACK WHILE SAWYER CONTINUED HIS EXPLORATION of the cabin, trying to make sense of everything that seemed to catch his eye. I assumed he was looking for evidence, but he appeared to be doing more than that. His comments suggested he was creating a psychological profile of whoever had put this cabin together.

He seemed convinced that the owner was responsible for the decor. I wasn't sure. After all, the caretakers were the ones involved in maintaining the property. Having met them, I wouldn't have been surprised at all if they had decorated the house in dead animals and obituaries. The caretakers weren't scary though, not in a threatening way at least. They were just strange, older people. People who hadn't grown up with the social customs of the city and were lacking manners.

I hoped that's all it was, anyway.

I followed Sawyer down the hallway to the bedroom. He walked in and immediately stopped in his tracks.

"Is that me?" he asked.

I blushed furiously, remembering that I had left out the sketchbook where I'd drawn him earlier. I ducked around him and snatched it off the bed, flipping it closed. When I glanced his way, he had a giant grin on his face.

"Come on," he said, holding out a hand. "Let me see."

I started to say no, then sighed. He'd already seen it. It wasn't as if I could pretend it didn't exist. Besides, I was a professional artist—it's not as if I'd been writing his name in a notebook and circling it with hearts. It was nothing more than a bit of practice.

"Here," I said, flipping back to the page with his image.

He took the sketchbook from my hand. "This is really good," he said, his face turning serious.

"Of course you'd think so," I said, unable to stop from rolling my eyes. The man was clearly in love with himself.

"No, I mean it." He paused, studying it with a thoughtful look on his face. "You're really talented. You'd known me for less than five minutes, but you... I don't know how to say it."

"Try," I said, curious about what he was thinking.

He looked at the sketch again in silence, then tore his gaze away from it to answer. "It's like you captured everything I was feeling some-how. It's not just a picture of me. It's...me. And also more than me. I don't know how else to explain it. But it's remarkable, really."

Nothing he could have said would have touched me more. It was exactly what I hoped to accomplish with my art. Even though I only illustrated children's books, I tried so hard to capture something real in every image. Something true. Something that told a story of what it meant to be human—to be alive in this painful, beautiful world.

That was way too personal to share though. So I simply said, "Thank you. You have an interesting face."

He chuckled. "I'm not sure that's a compliment."

"It is," I said, feeling suddenly shy. "I like faces that tell a story."

He looked back at me, holding my gaze, and my stomach flipped upside down. My breath caught in my chest. I felt pulled forward, as if we were magnets, drawn to each other. As if there was absolutely nothing I could do to stop it. There was some-thing happening between us—something I'd never expected. A connection, a knowing, a spark I hadn't felt in such a very long time.

It was also something I wasn't sure I wanted. Especially with someone like Sawyer, someone who was cocky and arrogant and who felt dangerous in more ways than one.

I shook myself, breaking the spell. "Well," I said, taking a deliberate step away from him as I moved toward the door. "If you're finished looking around—"

But my sentence was interrupted by the unmistakable sound of a door opening.

Sawyer frowned, then drew a pistol that I hadn't realized was hidden in a holster at his back. I opened my mouth to tell him about Penny, but he held a finger to his lips, warning me to be quiet. When I shook my head and tried to explain anyway, the man actually put his hand over my mouth.

I strongly considered biting it.

Instead, I rolled my eyes. Fine. Let him be the one to feel ridiculous this time, getting freaked out over the housekeeper.

I followed him, mildly amused as he stalked his way down the hall—despite the fact that I'd done the same exact thing a few hours earlier. He turned the corner into the kitchen and pushed open the barn door, moving into a shooter's stance.

Penny screamed bloody murder.

"It's alright," I said, gently placing a hand on Sawyer's forearm, nudging him to lower his weapon. I'd never expected him to actually point a gun at her, and I felt a tremendous stab of guilt over her terror.

"What are you doing in here?" he demanded.

Penny pointed at me, her hands shaking. "She said I could use the laundry room to catch up."

He looked to me for confirmation and I nodded.

"This is Penny," I said, introducing him. "She's a housekeeper here. There was an issue with one of the dryers, so she's using mine to finish her work."

He closed his eyes, pinching the bridge of his nose, then opened them and gave her a tight smile. "I'm very sorry for scaring you." Then he closed the door to the laundry room, holstered his weapon, and dragged me away from the kitchen.

"What are you—"

He put a finger up to his lips again as he pushed me through the front door. Then he grabbed my hand and pulled me out to the street, away from the cabin.

This man was unbelievable.

I wrenched my hand away from his and crossed my arms. "Are you out of your mind? Did you seriously just drag me out of my own cabin?"

"I don't want her to hear," he said, his voice low and tense. "Why did you agree to let her use your dryer?"

I stared at him, dumbfounded. "Because she needed to. And she was terrified of getting in trouble, so I said I wouldn't say anything."

He pointed at the other cabins. "We're only half full. Are you telling me there's not an empty cabin she could use?"

I chewed my lip, glancing around. He was right. There were several cabins that didn't have vehicles parked in front of them.

"Maybe," I admitted.

"It's very strange. You'd think she would get in more trouble for invading a guest's privacy than being behind on her work if there's a legitimate maintenance issue."

"That's true." It was something I hadn't thought of before, but Sawyer was right. Creating a positive customer experience was usually the primary goal of a place like this. Without big name recognition, small businesses desperately needed good reviews. "But she told me she thought my cabin was empty. That they don't normally rent it out unless they're full."

He gave me a dark look. "That's fine, but why keep coming back once she knew you were here?"

"I don't know."

"How'd she get in?"

"She uses the back door. She has a key."

He started pacing. "This place gets weirder and weirder."

"I can agree with you there," I said, shuddering. I'd already felt a little weird about Penny being in the cabin. After hearing Sawyer's perspective, I knew I wasn't overreacting by wanting her gone. It was too creepy.

He stopped pacing, and his face softened just a bit. "What are you doing for dinner?"

"Dinner?" I blinked, confused by his sudden change of attitude.

"You've been here for hours and haven't eaten. What was your plan?"

"I brought groceries. Was going to grill a steak, why?"

"Perfect." He grabbed my hand and started dragging me toward his place.

"You have got to stop doing that," I said, yanking my hand out of his grip.

He flashed me a grin. "Sorry."

I glared at him, knowing he wasn't sorry at all. But I followed him anyway. "What are we doing?"

"Grabbing my own steak," he said. "And bourbon, if you like. But we can eat at your place. I'm interested in seeing how this Penny woman comes and goes."

"She's probably almost done," I said, wondering if I should protest his idea to have dinner together. Every minute I spent with him left me reeling, either with unwanted feeling or with irritation.

"Maybe." He unlocked his cabin door. Before walking inside, he slipped an arm around my waist and pulled me to him, planting a hot kiss on my mouth before I even knew what was happening.

I froze for one split second before melting into him. His soft lips on mine, his rough beard against my skin, his strong arm cradling me against his firm chest—my body responded hungrily before my mind had a chance to catch up. But almost as soon as it started, he stopped.

He whispered, his breath hot against my ear. "Cameras. Just creating a story for why we're going to be hanging out together so much tonight." Then he pushed me into the cabin and closed the door behind him, putting that warning finger to his lips again.

I'd never felt so stunned in my whole life.

He strode casually toward the kitchen. "So was that a yes on the bourbon? I also brought potatoes."

"I-I like potatoes," I said before shaking myself and marching into the kitchen to confront him. "What. Just. Happened?"

He flashed a wicked grin. "There's a security camera facing each of our doors. Probably has audio too. Somebody—the caretakers or owner or both—will have seen us going into each other's cabins by now. Be careful what you say on your porch or near the front door."

I let out a breath. "There was no need to kiss me. We could just be new friends hanging out."

He leaned over the counter, those forest-green eyes gazing at me too deeply for comfort. "Olivia, you're the most beautiful woman I've ever laid eyes on. Who's going to believe I'm cooking you a steak dinner to be friends?" He winked. "It's just part of our cover. No need to get so serious about it."

I scowled at him.

"Well that's a first," he said, chuckling.

"What's a first?"

"First time I've ever called a woman beautiful and offered to cook for her only to get a scowl in return."

"In case you haven't realized it yet, I'm not like most women," I said between gritted teeth. "And you're starting to really get on my nerves."

"Just starting?" He laughed. "My mom would say that means you're my soulmate."

"Hardly." I took a deep breath and prayed for patience. "And by the way? I will be grilling the steaks. There's no way I'm letting a neanderthal like you ruin the filet mignon I've been looking forward to all day." I reached into his refrigerator and grabbed the porterhouse he already had marinating, then stormed off toward my cabin.

Chapter Ten

I grabbed the bottle of bourbon and headed after Olivia, wondering if I'd pushed things too far. She was right. There had been no real need to kiss her.

Except that I'd wanted to.

And based on the way she'd melted into me, I was pretty sure she'd wanted it too.

She was fascinating, and something about her made me want to keep coming back for more. There was an interesting give and take and an immense satisfaction in seeing her get all riled up. I didn't normally enjoy being scowled at, but I downright liked it when she glared at me.

She was feisty. Knew her own mind. Guarded her secrets in a way that made me desperate to uncover them. Besides that, the chemistry between us was so palpable I knew she had to feel it too. I'd seen it in her eyes, felt it when she kissed me back.

She wouldn't admit it though. She marched toward her cabin like she was marching off to war.

Then she deliberately changed her posture, relaxing, before stepping onto the porch.

Interesting. It appeared that, despite her irritation with me, she was taking the hidden camera thing seriously, even going along with the cover story. I did the same, making sure I looked easy and relaxed—like a man heading in for a date—as I followed her inside. In reality, I was on high alert. Something felt very off about this place, and I wasn't entirely sure why.

The dryer was still running, so Olivia and I avoided any kind of real conversation, knowing that Penny could come back at any moment to check on it. I got to work chopping the potatoes, offering to fry them up on the stove since Olivia insisted on cooking the steaks. She agreed. When she came back from lighting the grill, she appeared to soften a bit toward me.

"I thought you were going to insist on being the one to grill the steaks," she said, giving me a little smirk as she seasoned her filet. "You know, make me do the 'woman's work' in the kitchen while you get the fun part."

"Well, I'm not a total neanderthal," I said, winking at her.

She blushed. "Maybe that was unfair."

"Nah. I probably deserved it." That was the closest I could bring myself to apologizing, because the reality was...I wasn't sorry I had kissed her. Not at all.

And I didn't think she was sorry about it, either.

She gave me a long look, followed by a tiny smile. "I was planning on burning your porterhouse."

"Ouch."

"I've changed my mind."

"I'm grateful," I said, grinning. "Nothing worse than an overcooked steak."

"I take it you want yours rare?"

"Medium-rare," I said. "How do you take yours?"

She smiled again, and this time, it reached her eyes. "Same."

"Good to know. Hey, have we met before? I swear, there's something so familiar about you."

Her guard immediately came back up as that mask shuttered over her eyes. "No, we haven't. I'm certain I'd remember you."

"Are you ever going to tell me your last name?"

She ignored the question, picked up the steaks, and headed outside.

I stared after her for a moment. She was bound and determined to keep her identity a secret from me. Why?

There was no way I could ignore the pull of a mystery like that.

I noticed she'd left her purse hanging on one of the kitchen chairs. With an eye on the door, I slipped a hand inside and pulled out her wallet, flipping it open to look at her driver's license.

My jaw dropped as I realized why Olivia had been so familiar to me from the moment I'd seen her.

Olivia Mitchell. Judge Mitchell's daughter.

She had his piercing blue eyes and his evasive nature. And if that weren't enough, the address on her license was his—an address I'd memorized a very long time ago.

After sliding the wallet back into her purse, I walked to the counter and picked up the knife to continue chopping potatoes. For the first time in a long time—maybe ever—I regretted my dogged need for information. Had I allowed Olivia to keep her secrets, we could have had a fun weekend. Enjoyed this chemistry that was between us without strings, without complications, while I worked to figure out what happened to Grace.

But that was over now.

I had no business being here with Judge Mitchell's daughter. I shouldn't have even been talking to her, much less having dinner in her cabin. This could blow everything.

Best move would be to make an excuse, go home, and keep my distance from her.

But that creepy housekeeper was still coming and going, and Olivia was still a young woman stuck alone in cabin thirteen. I'd never forgive myself if something happened to her when I could have prevented it.

So I convinced myself one dinner wouldn't hurt. I'd make sure she never knew who I was and get her to pack up and leave tomorrow.

. . .

OLIVIA KEPT HER DISTANCE AND I KEPT MINE WHILE SHE grilled the steaks to perfection and I fried up the potatoes on the stove. The housekeeper came and went two more times, then tentatively stuck her head in the kitchen, said she was finished, and thanked me for helping keep her secret. I nodded and waited until she was good and gone before going in there and checking the back door. It led to a large porch with the grill on one side and a hot tub on the other. Olivia looked up from the grill, expecting me to join her, but I went the other way.

It didn't take long to spot the security camera pointing right at the hot tub, hidden in an old bird's nest where most people might not notice it.

I walked over to the grill and pointed it out to Olivia.

"Ew." She shuddered as she pulled the steaks off the grill and plated them. Then she headed toward the back door.

"Just be aware if you go for a dip in that thing," I warned as I held the door open for her. "Who knows what he might do with the footage?"

She nodded her agreement as I followed her in. "I'm sure it's just for security," she said. "I guess hotels probably have the same thing at their pools and hot tubs. I've just never really thought about it before."

"Probably. The porch is nice otherwise though," I said, pulling glasses out of the kitchen cabinet as Olivia added the potatoes to our plates. "Has a great view of the woods. Very quiet."

"Not sure I'll be able to enjoy it knowing there are cameras out there, watching my every move," she said, raising that single eyebrow again.

And once again, I had to fight the temptation to kiss it.

"Maybe not," I agreed. "Listen, I'm going to lock up the back door now that Penny's done. But first, I need to apologize." I'd been thinking about it ever since I realized who she was. I never would have kissed her had I known she was Judge Mitchell's daughter. I'd crossed a boundary that never should have been crossed.

"What for this time?" she asked, giving me a smirk as she leaned one hip against the bar. She was so graceful that she made it look like a ballet pose. Even now, all I could think about was pulling her back into my arms and tasting that sweet mouth of hers again.

But that could never happen. Thankfully, my self-control was back in place.

"For kissing you," I said. "I took advantage, and I'm sorry."

Her mouth twisted up into a smile. "It's alright. It, ah, wasn't a bad kiss."

This time, I was the one arching an eyebrow. And the self-control I'd put into place started to crumble. "You think that's good? I can do a hell of a lot better than that."

For one moment, she appeared tempted. But then her face relaxed into an easy smile and she shook her head. "No. I think we'd better just keep things friendly, don't you?"

Friendly. Right. I nodded. "Yeah. I won't cross the line again. I'm sorry."

"Is crossing the line something you make a habit of?" She stared at me with piercing eyes that demanded the truth.

I let out a loud sigh. "With women? No. Never. Gotta say, you're the first woman I've struggled to keep my hands off of. But in my job, I have to cross all sorts of other lines. Kind of goes with the territory. I guess right now it's bleeding over."

"You've never told me what you do."

"Neither have you," I pointed out.

"Fair point." She took a deep breath, studying me. "Tell you what. Go lock up, and I will."

So I locked the back door. For good measure, I slid a kitchen chair underneath the handle, hoping it would at least delay anyone who tried to come in that way. Olivia put our plates on the kitchen table and we settled in for a dinner where I asked so many questions about her job as a book illustrator that, by the end, she seemed to have forgotten I still hadn't told her anything about myself.

Chapter Eleven

Olivia

Sawyer was someone I couldn't figure out. He was delightful at dinner, asking me all sorts of interesting questions about my work—and never once telling me a single personal thing about himself.

Which, unfortunately, made me even more curious.

He was ridiculously attractive. And it wasn't just his looks, though he'd certainly won the lottery there. His entire energy was magnetic. It drew me in and left me wanting more.

Which, I knew, was a very dangerous thing.

He was attracted to me, too. I recognized the desire in his eyes. More than that, I liked it. Wanted to feed it. Wanted to see exactly what it might feel like for him to cross the boundaries we'd set and kiss me the way he had on the front porch. Because I knew that the fire between us would burn hot. It would be a raging passion.

But as I took a tiny sip of his excellent bourbon and answered yet another question about my painting process, I made the decision to shelve that thought. Getting involved with him was akin to playing with fire. And if you played with fire, you were certain to get burned.

When we had finished dinner and completed a quick cleanup, Sawyer asked if I was ready to go to the bonfire.

"Are we really going to that?" I asked, surprised. I'd forgotten all about it.

"Why? Would you rather stay holed up in here with me?" There was a challenge in his eyes, one that told me all I needed to know. If I stayed here with him, we'd both get burned sooner rather than later.

"Good point," I said, hiding my smile. "It's probably safer for us both if we go to the bonfire."

He reached out, tucking a loose curl behind my ear. It was a sweet intimacy he hadn't earned the right to, but for some reason, I didn't object.

"Probably," he said. "Safer for me, anyway."

His gaze held mine, and for a moment, I felt completely lost for words, entirely caught up in this radiating heat between us. When I finally found my tongue, all I could think to say was, "I'll grab my coat."

"I'll be waiting."

It felt like a promise—and a threat.

THE BONFIRE WAS ALREADY RAGING WHEN WE ARRIVED, with logs popping and crackling and sending sparks up into the night sky. Out here, away from the safety of the cabins, the woods felt darker. More mysterious. More dangerous. I shoved my hands into my pockets for warmth and eyed the surrounding forest, shivering.

"You okay?" Sawyer asked.

I nodded and gave him a smile. I hadn't wanted to come, but I had to admit that this felt fun. Between the dark shadows of the woods, the cold night air, the heat of the blazing flames, and the thick smell of woodsmoke, it felt like a completely different world. It felt wild and thrilling and like anything could happen.

And a new part of me, one I'd never really had a chance to explore, found that she kind of liked that.

Quite a few people had shown up to the bonfire, but it appeared to be an awkward party, with no one really talking to anyone else. Sadie was there in a chair pulled far away from a couple that I assumed were her parents. She gave me a shy smile and a little wave.

"Let's sit there," I suggested, pointing Sawyer toward the empty space beside her.

He agreed and carried over the camping chairs we'd brought.

"I'm surprised you came," Sadie said as I set up my chair.

"Why?"

"Because this is lame and you're not," she said under her breath, rolling her eyes.

I smiled. "I don't know. It's kind of fun. Fall bonfires are classic. Besides, I was told there would be s'mores. And I don't know about you, but I'm excited about that. I've never had one before."

Her jaw dropped. "You've never had a s'more?"

I shook my head. Camping vacations weren't exactly my parents' idea of a good time. I'd never had the opportunity.

"Then you are going to love this," she laughed. She leaned forward, grabbed a metal tin, and handed it to me. It was overflowing with chocolate, marshmallows, and graham crackers.

I pulled out one of everything, then handed the tin to Sawyer.

"Is that your boyfriend?" Sadie asked. Her eyes had lit up in pure admiration. Not that I blamed her. He was a beautiful specimen of a man.

From a purely artistic point of view, of course.

"Just friends," I said.

"Too bad." She sighed, then lowered her voice. "He's gorgeous."

"Don't let him hear you say that," I whispered back. "His ego is already the size of Alaska."

She giggled and winked before changing the subject. "Here. You can use this to toast your marshmallow. Like this." She handed me a long metal fork and showed me how to put my marshmallow on the end.

I toasted it, built my very first s'more, and nearly came undone when I bit into it.

"Good?" she asked with a knowing grin.

"Oh my goodness. I had no idea what I was missing out on."

I caught a glimpse of Sawyer watching me and turned toward him.

"What?" I asked, unable to hold back my smile. The bonfire, the s'mores —this was so much more fun than I'd imagined.

"You, uh. You've got something right here," he said before reaching out and wiping the side of my mouth, letting his thumb slide gently over my bottom lip.

I almost came undone again, this time for a completely different reason.

And when he took that thumb and popped it into his mouth, I lost my ability to speak.

"Chocolate," he said, still holding my gaze.

I blinked twice. "Um. Thank you." Then I turned back to Sadie, attempting to regain any semblance of control. "Are those your parents?" I asked, pointing at the couple sitting down from her. They appeared to be having a tense conversation.

"Yep." Her smile faded.

"Is everything okay there?" I also understood what it was like to live with parents who hated each other.

She sighed. "Not really. But I don't want to talk about it."

"That's okay," I said.

Before I even got the words out, her mom had caught us watching them. She immediately put on a polite smile and rose, coming over to introduce herself.

"Hi," she said, sticking out a hand for me to shake. "I'm Rachel, and that's my husband, Ethan. Sadie, is this the artist you were telling me about?"

"Yeah." Sadie crossed her arms and looked away.

"Thank you for being so sweet to our girl," Rachel said warmly. "She was very impressed with your work."

"Of course," I said. "I told her she's welcome to join me and sketch while I'm here. If that's okay with you."

"Yes! In fact, I'd love it. She could use some good influence in her life."

Sadie rolled her eyes, sinking deeper into her seat.

I felt a stab of sympathy for Rachel. She seemed genuinely concerned about her kid, and while I didn't know her well, I got the impression she was an involved, caring mom.

"I'll be hiking in the morning, looking for some interesting scenes to paint. Want to come?" I directed the question toward Sadie.

She glanced up at her mom, who subtly nodded. "Yeah. What time?"

"We can meet by the lake at eight, if that's not too early."

"Perfect," Rachel said, beaming. "That will give you something fun to do tomorrow. I'll go tell your dad." She smiled again—hesitant this time—then walked back to her husband and gave him the news.

He shot me a look, then seemed to protest under his breath.

Sadie just sighed. "Sorry. They argue about everything."

"I can relate," I said, giving her a conspiratorial smile. "My parents do too."

She leaned forward in her chair, a desperate expression on her face. "Did they ever divorce?"

"No," I said, sighing. "Though sometimes I wished they would."

"Yeah." She looked down, gripping the sides of her chair. "I know what you mean. I used to hope they'd make up and be okay, but now—" Her cell phone buzzed and she cut off, grabbing it. "Finally! I'll be back." She jumped up and headed toward the cabins for privacy.

Rachel's face fell. Ethan lifted his hands as if to say, "What did you expect?"

I was watching them when Adam—the all-black-wearing guy who'd invited us to the bonfire—came up and blocked my view. He slapped me on the shoulder and reached out to shake Sawyer's hand.

"Aw, man, I'm glad you guys made it," he said. "Hey, Eve, come over here! Let's hang with these guys." He plopped down in the chair Sadie had vacated.

I found myself wishing she hadn't left.

Eve came over and sat on his lap since there wasn't another chair empty. "How long have you guys been together?" she asked, eyeing us both.

"We're not," I said.

"Well, the weekend just started, am I right?" Adam said, reaching around me trying to fist-bump Sawyer. Sawyer gave him a polite smile and didn't respond, leaving Adam's fist hanging in midair.

Adam ignored the slight and kept going with his chirpy attitude. It seemed whatever substances had slowed him down earlier had worn off —or perhaps he'd taken something to speed himself up. Whatever the case, he was significantly more energetic than he had been when we'd met him.

"So, for fun, I thought we could tell the Hidden Gem ghost stories tonight," he said, his face lighting up in glee.

"Ghost stories?" I asked, amused. Adam was a grown man, and I thought it was hilarious that he was excited by something so juvenile.

"Oh yeah," Eve jumped in, her face dead serious. "This place is totally haunted."

"Totally," Adam agreed, nodding. "It's why we're here."

Sawyer leaned forward in his chair. "Let me guess. You're ghost hunters?"

Adam grinned. "How'd you know?"

Sawyer didn't return his smile. "I saw you unloading equipment earlier."

Eve's eyes brightened. "You guys could join us, you know. We're shooting video for our channel. It would be so fun to add another couple to the mix. We could cover twice the ground!"

Sawyer shook his head. "No, thanks."

"I don't know. It sounds kind of fun to me," I said, taking the opportunity to tease him. He was clearly uncomfortable with the ghost hunting thing, and I liked seeing him off his normal stride.

Besides, this bonfire was turning out to be a kind of fun I'd never really experienced. What if ghost hunting was the same way?

Before he could respond, Adam pushed Eve off his lap and called for attention. When everyone stopped their quiet conversations and looked up at him, he spoke.

"Who here has heard about the ghosts of Hidden Gem Lake?" he asked, raising his red plastic cup as if in toast.

A few hands went up. Eve raised hers, of course, as did Ethan, Sadie's dad. A sulking teenage boy raised his, along with a jovial-looking man I presumed to be his father. The woman beside them raised hers, too, with an amused smile on her face.

And then, Sawyer raised his.

I sent him a questioning look and thought I saw a flash of guilt on his face.

"It's a great story," Adam said, grinning before taking a long swig from his cup. He started walking slowly around the fire.

The flames sizzled and popped, illuminating his face and casting dark shadows behind him. I watched, feeling a strange sensation—as if we'd entered into a new realm, one touched by magic, where anything could happen.

After completing his circle, he began telling his story in a clear, powerful voice meant for the stage. "Over a hundred years ago, this land belonged to a man named Abel MacLaine, who fell in love with a young woman named Grace. She was a beautiful girl—blonde hair, blue eyes, a real beauty. It was said that she could have had her pick of men. People laughed at Abel, saying he didn't have a chance with her. He was rough around the edges, a real wilderness man. But Grace loved him. And when he asked her to marry him, she said yes."

I stared at Sawyer, who refused to meet my gaze. *Grace.* That was a strange coincidence indeed.

"What happened?" Rachel asked, mesmerized by the story.

Adam took his time before he answered, obviously enjoying the drama of it all. "Grace had an older sister named Ethel. Ethel and Grace were about as different as different could be. Grace was small and dainty. Ethel was tall and clumsy. Grace had golden hair and a creamy complexion. Ethel's hair was red and her nose was covered with freckles that wouldn't fade no matter how many times she scrubbed her face with buttermilk. Everyone knew that Ethel was jealous of Grace. But that jealousy grew out of control when Abel asked Grace to marry him."

"Was Ethel in love with Abel?" Sadie asked, startling me. I'd been so entranced by Adam's tale I hadn't even noticed her slipping back to the group.

Adam shrugged. "I don't know if she loved him or not. All I know is that she was a spinster who was jealous of her sister's happiness and was determined to stop it."

"So, what happened?" Sadie leaned forward, eagerly awaiting his answer.

Adam gave her a long look, taking his time before answering. He was clearly a natural storyteller who knew how to build suspense. Even I was on the edge of my seat, waiting for him to continue.

"Ethel pouted during the engagement, especially when Abel built a beautiful cabin for him and Grace to live in. See, Ethel was still stuck at home with her parents, having never received a marriage proposal. And she knew that, at her age, one wasn't likely to come. The thought of her sister moving out and having such a beautiful home was just salt in the wound.

"On the day before the wedding, the whole family came out to move Grace's things in. Ethel came and pretended to help. But with every hour that passed, she became angrier and angrier, until finally, she was seething with rage."

My stomach sank. I pinched Sawyer's arm to get his attention.

"Ow," he said, looking back at me.

"It's cabin thirteen, isn't it?" I whispered. "The one Abel built for Grace?"

He nodded as Adam continued his story.

"Ethel stormed off after slamming down a porcelain teapot so hard it shattered. Came back an hour later and apologized, said she was emotional about losing her sister, that was all, and that if they spent some quality time together, she'd feel better. Suggested they go swimming in the lake."

Adam made one more slow loop around the fire. "Both sisters went in the water." He paused, spinning slowly as he made eye contact with everyone in turn. "But only one of them came out."

Sadie and Rachel both gasped in unison.

"She killed her!" Sadie said, her eyes wide with shock.

Adam's lips twisted in a sly smile as he shrugged. "No one for sure knows what happened. Ethel claimed it was an accident, and though not everyone believed her, there was no proof otherwise. She said Grace got a cramp and couldn't swim back to shore. Claimed she tried to help her but was a weak swimmer and couldn't."

"Tell them what happened after that," Eve popped up, enjoying Adam's story as much as everyone else.

"Abel was heartbroken. But, thankfully, Ethel was there to comfort him. They shared their grief together and formed their own kind of bond. It wasn't the kind of love he and Grace had, but it was enough for Ethel. After a year, he asked her to marry him. She said yes, of course."

This time, I popped in with a question. "Did they live in cabin thirteen?"

Adam shook his head. "Nope. Abel said he'd put all his dreams for Grace into that place and couldn't possibly live there with another woman. He built a second cabin to share with Ethel. It's the one the caretakers live in now. He didn't want to even see the lake from his windows. Cabin thirteen was abandoned and fell into disrepair until he and Ethel died. But that's another story." He winked.

"Tell it!" Sadie said.

The teenage boy gave a little laugh, but the look he gave her was good-natured. She blushed when she looked back at him, but then she smiled.

A connection, I thought, though I wasn't sure if that was a good thing. He seemed angry, and she didn't need any more of that.

"Alright," Adam said, laughing. He resumed his stroll around the fire, gearing up for another story. "Abel and Ethel lived in the caretaker's cottage until they were in their sixties. Then one day, something happened. The only witness was a young girl who was here helping Ethel with her sewing, as Ethel's eyesight had started deteriorating. She said Abel stormed into the cottage, yelling, asking Ethel how could she."

"How could she what?" the teenager asked—glancing at Sadie in a way that made me think he was trying to win brownie points.

"The girl didn't hear," Adam answered, shrugging. "Abel grabbed Ethel by the arm and dragged her out of the house. The girl followed behind at a distance, not wanting him to notice her. He dragged Ethel all the way down the road to the lake, pointed at it, and screamed at her. The girl couldn't make out everything he said, but she swore she heard the words 'ghost,' 'killed,' and 'her.'"

I shivered again, trying to remind myself that it was just a story. But here, underneath the black sky, surrounded by a shadow-filled forest, and the raging flames of the bonfire, everything felt entirely too...possible.

Adam continued. "The girl said Ethel's face turned white and she started shaking, looking around like she was terrified. The girl was frightened and ran away. Told her parents, who came to see what was going on. When they got here, Abel and Ethel were both dead."

"Dead?" Sadie's jaw dropped.

Admittedly, mine did too.

Adam nodded, a satisfied look on his face. "It was a mystery, never to be solved. There was no obvious cause of death. Both bodies were by the lake, almost like they'd both had heart attacks where they were standing. They were buried here on the land."

I felt the color drain from my face. "Buried here?"

He looked my way and grinned. "Yeah. Their graves are back behind the caretaker's cottage."

"This is so creepy!" Sadie said, twisting the edges of her sleeves.

"It gets better," Eve said, jumping up to join Adam. "After their deaths, they found Ethel's journals. They were full of times when she thought she'd seen her sister's ghost. People who'd been around back then said it was just her guilty conscience. But when their son inherited the land and started rehabbing cabin thirteen, all sorts of strange things started happening."

Adam slung his arm around Eve's neck. "Yep. Over the years, there have been stories about odd things happening here, especially in cabin thirteen. Items moved, unexplained noises, the smell of lavender. Some people claim to have seen the ghosts of all three of them. And then there have been the deaths."

"Deaths?" The teenage boy's voice squeaked in a way that clearly embarrassed him—until Sadie shot him an empathetic smile.

Adam nodded. "Oh yeah. Like I said, this place is totally haunted. There's been a string of crazy deaths, all happening here on the property. Get this—last year, a girl named Grace actually drowned in the lake, just like Ethel's sister!"

Sawyer spoke up, his voice cold. "I'm surprised you find death so amusing."

Adam looked like he wanted to roll his eyes. "Aw, man, all respect and everything to those who died. But places like this are what I live for. It's a real-life haunting, man! A serious one, with real danger! Who knows? Someone could even die tonight."

"You'd deliberately bring your fiancée somewhere she might be in danger?"

Eve blew it off. "Adam will protect me. He knows everything about ghosts."

But all I could think about were his words.

"Someone could die tonight."

CHAPTER TWELVE

THE MAN BESIDE THE TEENAGER STOOD UP, OBVIOUSLY trying to break the tension. "Whoa, no need for anyone to get freaked out," he said, grinning. "Adam, maybe no more beer, okay? Nobody's going to die tonight. It's just a ghost story. You know how these things get twisted and blown out of proportion."

"No," Adam insisted, shaking his head. "This is the real deal."

The man held up his hands. "Hey, man, I know you're here to ghost hunt and you're into that whole thing. But there are kids here, and not everyone likes a good scare. Let's maybe change the tone for a bit, alright?"

I spoke up. "I think that's an excellent idea."

The man crossed to our side of the fire, sticking a hand out for me to shake. "The name's Joseph. That's my wife, Meg, and my son, Joey."

I shook his hand, taking a second to study the family. Physically, Joseph and Joey looked like twins twenty years apart. Thin builds, curly brown hair, and a bit of scruff like they'd both decided to attempt growing a beard for this getaway. But personality-wise, they seemed to be complete opposites. Joseph was friendly and smiling. Joey looked like he'd slug you if you even looked at him the wrong way.

Meg—a brunette with a pretty face and a killer body—seemed to have more in common with Joey than her husband. She'd made no attempts to talk to anyone at the bonfire, smiling only when Adam had brought up the ghost stories. Her leg twitched like she was desperate to get up and escape all this family bonding.

"This is Olivia," I said, introducing her to Joseph as if she were mine. Frankly, unlike her, I hoped people assumed we were there together. It made it less suspicious that I was there alone.

Joseph grasped Olivia's hand, giving her a warm smile. "Nice to meet you guys. You know, all this ghost story stuff is just good fun. Don't let it get to you. We're going to have a great weekend."

"I hope so," Olivia said, her smile strained.

She'd been blindsided by the history of this place, and it was clear by her guarded posture and pained expression that it scared her.

At least now, maybe she'd trade cabins with me.

Joseph turned back to me. "You fish? I've heard the lake's full of trout. I'm going to do some fishing in the morning and try to catch our dinner."

His wife let out a sharp laugh from across the fire, rolling her eyes.

A pained expression briefly crossed Joseph's face.

"I fish some," I said. "I didn't bring my gear though."

"Oh, I've got plenty! You want to join, just come on over. I brought enough to share."

"Maybe I'll do that."

He brightened, shaking my hand again before walking back over to his family. He sat down by his wife, who subtly moved her body away from his.

Meanwhile, Olivia had scooted closer to me. I glanced over and noticed she was still wound tight, biting her bottom lip as she looked around like she expected a ghost to jump out of the woods at any moment.

"You ready to get out of here?" I asked, nudging her knee with my own.

She looked over at me and nodded, her eyes still wide.

I stood and put out a hand to help her up, then grabbed the camping chairs and tucked them under my arm. But as we started to walk away, the caretakers pulled up in their truck, flagging us down.

"Hold up," Felix called as he swung out of the cab and hobbled his way toward the fire. "We've got something to say. Easier to tell everybody at once." His face was hard.

Olivia and I exchanged glances as we headed back to the group.

"There's a storm coming," he announced. "Blew up out of nowhere. Looks to be a bad one. They're calling for seventy-mile-an-hour wind gusts, so make sure you don't leave anything outside tonight. All these chairs need to be picked up and put away, you hear?"

"Aww, that's a shame," Joseph said, standing and gesturing for his family to do the same. "We were having such a nice time."

Olivia looked at me, even more uncertain. "That doesn't sound good. Maybe I really should just pack up and drive home tonight."

"It's too late for that," Deb warned. "The storm will be here soon, and you don't want to be on those gravel roads when it comes. You're liable to get stranded and be in worse shape than you will be here, that's for sure."

"You know what this means," Adam said, clapping his hands. "Storms bring the electrical energy ghosts need to communicate. We'll see one for sure tonight!"

Felix and Deb exchanged glances. Deb started to speak, but Felix cocked his head and gave her a warning look. She clamped her mouth shut and crossed her arms.

Rachel stood, suddenly realizing Sadie had disappeared again. "Honey," she said, grabbing Ethan's arm. "Sadie! She's not here. We have to find her."

He jumped up. "Wait a sec." He pointed at Joseph. "Your son's gone too!"

Joseph and Meg both looked around, confused, before realizing he was right. Joseph grinned. "That's my boy. He's quite the ladies' man!"

Rachel turned white. "We have to find them."

I stepped forward. "I'll help look."

"I will too," Olivia offered.

"Come on, Eve," Adam said, tugging at her arm. "Let's go set up our equipment."

"Aren't you going to help find the kids?" Rachel asked.

"Yeah," Ethan added. "We could use all the help we can get."

Adam waved them off. "I'm sure they're fine. They're probably getting it on in one of your cabins. You'll find them." He pulled Eve away as she shot an apologetic look over her shoulder.

Rachel stared at them, disgusted.

"Let's split up," Ethan suggested. "I heard Sadie mention wanting to see the waterfall at the end of the trail. I'm going to look there."

"I'll check our cabin," Rachel said. They hurried off in opposite directions.

"And I'll check ours," Joseph said, looking to his wife for confirmation. "That's probably where they are, if I know Joey."

Meg nodded. "I'll look around here, I guess, see if they just slipped off and found a spot to cozy up."

"We'll look down by the lake," I offered, grabbing Olivia's hand. This time, she didn't yank it away.

"Good luck to you all," Felix said. "We're heading back to our house before the storm hits."

Meg grabbed his arm. "You aren't going to help look? There are kids missing."

Felix just shrugged. "Not our responsibility, is it? Shoulda kept an eye on them teenagers before they snuck off to do God knows what. Come on, Deb." They started walking back to the road without looking back.

Olivia gripped my hand. "I hope Sadie's okay."

"Me too."

Because I was getting a real bad feeling about things. And if there was one thing I'd learned over the course of my career, it was to trust my bad feelings.

"Stay close to me," I murmured under my breath, taking the lead as we walked toward the lake.

Olivia looked up at me and swallowed hard, nodding. She never dropped my hand, so I didn't let go, either.

"It's spooky out here," she said as we got farther from the light of the fire.

"Don't let the ghost stories get to you," I said. "This is the same place it was earlier today."

"Right," she said, her tone laced with sarcasm. "A place where your friend died mysteriously. That makes me feel so much better."

I chuckled. "It wasn't meant to. I'm just saying you shouldn't focus on supernatural threats when there might be real ones."

"Unless a ghost is the real threat," she countered. "Don't you think it's really strange that the original Grace was a beautiful blonde woman, and that she drowned in the lake just like your friend?"

"It's definitely a strange coincidence," I agreed.

"More than strange." She stared ahead at the lake in front of us. The trees surrounding it were nothing but a black silhouette casting dark reflections onto the surface of the water. The moon had risen, full and bright, illuminating the shelf of storm clouds moving in.

Even I had to agree it was an eerie sight.

I headed straight for the boathouse, knowing that an empty building was a prime make-out spot for teens. It was an old building—rough wood planks built on a foundation of piled up boulders in the water. The roof was sagging, like one bad storm could make it cave in.

"I hope they aren't in there," Olivia said, worried.

I dropped her hand to inspect the door. Padlocked.

"They're not, unless they entered through the water," I said, glancing up at the windows. They were small—too small for the teens to slip through—and didn't appear to have been opened in quite some time.

"That seems like that would be a terrible idea."

"You afraid of the water?"

"At night? Yes. Actually, during the day, also yes," she said, giving a tiny laugh. "I've never been much of a swimmer."

"Maybe I could teach you," I said before thinking it through. Here I was, still thinking I might have a chance with Olivia, but I needed to get my head on straight and remember that she was Judge Mitchell's daughter. Pretty soon, we wouldn't even be friends, much less anything else.

"Maybe," she said absently, still staring out at the lake. "I don't see anyone out here. Maybe we should look somewhere else."

"We should check the kayaks."

"The kayaks?"

I flashed her a grin, pointing at the kayaks lined up on the other side of the boathouse. "If I was a teenager looking for a place to make out and couldn't get into the boathouse, that's where I'd go."

That eyebrow arched up and she smiled for the first time since the ghost stories. "Yeah, I bet you would."

We hurried over and searched the kayaks, separating to cover ground more quickly. The clouds were building, and the winds had already picked up. They howled through the trees, echoing over the lake. This was going to be a monster storm. We needed to find the kids fast. This was not the kind of thing anyone needed to be out in.

"They aren't here," Olivia called from the last kayak, clearly worried sick.

"It's okay," I said. "We'll—"

But my words were cut off by Rachel running toward us, waving. "We found them!"

"You did?" Olivia rushed forward.

"Yes." Rachel practically sagged in relief. "It was like Ethan said. They had walked to the waterfall. They were already on their way back when he headed down the trail. I just wanted you to know so you wouldn't keep searching."

The first bolt of lightning cracked the sky.

"We'd all better take cover," I said. "It's moving in quick."

"Agreed. Thank you again," Rachel said. "See you guys in the morning." She turned and ran toward her cabin, pulling her jacket over her head as the first raindrops began to fall. Within seconds, the drops became heavy sheets of rain, soaking us to the bone.

"Come on," I said, grabbing Olivia's hand again. "What did you decide about switching cabins?"

"At this point, I think I'll just stay in mine," she yelled as we dashed toward number thirteen. "All my stuff is there, and I'm going to want dry clothes."

It was too loud to even answer as thunder crashed and the wind roared. So I waited until we made it under the cover of her porch. Even there, the noise was deafening as the rain pelted the metal roof.

"Are you sure you want to stay here after everything?" I yelled over the torrent. "I don't mind carrying your stuff to mine."

She shook her head, shivering. Raindrops clung to her eyelashes, and her lips quivered from the cold. I couldn't look away, entranced by her beauty.

She stared at me for a split second, then threw her arms around my neck and brought those lips to mine. I was caught off guard but quickly recovered. I dropped the chairs I was carrying and put my hands on her waist, pulling her tight against me as she let those luscious lips part ever so slightly. I took full advantage, deepening the kiss until she suddenly broke away.

"Purely tactical," she stage-whispered in my ear. "Can't forget about the cameras."

She gave me a wink and disappeared inside, closing the door and leaving me gaping on the porch.

"Lock up," I hollered when I'd recovered my senses.

"Already have." Her musical voice came through the door.

I tested it anyway to make sure. Then I pulled the hood of my jacket over my head to walk back to my cabin alone.

The rain drove down in sheets, drenching the ground and turning the dirt path to mud. Thunder echoed through the valley, and fierce winds ripped through the trees.

I breathed a sigh of relief that we had found the teens before it had started. Nobody should be out in this.

But when lightning lit up the sky, I saw two figures—one male, one female—huddled underneath the awning of the boat shed. It was too dark to make out who it was, but their body language suggested they were in the middle of a heated argument.

Adam's words echoed through my mind: *"Someone might die tonight."*

Chapter Thirteen

Olivia

I CLOSED MY EYES AND LEANED AGAINST THE DOOR, fighting a smile as I listened to Sawyer walk away. I'd caught him off guard with that kiss. Fair payback after the way he'd surprised me.

Sawyer had kissed back—with passion and electricity I'd never felt before. I had nearly lost my senses and forgotten to pull away, until a bolt of lightning had made me jump.

Though part of me regretted ending the encounter, the look on his face when I'd told him it was purely tactical was pure gold. Take that, Sawyer Reed. Two could play at this game.

When I opened my eyes and remembered where I was, my heart fell. Sadie's disappearance had been such a distraction that I'd forgotten how creepy this place really was. It was so much worse now, alone here in the dark save for the blank stares of the countless animals mounted on the wall. Dozens of lives ended, frozen in time, watching me as if they were waiting for me to join them. Antlers scattered like trophies of death, a stark reminder of how fleeting life was—and how there were those among us who enjoyed the thrill of the hunt, the power of a kill.

Beyond that, there was a deep sadness in knowing why this cabin had been built and the heartache it held. I'd always smiled at ghost stories, enjoying a good scare and taking them all in fun. But Adam's story about this land and the people who'd lived here felt too real. Like I could almost feel Ethel's bitterness and Abel's heartbreak. Like Grace— Abel's Grace—was trapped here too, like these animals on the wall. Watching. Waiting.

I shivered as a cold chill went down my spine.

Shaking myself, I went to my room and peeled off my sopping-wet clothes, drying off with a towel before putting on warm pajamas.

A less stubborn woman would march herself over to Sawyer's and agree to switch cabins—or ask to stay in his with him, which, admittedly, was a tempting thought for several reasons. But I couldn't let a silly ghost story scare me into making a mistake like that. Besides, I was here and dry. There was no sense in going back outside in this.

So I gave myself a pep talk, then checked all the windows to make sure they were locked. Next, I checked the doors, smiling when I saw the chair Sawyer had shoved under the back entrance Penny had been going in and out of. Despite his arrogance, he was a thoughtful guy with a protective nature, and I found myself liking him more and more.

With the locks secure, I walked over to the shelf with the obituaries, wondering if it would be disrespectful to set them face down. It was a silly thing, but I already felt uncomfortable with all the animals staring at me. The human faces in the obituaries were even worse—especially the one of Grace, Sawyer's friend.

What had happened to her? I studied the newspaper clipping, willing it to give me answers. People drowned. It was just a fact of life in a land blessed with water. But for someone named Grace to drown in the same lake that was supposedly haunted by a Grace who had drowned there a century before? That was beyond weird.

When I'd originally seen the obituaries, I'd felt comforted that there wasn't a clear pattern to the victims. But when I looked at them now, I began to wonder if there was a pattern we just hadn't seen because I didn't know the story. Three of the women were young blondes. Two were older women in their sixties. Two were older men. And one was a young, handsome man—an outdoorsy type, by the description, who'd died in a freak fall while hiking.

Could they represent Grace, Ethel, Abel, and a young version of Abel? The Abel that Grace had never been able to marry? Or...the Abel that had never truly loved Ethel?

Could a ghost commit murder?

The very thought made the hair on the back of my neck stand straight up.

"Stop it," I spoke aloud. "You're making up a pattern where there is none. Ghosts—if they're even real—can't possibly kill people."

The worst I'd ever heard of a supposed ghost doing was knocking over some books or making a person feel cold. I had absolutely nothing to worry about.

Still, I placed the obituaries face down. I needed to put all of this out of my mind as much as possible.

After that, there was nothing left to do. I wanted a shower, but I knew that showering during a thunderstorm was just asking for trouble. I didn't feel like painting or doing anything productive, really. My mind was too scattered, thinking of ghosts and heartbreak. So I tucked my gun underneath my pillow, hunkered down inside my bed, and tried to sleep. But with Adam's stories playing on repeat in my mind, sleep was hard to find.

A LOUD CRASH OF THUNDER WOKE ME IN THE DEAD OF night. I sat up, my heart pounding, and checked my watch. It was just after midnight, and the storm hadn't let up at all. If anything, it had strengthened.

With the way my heart was racing, I knew I would be unable to sleep. I slipped out of bed, grabbed a blanket to wrap around my shoulders, and padded down toward the kitchen. I'd noticed a basket of continental breakfast items on the counter. Maybe I'd find an herbal tea that could help me wind back down.

I flicked on the kitchen light and thumbed through the teas in the basket. Earl Grey, Orange Pekoe, English Breakfast—ah. Finally. There was a bag of chamomile. I put on a pot of water and placed the teabag in a coffee mug, then stood to wait, yawning even as the aroma of the dried herbs hit. Chamomile had been my "sleepy" tea ever since I'd been a child. One whiff of it was enough to start calming my nervous system.

I picked up the cup and took another whiff of the dry tea bag, yawning again—then froze.

Lavender.

My trembling hand lowered the mug to the bar. No. It couldn't be lavender. It was just the chamomile. Both plants had sweet, floral scents. Maybe I was overly tired.

The water started to boil. I quickly turned off the burner and poured the hot water over the teabag, grateful when the distinctive aroma of chamomile bloomed, displacing what I'd smelled before.

I moved to the sink to check the cabinets for sugar or honey. A flash of lightning illuminated the landscape outside the window—and I screamed when I saw the silhouette of a man standing just off the porch, staring through the glass at me. It was over in an instant, as the world went dark again. I froze, staring, until the storm lit up the yard once more.

He was gone.

I stood there for half an hour, watching. Waiting, though for what I wasn't sure. When all was quiet and the storm finally began dying down, I checked all my locks again, then went back to bed.

For good measure, I locked my bedroom door, too.

SOFT LIGHT SPILLED IN THROUGH THE SHEER CURTAINS when I woke. I sat up and stretched like a cat, smiling, before going to the window to look. The sun was starting to rise, painting the world with the hazy tones of dawn. Everything felt soft, fresh, and reborn. I loved early mornings and the promise they held.

But more importantly, I'd made it through the night without any ghostly encounters. I felt a bit silly thinking about my fear the night before. Now, the storm was over, I could leave if I wanted, and everything was going to be okay.

I pulled off my sweats, tossing them into my suitcase before grabbing fresh clothes and heading to the bathroom. My hair smelled of campfire smoke, and I had smudges of ash on my face that had gone unseen in my hurry to get to bed the night before. I glanced at my watch, checking to make sure I had plenty of time before I needed to meet Sadie. A long, hot shower was exactly what I needed to feel like myself again.

I turned the faucet to hot, letting steam fill the bathroom, then stepped into the shower and let the warm water wash over me as I hummed a favorite song, reveling in the clean scent of soap and shampoo. When the water turned cold, I reluctantly turned off the tap and dried off. I threw on my clothes, along with sunscreen and lip balm, and quickly dried my hair. Then I headed to the kitchen to grab a bite to eat.

I could feel that something was wrong the minute I walked into the living room.

"Hello?" I called.

Nobody answered.

I scanned the room, searching for movement, but it was clear nobody was there. It was just a feeling—a feeling of fear that had crept up my toes and wrapped around my legs like vines strangling a tree.

It took a moment before I realized what had changed. The obituaries were back in place. Eight photographs of dead people stared accusingly at me from the shelf.

I stood staring, frozen, until a timid knock made me jump. For a second, I wondered if it was paranormal. Was something here trying to communicate?

Then it happened again and I realized someone was at the door. I put my hand on my chest and let out a breath, trying to get my heart rate to return to normal.

This place was getting to me, and Sawyer was right. I needed to pack up my bags and head back to the city. Or...somewhere. Anywhere but here.

I walked to the door and answered it, finding Sadie on my porch. Her face was red and her eyes were swollen, like she'd been sobbing. She stood with her hoodie pulled over her head and her arms crossed in a protective posture.

"Oh, sweetie. What's wrong?"

"Nothing." She sniffed, pulling those arms tighter. "I'm here to draw."

"Right." With everything that had just happened, I'd almost forgotten. "Let me grab a bite to eat. Then I'll get my gear. Do you want to come in for a minute?"

She nodded and walked past me, plopping down on the couch.

I headed to the kitchen. "Do you want a granola bar, or some water, or something?"

"No, thanks."

"Okay. Make yourself at home. I'll be right back." I pulled a granola bar from the counter and scarfed it down. Then I went to my room and grabbed my *plein air* watercolor kit.

On impulse, I grabbed some extra brushes and a few more sheets of watercolor paper in case Sadie wanted to give painting a try.

"Alright, we can go," I said, walking back toward the living room. "But just for a couple of hours. I think I'm going to check out today and head home."

"Because of the ghost stuff?" Her face was serious.

"Yes. I know that sounds silly." I blushed.

She shook her head, then glanced around. "I don't think it's silly at all. This whole place is creepy. And I swear I can smell lavender in here, like he was saying."

"Right?" I was astonished—but grateful to have it confirmed by someone else. "I thought I was losing my mind last night."

"No, I totally smell it. This cabin feels spooky."

"Is yours decorated like this?" I asked, curious.

"You mean with all the dead animals?"

"Yeah."

She nodded. "Yep. You should see our bathroom. The entire wall is covered in fish jaws."

"Fish jaws?"

"Yeah. Like the open jaws, with all the teeth. They're nailed over the wall. There's even a big set nailed up around the light switch so you have to stick your hand through it to turn on the light."

"That's...really weird."

"Isn't it? But at least we don't seem to have a ghost." She giggled, finally relaxing a little bit. "I wish I could leave today too."

"It's hard not having the choice, isn't it?" I understood that well.

She nodded, sighing. "Yep. I'm counting down the days until I turn eighteen and can do whatever I want. Like you."

This time, I was the one to sigh. If only it were that simple. I was several years past eighteen and still had very little real control over my own life. But there was no need to burst Sadie's bubble.

"Come on," she said. "Let's go have some fun before you leave and I'm stuck here without you."

"Okay." I gave her a little smile. "How was the waterfall last night? Worth painting?"

Her eyes lit up. "Yeah, I think so. It was pretty dark, but what we could see with the flashlights was really cool. It's not a big waterfall or anything, but still pretty neat. Had some big boulders out front, and there's a little gazebo thing out there, where you can sit and watch it. It's pretty."

"Even better. I love a covered place to paint. Let's check it out," I said. "I got some nice sketches of the lake yesterday. I want to do something different this morning."

"Okay." She agreed and we headed out, locking the cabin behind us.

"You take the lead," I said when we got to the trailhead—trailhead being a generous word for what was in front of us. The caretakers were too old to take care of this place properly, and while someone had done a cursory job of keeping a thin trail in place, it wasn't wide enough for us to walk side by side.

"It's not far," she said. "Just five minutes."

"Perfect."

But we only made it two minutes down the trail before Sadie stopped suddenly—and screamed.

Chapter Fourteen

Sawyer

After a night spent tossing and turning with my body on high alert, I finally dozed off near sunrise only to wake soon after with someone pounding on my door.

"This is not my idea of a getaway," I grumbled as I rolled out of bed and walked to the living room, wiping the sleep—or lack thereof—from my eyes.

"What?" I spat as I threw the door open—immediately softening when I saw Olivia and Sadie standing there.

Olivia's eyes went wide before straying downward, taking in the sight of my bare chest. She opened her mouth as if to say something, but nothing came out.

"Like what you see?" I asked, grinning as I purposely propped an arm up on the doorframe, flexing. But my grin faded when I realized something was wrong.

Terribly wrong.

"Come inside," I said, opening the door for both of them. Whatever it was, I didn't want them saying it on the front porch in front of the cameras.

Olivia reached for Sadie's hand and pulled her into the cabin. I shut the door behind them and turned, crossing my arms in front of my chest.

"What happened?"

Sadie burst into tears.

Olivia glanced at her, then back to me. "Can we talk privately?"

I nodded and gestured toward the back bedroom, waiting for Olivia to walk first so that I could follow her. I didn't mind her seeing my chest, but the scars on my back tended to raise questions. Questions I wasn't in the mood to answer.

When we got to my room, Olivia started pacing, clasping her hands together like she was praying for a miracle.

I closed the door and leaned against it. "What's going on?"

She let out a shaky breath. "We went on the trail to the waterfall, planning to paint. Sadie was in front, but she stopped and screamed. I pushed past her to see what the matter was—Sawyer, it was Ethan, her dad. I think...I think he's dead."

"You think? Or you know?"

She swallowed hard. "I mean, I know. He's dead. It just feels so... final. To say it like that."

"Did you touch him?" I needed to know how sure she was—and if she'd messed up any evidence.

She nodded. "To check his pulse, yeah. Though I really didn't need to." She turned green.

"Sit," I said, steering her to my bed and gently pushing her down by her shoulders.

She sank down, pressing her hands together between her knees like she could somehow stop them from shaking. "I didn't know what to do. I told Sadie to stay back. That we'd go for help. I don't know... I don't know if she realizes. She didn't want to leave, but I told her she had to. I didn't want her to see him like that."

"You did the right thing. Have you called the police?"

She shook her head. "I tried while I was there beside him. I couldn't get a signal. I just came here. I didn't know what else to do."

"Everything's going to be okay," I said, kneeling in front of her and taking her hands in mine. They were as cold as ice. "Stay here with Sadie. I'll go take a look. Tell her I'm going to help him. She doesn't have to know yet, okay? I'll call the police when I'm out of earshot."

She nodded. "Okay."

I grabbed a sweatshirt from my bag and pulled it over my head, then reached for a pair of jeans. "You planning to sit there and watch me change? Hoping I'll put on a show?" I asked, throwing her a grin.

She sat back, startled. "Oh. Um. Sorry. No. I'll just go sit with Sadie."

I chuckled as she fled the room before I removed my sweatpants, tossing them to the side. I pulled on the jeans and grabbed my holster and my pistol from my nightstand. Then I threw on some boots and picked up my cell phone, shoving it into my pocket. Finally, I grabbed my backpack, knowing I might need some of the supplies in it.

Sadie was still crying when I returned to the living room.

"You're going to help him, right?" she asked, looking up at me from where she was huddled on my couch with the most pitiful eyes I'd ever seen.

"I'll do whatever I can," I promised. "Tell me where he is."

She rattled off the directions to the trail, and I nodded.

"Stay here," I said, directing it to Olivia. "Lock the door behind me. There's food and drinks in the fridge. Help yourself to whatever you need. I'll be back soon."

I stepped outside into the fresh air, walked away from the cabin, and pulled out my cell phone. I hated to report something I hadn't confirmed for myself, but I knew that Olivia could have been wrong about Ethan. And if he was still alive, the faster we could get a medic out here, the better his chances would be.

Not to mention the fact that it was better for me to stay as uninvolved as possible. Turn this over to the authorities, show them the respect they were due and all that. The local sheriff was already annoyed with me. No need to make things worse.

I frowned when the call failed. No signal.

Two more tries with the same result.

So I headed toward the trail, wondering how I kept getting myself into situations like this.

ETHAN WAS FAR BEYOND HELP WHEN I ARRIVED. THAT WAS clear before I even got close enough to touch him. I felt a quick moment of anger and frustration for the life lost. But then the switch flipped, the one that shut off my emotions so I could tap only into the part of my brain I needed to handle the situation. To think of the person in question as an object instead of a human. It was a switch I'd had to flip too many times in my life.

I was just glad I still knew how to turn it on and off.

Before getting close enough for a good look, I slipped on a pair of gloves and pulled out my camera, shooting a few shots from where I stood.

Ethan's body lay sprawled out in a large puddle of blood, suggesting he'd died here. His posture was natural, and there were no blood trails or anything else to indicate that his body had been moved.

I moved closer, squatting beside him. He wore the same clothes he'd worn last night to the bonfire, and they were soaked, suggesting he'd been here during the storm.

The stiffness in his body suggested the same.

I wasn't a medical examiner, but I'd seen more dead bodies than I could count. He appeared to be in full rigor, which meant he'd been dead at least four hours. Probably more.

There were two bullet wounds to his chest, another to his left shoulder. Small caliber handgun, by the look of it. Something small and easy to conceal. His glasses were broken, and there was a small cut on his right cheek. It was barely noticeable, but the shape and location made me think he'd been punched in the face before getting shot.

I sat back on my heels, thinking.

Last night, when Sadie and Joey had been missing, Ethan had said he would check the waterfall. Everyone had heard it and knew where he would be—including the caretakers. But when Rachel had told us to call off the search, she said Ethan had found the kids. So, presumably, he had returned with them. Why would he have come back out here again later?

Unless Rachel had been lying and he'd never returned at all.

Regardless of what had happened, one thing was clear—this was the work of a human, not a ghost. And the first thing I needed to do was alert the local authorities.

I stood and pulled out my cell phone, attempting to call 911 again. Still no luck. I'd have to return to the cabin area to try to find a working phone—which meant leaving Ethan's body behind.

Something that went against every instinct in my body.

This was a crime scene. It needed to be locked down and preserved.

I couldn't just stay here, hoping someone showed up though. So I pulled out my camera and snapped a series of pictures of the body and the surroundings, keeping my eyes open for any other potential clues.

I found the bullet casings ten feet from the body. Nine mil, with a rectangular firing pin strike that suggested it was a Glock.

Just like Olivia's, I thought with a sick feeling. It was a popular model though. I owned a couple myself.

Three badly grouped shots at close range suggested the shooter wasn't particularly proficient with the firearm. With any skill, it would have taken only one to do the job.

I photographed everything. Then I roped off the trail a few feet from his body, hoping it would stop any other hikers from coming across him. With one last look, I headed back toward the cabins to find a phone.

I TRIED MY PHONE ONE MORE TIME WHEN I GOT BACK TO THE cabins, hoping the problem had been fixed while I was gone. Still nothing. I sighed, realizing I'd have to talk to Olivia and Sadie before hunting down a phone elsewhere.

I knocked on the cabin door, waiting for Olivia to answer.

"Who is it?"

"It's me," I said.

She opened the door and gave me a questioning look.

My lips flattened and I gave a tiny nod.

She closed her eyes and leaned into the door, bracing herself.

"He's dead, isn't he?" Sadie's voice came out in a sob.

"I'm sorry," I said, nodding. I came in and closed the door carefully, then took the seat across from Sadie. "He died last night. There was nothing you could do."

"I don't understand," she cried. "Was it the ghost?"

Olivia and I exchanged glances as she took the seat by Sadie and rubbed her back in an attempt to comfort her.

"No," I said. "It wasn't a ghost. Sadie, I need to ask you some questions, but first, we need to call the police. I can't get a cell signal. Olivia, will you check yours again?"

"I've been checking every five minutes," she said, shaking her head. "I still don't have a signal, either."

"What about yours, Sadie?"

She pulled out her phone and typed in the password with tears streaming. "I doubt it. I could barely get a signal yesterday." She tried calling 911, shaking her head when it failed. "Mine won't work, either."

"Alright. I'll go to the caretaker's cottage. They're so old school they probably have a landline."

"Can you come with me to tell my mom first?" Sadie's voice was small and sad.

"Of course we will," Olivia said, looking to me for reassurance.

I started to say we should split up, knowing that time was of the essence. But Olivia's face stopped me. This was something she didn't want to handle alone. Not that I blamed her. Telling someone their husband was dead was one of the worst feelings in the world.

"Yeah. We'll take you to your mom. Then I'll go make the call. But first, Sadie, can I ask you something?"

She nodded, sniffling.

"Last night, you and Joey were at the waterfall, right?"

"Right." She blushed.

"Did your dad come find you there?"

"Yeah." Her blush turned darker. "He did."

"What happened then?"

"He chewed us out. Said we scared him half to death and had no business sneaking off like that. He was really upset. Told us a big storm was coming and we had to hurry. Then he took me back to the cabins and told Mom where I'd been."

So he'd made it off the trail the first time. Why on earth had he gone back during the storm?

"Hmmm," I said. "Do you know why he went back? Did you leave something out there?"

She got a confused look on her face. "I didn't, no. Maybe he did? I don't know. Mom said they needed to tell everyone they could stop looking. When they got back, it was already storming pretty bad. They had a huge fight and were still fighting when I went to bed. When I got up this morning, I asked Mom where he was and she wouldn't talk about it."

Interesting.

"Do they fight a lot?" A stab of guilt hit. I shouldn't have been interrogating a minor without her parent present, especially considering the circumstance. But I wasn't a law enforcement officer, and I needed to know.

She nodded. "Lately, yeah. I thought things were starting to get better, but then stuff happened and everything got worse. I think this trip is one last-ditch effort to make it before they divorce. Or was." Fresh tears filled her eyes as the truth hit her again. "I wanted them to divorce. Wanted the fighting to stop. But I didn't want..."

"Oh, Sadie." Olivia hugged her, rocking her like a mother would rock a baby. "Of course you didn't."

Chapter Fifteen

Olivia

I was completely numb as we plodded down the gravel road toward Sadie's cabin, silent except for the sound of our boots crunching on the wet rocks. It felt like a funeral march. How could this be happening? It was unreal.

Murder was something I saw on the news or on true crime documentaries. Always on a screen, where it felt walled off from my real life. Until recently, it was the kind of thing that happened to other people—not me or anyone I knew.

Yet here we were. What had begun as a vacation getaway had turned into something completely different. How was it that just yesterday I had driven down this road, excited by the changing leaves and the anticipation of a peaceful week spent painting? It felt like that was a different life altogether. That somehow I'd fallen out of my real life and into this very different one, where everything felt surreal and horrifying and heartbreaking at the same time. Sadie's dad was dead. *Murdered*. And somehow I had become part of it.

I dreaded seeing the look on Rachel's face when she heard she would never see her husband alive again. My heart shattered into pieces just thinking of it.

I was so grateful for Sawyer. He led the way, his face stoic. When we got to the cabin, he was the one to knock on the door. And when Rachel invited us in, obviously nervous about why we were there, he was the one to gently tell her what had happened.

A version of it, anyway.

"You might want to sit down," he said, placing a hand on her elbow and gently guiding her toward the oversized leather loveseat that sat beneath a moose head.

"Why? What happened?" She shifted her eyes to Sadie, scanning her up and down as if to make sure nothing had happened to her. It was an understandable assumption, considering Sadie's swollen eyes and tear-stained cheeks.

Sadie sat in the chair across from her mom instead of taking the seat next to her, so I took it instead, putting a hand on Rachel's back for support. She looked at me nervously, then back to Sawyer, who remained standing in front of her.

"I'm so sorry, Rachel. Ethan was killed last night."

"What?" Her voice sharpened and her back tensed beneath my hand as she shook her head in denial. "What are you talking about? You're wrong. You have to be. Where is he? I need you to take me to him." She jumped up, moving toward the door.

Sawyer held out an arm to block her, gently moving her back toward the couch. "We can't. I'm sorry."

Her face crumpled, and her body sagged as she stared at Sawyer and saw the truth in his eyes. "I don't understand. What happened? Did he fall or have some kind of accident? Why can't you take me to him?" She sank back down onto the sofa.

"No." Sawyer's voice was kind but firm. His eyes narrowed as he focused in on her, speaking deliberately. "I know this has to be hard to hear, but Ethan was stabbed to death. We found his body on the water-fall trail. It wasn't an accident. It was murder. And that area is now a crime scene."

"What?" She covered her mouth with a shaky hand before letting out a sob.

I threw Sawyer a questioning glance. I hadn't looked closely, but I'd thought Ethan had been shot. The round holes in his shirt looked like bullet wounds to me. But Sawyer's face betrayed nothing.

Maybe I'd been wrong. Maybe he'd been stabbed with something that made a round hole.

Rachel sobbed while Sadie avoided looking at her. I fought back tears of my own, trying to be strong for them. I didn't even really know the man, but the pain in the room felt palpable and Rachel's grief was almost too much for me to bear.

"I'm truly sorry for your loss," Sawyer said. "I know this is a shock. We'll try to help you with whatever you need."

If she heard him, she didn't give any indication. She buried her face in her hands, her body wracked with soft sobs, while Sadie cried quiet tears of her own.

After a few moments, Sawyer spoke again. "We need to call the police. The storm must have knocked out our cell reception. Mind if I try yours?"

Rachel looked up, momentarily confused, then seemingly strengthened by having a task to do. "Yes. Yes, of course. The police." She shook her head. "I'm sorry. I didn't even think. Yes, we need to call the police right away." She picked up her cell phone from the coffee table in front of us and typed in her passcode before handing it to Sawyer.

He took it and attempted to make the call, frowning when it failed. "Yours isn't working, either. I'll head to the caretaker's cottage now to see if they have a landline or some other means of communication. Olivia, do you mind staying with them, making sure they're okay?"

"Of course," I said, but Rachel shook her head.

"No. Thank you. I really appreciate it. But I think maybe we need to be alone for a bit. I need... I need to process this." She looked up at Sawyer again. "Are you sure? There's no chance you're confused about who it is?"

"It's him," Sadie said, her voice so raw it was almost unrecognizable. "I saw him."

"Oh, baby." Rachel's body sagged again. "I just can't believe any of this. It's got to be a bad dream."

"I'm so sorry," I said. "Are you sure you don't want me to stay?"

Rachel glanced at me, then at Sadie. "No. I think Sadie and I need to be alone. But thank you." Her voice wobbled.

"We'll come back here to check on you guys after we talk to the authorities," Sawyer said.

Rachel nodded.

With nothing left to say, we left them alone in their grief.

SAWYER AND I DIDN'T SPEAK UNTIL WE GOT INTO HIS SUV and headed down the shady lane to where the caretakers lived. As he drove, I studied him.

"You're good at that," I said. "I didn't know how to break the news."

"Not my first time." He stared at the road ahead. "It's best to just say it, get it over with."

"What do you do for a living?"

He paused before answering. "I'm in between jobs at the moment."

His evasiveness annoyed me—even though I'd been guilty of the same. "What did you used to do?"

He chuckled. "If I told you, I'd have to kill you." Then he glanced my way. "Sorry. Bad joke, considering the circumstances."

"Yes," I agreed. "It was. Can I ask you something else?"

His face became guarded again. "What?"

"Why did you tell her Ethan was stabbed? I was sure he'd been shot."

This time he smiled. "You're observant. And you're right. He was shot."

"Then why lie?"

He took a deep breath and shifted his hands on the steering wheel, frowning. "When a spouse kills their partner, they know they're going to get a notification, right? So they practice for it. Practice the shock, the grief, the reaction. But what they don't practice for is misinformation. I knew if Rachel had killed her husband, she'd know he'd been shot. So my saying he'd been stabbed would be confusing, and she might screw up and let something slip."

I jerked my head. "Wait. You think Rachel killed Ethan?"

"The spouse is always the primary suspect." He shrugged. "Plus we know they were fighting, and she doesn't have an alibi."

"She doesn't seem like the type." I couldn't picture it. Rachel was too sweet.

He glanced my way. "They never do."

"So do you really think she did it?"

He frowned again. "I'm not sure. She did act confused, but she was acting confused before that—like she didn't understand or fully believe he was dead. It's a common reaction. It's also something she could have practiced. There wasn't any sort of obvious slip-up or facial change when I mentioned the cause of death. That's a point in her credit. But she could also be an excellent actress."

"So you lied to her and it was pointless?" It annoyed me that he'd lie to a grieving widow just to see her reaction.

He shrugged. "Information is information."

"What are you going to say when she finds out the truth?"

"If she's innocent, she probably won't even remember what I said. But if she does, it's an easy enough mistake, right? You find a body, you panic. All the focus goes to seeing if the person is still alive, and if there's anything that can be done. You see a few bloody wounds in a panicked state like that and you could easily misidentify what caused them." He shrugged.

I studied him. "I bet you didn't panic at all, did you?"

"No."

"Do you ever panic?"

He turned to look at me. "No, not really." He shrugged casually. But there was something in his eyes—something that told me he wasn't being entirely honest.

The man had a habit of lying.

We pulled up to the cottage and got out. Tree limbs and branches were scattered across the yard, and Felix and Deb were both outside, cleaning up the mess. Felix straightened as we walked up, sticking out a hand to shake Sawyer's.

"You guys have got quite a mess up here," Sawyer commented. "Need a hand?"

Felix's chest puffed out. "I may be getting on up there, but I'm still able-bodied enough to handle a few limbs."

"Never said you weren't. But a couple extra hands makes the work go quicker."

"Oh, take him up on it," Deb said crankily, swiping her sweaty forehead. "Otherwise I'm bound to hear you complaining of back pain all night long."

"Better than having to hear you all night," Felix muttered under his breath. "Fine, fine. You can help."

"I'd be glad to," Sawyer said. "But first, I need a favor. Do you have a landline? I need to make a call and our cell phones aren't working."

Felix snorted. "Landline? What do you think this is, the nineteen hundreds? Of course we don't have a landline. We've got cell phones, same as you. And they're all out. The storm took out the only tower in the area."

Sawyer grimaced, then started grabbing limbs, tossing them easily into the pile Deb and Felix had already started. "Well, that's no good. I'll help you here. Then we're going to need to drive into town."

Deb laughed. "Won't be doing that, neither."

"Why not?" I asked.

"Road's closed," she said. "Got a big tree down. Plus the creek's swelled up and the gravel got totally washed out down by the turn. Going to take a few days to get things taken care of."

"Took a week last time this happened," Felix added.

I shot Sawyer a look. His face had gone hard.

"We've got to get a message out somehow. There was a death here last night, and we need to contact the police."

"A death?" Felix dropped the limb he was carrying and walked over to Sawyer. "What death?"

"Ethan, one of your guests. He was shot. We found his body on one of the trails."

Deb clucked her tongue. "People are always killing people, aren't they? I hope it was his wife."

Felix sighed. "Well, I guess this will wait. We should probably move the body first."

"Yeah," Deb said, nodding. "We've got that freezer out back nearly empty. I'll move the last of the venison over. Then we can put him there to keep until the road's open."

Sawyer's knuckles went white on the limb he was gripping. "You can't put a murder victim in a freezer."

"Why not?" Felix demanded. "That's what they do at the morgue, isn't it?"

"Because you could destroy evidence." The limb snapped in his hands. He acted like he didn't even notice. "We've got to get the authorities out here before the body is moved. Surely you have an ATV or something? A HAM radio? Anything?"

Felix shook his head. "I'm afraid not. Don't worry. It's not the first time this has happened. We'll take care of things." He clapped Sawyer on the shoulder. "Can't leave him out there. If we do, a bear or a cougar's likely to get him and destroy all that evidence anyway. Don't worry. We'll put on our gardening gloves."

Sawyer just stared at him. "Gardening gloves?"

Felix nodded. "Keep things proper like. That way, our fingerprints don't mess anything up."

Sawyer blew out a breath. "Give me an hour. Let me see if I can figure out a way to call the sheriff."

Deb shrugged. "Suit yourself. It'll take us a while to get ready anyway, right, Felix?"

"Right." He nodded like they were discussing something as simple as getting ready for dinner at a restaurant. Not moving a dead body into an empty freezer.

"Come on," I said, putting a hand on Sawyer's bicep and tugging him gently. I could tell he was about to blow, and the last thing we needed was to make these people angry if we were stuck here with them for several days. "Let's go see if anyone else has a working phone."

He clenched his jaw and nodded, following me to his vehicle. When we got in, he turned toward the direction of the entrance.

"What are you doing?" I asked.

"Going to look for myself. Maybe I can strap a chain on the tree, move it out of the way. I'm not worried about the gravel. This thing can handle some off-roading."

But it didn't take long to realize Deb and Felix were right. The tree that had fallen on the road was massive, and on the other side of it was a creek that had turned into a raging river.

Sawyer gripped the steering wheel, staring at the sight in front of us.

"Olivia, we've got to figure out who killed Ethan."

"I'm sure the police will figure it out when they get through," I said, trying to comfort him.

He turned to me. "Don't you get it?"

"Get what?"

"We're trapped here—with a killer."

Chapter Sixteen

I backed my SUV down the road until I could turn around and head toward the cabins. My mind raced as I tried to think of a way out of here.

There was still Richard—he might own a landline or an ATV. Hard to believe a hunter like him wouldn't.

Worst case, I could hike out of here, try to get help. But without a map of the region, I'd only be making educated guesses about where to head. And it meant leaving Olivia alone here with a killer on the loose.

That did not feel okay.

"What now?" Olivia asked, breaking my thoughts.

"I think our best bet is heading up to Richard's house and seeing if he has an ATV." I glanced over and saw her shudder. "You don't have to go. I can take you back to your cabin or drop you off with Rachel and Sadie."

She gasped. "But you think Rachel might be a murderer!"

"She might be. But in a way, that's the best-case scenario. If she killed her husband, it's personal. *Deeply* personal. She's not the type to kill randomly. So as long as you act like you don't suspect her, you'll be fine."

Olivia blew out a breath, obviously thinking things over. "I haven't had a chance to tell you about last night yet."

That got my attention. "What do you mean? What happened?"

She brought her fist to her mouth, biting a fingernail, before realizing what she was doing and carefully placing her hands back on her lap. I got the impression that biting her nails was an old habit she'd fought hard to break and that it came back in times of stress.

I understood that. Had a few habits like that myself.

"This is going to sound insane," she admitted.

"Try me." I pulled over in front of her cabin and parked the car but made no move to get out.

"Last night, I...I got up in the middle of the night to make tea."

"Our definitions of insanity are not the same," I said, chuckling.

"I smelled lavender."

I drew a blank for a sec until I remembered the ghost stories. "I see. Look, I know that probably freaked you out, but it's not a big deal. The power of suggestion makes the brain do all sorts of weird things."

"That's not all," she said, swallowing hard. "I was standing there, trying to figure out the lavender thing, when lightning flashed nearby. I was right in front of the kitchen window. When everything lit up, I saw a man standing there."

"Was it Ethan?" I asked, leaning forward. If she knew what time she'd seen him, that would give us a better timeline on his death.

She blinked a couple of times. "Ethan? I don't know. I...I thought it was Abel."

"Abel, as in...a ghost?" I had a hard time keeping the skepticism out of my voice.

"I mean, that's where my mind went under the circumstances." She blushed. "We didn't know about Ethan at that point."

"Could it have been Ethan though?"

"Maybe?" She seemed very unsure. "It was such a quick flash. He was gone the next time I could see anything."

"Are you sure it was a man?"

"Not positive, but that's definitely the impression I got. The stance was masculine. Threatening. I don't know how to describe it." She shivered again.

"What time was that?"

"Just after midnight."

"It could have been him," I pointed out. "He would have had to pass by your cabin on his way to the waterfall trail. You may have been the last person to see him alive. That's great. Gives us at least a potential idea of the timeline. I just don't understand what he was doing out there last night."

"Me either. It was absolutely pouring, and the storm was terrible. Who in their right mind would be out walking behind the cabins during that? Are you sure we aren't dealing with a ghost?"

"Ghosts don't use bullets," I said, chuckling. "Humans do."

She tilted her head, granting me the point. "But something else happened last night."

"What was it?"

She twisted her hands in her lap, rubbing her thumbs together. "Before bed, I put all the obituaries face down. They freaked me out."

"I don't blame you."

"This morning, they were standing up again."

My jaw dropped. "What?"

She nodded. "All eight of them. They were back in place."

I studied her face. Nothing about her expression indicated that she was lying, and I was well aware of the stories surrounding this place. There were entire sub-forums online dedicated to cabin thirteen and the experiences people had there. Everything Olivia was saying was right in line with the rest—apparitions, items being moved, ghostly voices, and the smell of lavender. A few people even reported being touched or feeling threatened.

"Any chance you were sleepwalking?"

"I never have."

"Huh." I sat back in my seat, thinking it over. I refused to jump straight to a paranormal explanation. It wasn't that I was completely unwilling to consider the possibility. I'd seen enough in my life to know better than that, and in a place with nearly a hundred years of stories, there was bound to be a grain of truth in there somewhere. But I also knew that people had a natural tendency to believe something was paranormal simply because they didn't have a better explanation.

I lived for finding the truth.

"Did you leave that chair behind your back door?"

She nodded. "Yes. And I checked all my windows before bed. They were locked."

"Alright. When I talk to Richard, I'm going to ask him about the camera mounted out front. See if we can check the footage. Maybe the housekeeper came in early for some reason and put them back."

"While I was sleeping?" Olivia's face wrinkled up in doubt. "I don't think that's possible."

"It's entirely possible. Unlikely, maybe, but possible. The storm probably kept you from resting well until it was over, and you could have been making up for it by sleeping extra deep this morning."

"Maybe." She was clearly skeptical of the idea.

"I'd like to completely rule out human involvement before jumping to a paranormal explanation. Besides, if someone entered your cabin without your knowledge, that's a whole lot more dangerous than a ghost moving objects around. Especially considering the murder last night. We need to know what happened."

She blinked again. "I hadn't thought of it like that."

"So," I said, aware that the minutes were ticking down on the hour Felix had granted me. "What do you want to do? Go with me to see Richard, stay at your cabin—or mine, which you're welcome to do—or should I take you to Rachel's?"

She looked at cabin thirteen, biting her lip before turning back to me. "Take me back to Rachel's. We promised to check on them and let them know what was going on. But you'll pick me up when you're done?"

Her eyes were wide, and I could tell she was freaked out.

"Yes. I promise."

"Okay." She took a breath.

"Listen," I said, swinging around to head toward Rachel's. "Don't interrogate her. I don't want her to get any hint that we've considered she might be part of this. But if you notice anything weird, just make note of it. Keep yourself safe. I'll be back soon." I threw the SUV into park again and eyed Rachel's cabin. I had to admit I felt nervous leaving Olivia here even though logically it was safe.

"Thanks, Sawyer." She paused before opening the door. "I'm really glad you forced me to be friends with you."

"Forced?"

"Oh, yes." She nodded, giving me a playful wink. "You were quite annoying, actually. But I'm really glad I have someone out here I can trust."

The weight of her words hit me. "Same," I said, attempting a smile.

She smiled and turned for the door.

I waited and watched her go in, thinking. Olivia trusted me. But could I fully trust her? Ethan had been shot by a small-caliber handgun, and so far, I only knew of two people out here who had one of those: me.

And Olivia.

THE GRAVEL LANE WOUND AROUND THE CABINS, THE EDGE of the lake, and up the hill on the other side. It was a pretty drive, one I'd have enjoyed if I wasn't so focused on the task ahead of me. As it was, all my thoughts were zeroed in on the man I was about to meet: Richard Moore, the reclusive owner of Hidden Gem Lake and Resort. I'd done my research on him before ever making the trip. Richard had a reputation, although not many were willing to talk about it. I'd gotten a clear enough picture though.

I began the sharp ascent up his driveway. He'd clearly put his house up here to make a statement—this incline was no joke. Building here had to have been tricky and would have increased the expense. Not to mention how ridiculously inconvenient this trek must be during winter. But the house looked impressive from down at the lake—I had to give him that. The location also gave him a great view of everything below while ensuring his own personal privacy.

I heard the sharp bark of a large dog as I approached. Great. I loved family dogs as much as the next guy, but guard dogs were a different thing altogether. And with what I knew about Richard, I imagined that his dog was probably extra mean.

Good thing I knew how to handle mean.

I pulled up to the front of the house and jumped out, heading for the front door. The barking increased but didn't come closer—that, at least, was good.

I ignored the doorbell and used my fist to knock on the door. Loudly, to make a point.

Sixty seconds later, the man himself answered, wearing a thin smile. "Yes?" he asked, skipping pleasantries. He looked older than the pictures I'd seen. I knew from research that he was in his late forties, but if I'd seen him on the street, I would have assumed fifties. His face wore the mark of a hard life, with rough sun-damaged skin, dark circles under his eyes, and hair that had gone gray early.

"Good morning," I said, giving him an easy smile. "I'm Sawyer Reed. I'm staying in one of your cabins. Do you have a working phone or internet or anything up here? My cell isn't getting reception and I need to make a call."

"If you need assistance, you should speak to the caretakers," he said pointedly. "That's their job."

"I understand," I said, nodding. "But I already have. Their phone isn't working, either. And we've got an emergency situation down there."

"What kind of emergency?" His sharp eyes flickered with curiosity.

"The murder kind."

His facial muscles ticked before a mask slid into place. "Murder? That's terrible. A guest?"

"Correct. Can I come in?"

He studied me for a second before giving a slight nod and opening the door, welcoming me inside. His own living room was decorated similarly to Olivia's, with game mounted on every wall. It was a dark, masculine space. All straight lines and hard furniture, with none of the comforts that softened the cabin spaces and made them at least somewhat inviting.

"Have a seat," he said before closing the door and slowly making his way toward what appeared to be his favorite spot—a large straight-back leather chair that reminded me of a throne.

Here, it was clear he considered himself to be the king.

He dragged his right leg slightly as he walked. When he noticed me looking at it, he gave me a little smile. "Old war injury. Still have a bit of shrapnel they couldn't take out."

I gritted my teeth and forced myself not to call him on what I knew was a lie. "Sorry to hear that."

"My only regret is that it ended my time of service," he said with false modesty. "I would have served my whole life if given the chance."

"I'm sure that was hard," I agreed. Never mind the fact that I knew the truth—that he'd never been injured. Not in war, anyway. He'd been discharged from the army for insubordination, and no one who'd served with him had anything good to say about the experience. "So, about that phone?"

He sat down and shook his head. "Sorry. My phone is down too. You said Felix and Deb have been notified about the death?"

"Yes."

He nodded. "Good. They'll take care of the body until Sheriff Patterson can get out here. What makes you think it was murder?"

I gave him a level look. "Two to the chest usually isn't an accident."

He blinked twice before chuckling nervously. "No, I guess it isn't. Who was it?"

"First name's Ethan. I don't know his last name. His family is in cabin five."

He shook his head. "He's the one with a teenage daughter, isn't he? So sad. Where was he found?"

"Waterfall trail."

"Hmmm." His eyes narrowed. "Terrible timing with the storm. Any evidence likely got washed away, and it could be days before we can get the sheriff out here."

"There's always evidence," I said evenly. "And that leads to my next question. Since we don't have a way to call, can I borrow your ATV and a map of the area? I'm sure, being the avid hunter you are, that you have one. One of the trails out here should lead to another road, yes? That way, we can get to the authorities today."

He drummed his fingers on the arm of the chair. "I'm not in the habit of loaning my stuff to strangers."

"Sure. But we're talking about a murder. Seems like a good time to make an exception."

He mused for a moment. "For all I know, you could be the killer, looking for an escape plan. Letting you leave here on my ATV might legally make me an accomplice. I'll check in with Deb and Felix. If it really was murder, then I'll take the ATV and talk to Sheriff Patterson myself."

It wasn't what I wanted. But it was something.

"Alright," I agreed. "Now, my next question. I know you have cameras up. Do you have any on the trails?"

There was that flicker in his eyes again. I'd hit on something. But he put his mask right back up and shrugged. "A game camera or two, to keep an eye on my hunting spots. But none on the waterfall trail."

"Gotcha. One last thing. I need to see the footage taken last night on the front porch of cabin thirteen."

His eyes narrowed. "Why?"

"Someone entered that cabin without the occupant's permission. I want to know who."

I could see instantly I'd made a mistake. Anger flashed on his face. "I assure you that none of my staff would enter a guest cabin in the night unless there was an emergency. And even then, they would make themselves known. What makes you think someone went in there anyway?"

"When the occupant awoke, she discovered that items in the living room had been moved."

His face instantly relaxed and he chuckled. "I don't know if you're aware, but that cabin is haunted. Things get moved around sometimes." He lifted his hands and shrugged.

"I'd still like to see that footage."

He shook his head. "Absolutely not. Those cameras are up only for the security of the guests here. It would be a violation to show you footage of someone else's cabin. I'll review it myself for your peace of mind, but I can already tell you there won't be anything on it. There's a long history of strange things happening in that cottage, but it's not a human causing them."

"I'm not sure I believe in ghosts."

"You will, Mr. Reed. Before the week is over, you will."

CHAPTER SEVENTEEN

Olivia

DESPITE THE CRISP MORNING AIR, MY PALMS WERE SWEATY as I walked up to Rachel's cabin knowing there was a chance she had killed her husband last night. But when Sadie opened the door, my feelings instantly changed.

Her face was puffy and red, and my heart instantly broke for her—then broke all over again when she let me inside and I saw Rachel curled up in the corner of the couch, crying softly. The room was dark, as if neither of them could bear the light. Grief hung heavy in the air, like a palpable presence from which there was no escape.

Sadie didn't say a word to me. She just walked down the hallway and disappeared.

I stood frozen for a moment, unsure of what to do. Then I remembered my great-grandmother, the only person I'd ever known who seemed to naturally know how to tend to other people. If she were here, she'd know exactly what to do.

And from what little I remembered of her, I knew that it would probably involve food.

"I just came to check on you, maybe sit with you for a bit," I began. "Could I make you a cup of tea? Or something to eat?"

Rachel sat up, sniffling as she grabbed another tissue, dabbed her eyes, then threw it to the ground with the rest of them. "I don't think I could eat," she said. "I'm sorry. I know I have to pull myself together. This is just such a shock."

"I can't even imagine." My heart went out to her. She didn't seem like a murderer at all—just a grieving woman who was lost and dealing with unexpected tragedy.

I looked around, hesitating, then decided not to take no for an answer. I turned the light on, immediately brightening the space, and picked up all the tissues from the floor, tossing them into the wastebasket. Then I found a pot and began heating water before riffling through the basket on their counter to find some suitable teabags.

Rachel watched me, then seemed to shake herself. She stood up and smoothed out her wrinkled sweater, then disappeared into the bathroom. When she came back, she'd washed her face. Her eyes were still red, but there was light in them again.

"Here," I said, passing her the cup of tea I'd just made. "Sit down and drink this. I'm going to make you something to eat. You have to take care of yourself. Sadie needs you to be strong."

Rachel took the cup automatically but set it down on the table without taking a sip. She looked somewhat dazed. "Where is Sadie?"

"I think she went to her room."

She stared down at the teacup. "She said she wished it would have been me."

"What?" I put down the cup I was making for myself, caught completely off guard.

Her voice wobbled as she repeated it. "Sadie said she wished I would have been the one to die out here."

"Oh, Rachel." I sat down and reached a hand out, squeezing hers. "She didn't mean it. She's just in shock."

Rachel covered her face with her hands. "Oh, she meant it. She's always been closer to Ethan. They're two peas in a pod. Plus, everyone loves him. He's always been the charming, popular one." There was the tiniest bit of resentment in her voice.

"She loves you, too," I said, believing—hoping—it was true.

"Not the way she loved Ethan. I've always been her second choice. Always felt like I was on the outside of my own family, especially since I went back to work last year. But she didn't used to hate me. Not until a few weeks ago."

"What happened?" Sawyer's words about not interrogating Rachel came back to me. But this wasn't an interrogation, I assured myself. Just normal conversation.

Well, as normal as conversation could be considering the circumstances.

"I don't know." She dropped her hands and shook her head helplessly. "Honestly, I don't. Sadie just got angry. I figured it was hormones, but it lingered this time. After about a week of the silent treatment, I tried to talk to her. She said she knew what I'd done and that she'd never forgive me."

I frowned. "Never forgive you for what?"

Rachel shrugged. "That's the thing, I have no idea. She refuses to discuss it with me. I'd put some restrictions on her dating life that she wasn't happy about, and I keep tabs on her phone. But it's not as if that was a secret. All I can figure is that her hormones have hit crisis level and she's going to despise me until she's an adult." Rachel's voice broke.

"You guys will figure this out," I said, though it sounded hollow, even to me. My mother and I certainly hadn't. But our problems stemmed from the dysfunctional dynamics between her and my father. If he had died, we might have had a very different relationship. Maybe there was hope for Rachel and Sadie.

"We have to figure it out," Rachel said. "We have no choice. We only have each other now."

A worrisome thought crossed my mind. Could Rachel have killed Ethan because she was jealous of his relationship with Sadie and wanted to get him out of the picture? Her resentment made me wonder. That didn't fit with the grief I'd seen when I walked in though.

Unless the tears were from guilt.

· · ·

I put together a simple brunch of sandwiches and fruit, then told Rachel I'd check on Sadie and see if she'd come eat with us. I knocked lightly on Sadie's door before cracking it open. "Can I come in?"

She nodded, pulling her knees into herself. She was sitting on her bed with her hoodie pulled over her head, staring at her phone.

"Are you okay?" I asked.

"Not really."

I sat down on the end of the old daybed, running a hand over the faded quilt. "Yeah. That was a stupid question. I'm sorry."

"It's okay." She kept her eyes downcast. "I just can't believe he's gone."

"I know."

She looked up, her eyes full of grief and unanswered questions. "What's going to happen now?"

I let out a breath, not wanting to lie but also wanting to avoid the horrible truth about what the caretakers planned to do with her dad's body. "The road is blocked. Sawyer is trying to figure out a way to call the police, but so far, we haven't had any luck. I don't guess your phone is working yet?"

She shook her head. "No. I was just looking at old pictures."

"Your mom said that you and your dad were really close."

"Yeah." Her voice trembled. "I don't know what I'm going to do without him."

"I've never been through that," I confessed. "I imagine it's going to be really hard. But even though it doesn't feel like it right now, I think it will get easier. Someday."

She glanced at the door, then lowered her voice to a whisper. "Do you think my mom killed him?"

"What?" I was completely caught off guard and had no idea what to say.

"Sawyer said he'd been stabbed. So it's either got to be one of the ghosts or my mom, right? I mean, Dad didn't even know anyone else here." The words spilled out of her like she'd been holding them back and was relieved to finally voice them.

"Do *you* think it was your mom?" I felt guilty even asking the question.

Sadie's face grew dark. "Maybe. She's not a good person."

"What makes you say that?"

But before Sadie could say anything, Rachel knocked on the door. "Girls? Are you coming to eat?"

"Be right there," I said with my heart pounding. I shot Sadie a look, but she avoided my eyes, like she already regretted what she'd said.

WE WERE JUST FINISHING OUR BRUNCH WHEN SAWYER arrived.

"Any luck?" I asked under my breath as I let him into the cabin.

He shook his head. "Not really, but I'll explain later."

Rachel stood, looking much more composed than she had when I first arrived. "Thank you for what you both have done. We really appreciate it. Has the coroner made it yet? We really need to pack up and get home so we can start making arrangements, but I don't want to leave until I know Ethan's been taken care of."

Sawyer shot me a subtle warning look to not say anything. "Not yet. There's a tree blocking the road. The resort owner has an ATV and is heading to the sheriff's station via an alternate route. So I'm afraid you guys are stuck here temporarily."

Rachel blinked several times. "Stuck here?"

"For now. None of our vehicles can get through until they move the tree."

She sat back down, looking deflated. "I don't know what I'm supposed to do."

Sawyer crossed the room and took a seat at the table with her. "Just stay here and take care of Sadie. Listen, I don't want to worry you too much, but the fact that Ethan was killed means that there's a murderer here. Right now, the most important thing you can do is to keep Sadie safe."

Rachel's eyes went wide. "I-I hadn't really thought about that."

"Can you think of any reason why someone here would want to kill your husband?"

"No," she said like the very idea of it shocked her. "Everyone loved Ethan. Besides, we don't know anyone here."

"Did he get into any arguments with anyone after you guys arrived?"

"No—well..." Her voice was hesitant.

I sat beside her. "If there's anything at all, please tell us. Even if you think it might not be important."

"Well," she said, swallowing hard. "He was really upset about Sadie and Joey sneaking off last night. He was harder on Sadie than he normally is, and she was pretty upset with him. I know Joey and his parents heard some of it. I think they were offended. Joey yelled out that Sadie's not a kid and that she can do what she wants."

"Hmmmm..." Sawyer's face was thoughtful. "That's interesting, but that's a pretty thin reason for murder. He was found on the waterfall trail. Do you have any idea why he headed back out there last night?"

Rachel shook her head slowly. "No. Not exactly."

"What do you mean 'not exactly'?"

She sighed. "We had a big fight after we got back. I told him he'd overreacted, that they were just being kids and having some fun. He was furious that I took Sadie's side instead of backing him up. Normally, I try to smooth things over and keep the peace, but I guess I was feeling stubborn. I refused to back down. He blew up and said he'd go sleep in the car, that he wasn't going to stay where he wasn't welcome. I thought that's where he went and that he'd show back up when he got hungry for breakfast."

"So no reason that you can think of for him to go out on a trail?"

"In that storm?" she asked, incredulous. "I couldn't even believe he wanted to be out in the car during that thing."

Sawyer made a face showing agreement. "What time did he walk out?"

Rachel's eyes drifted toward the clock like she was trying to remember. "I guess it was close to eleven. It was almost ten when we got back from looking for the kids, and it felt like we argued forever."

"Good to know," Sawyer said. "That helps with the timeline."

"Oh my God." Rachel's face turned white. "They're going to think I did it, aren't they?"

"Why would you say that?"

I'd only known Sawyer for a day, but I could see the spark in his eyes even as he kept the rest of his face completely neutral.

"Because I'm the wife. Because we'd been fighting." Rachel started shaking.

"They'll find out who really did this. Everything will be okay," I soothed.

"You don't know that." Her voice trembled. "If I go to jail, Sadie will be on her own."

"Just try to think," Sawyer said. "Is there anything else that might help? What does Ethan do for a living?"

"He's—he was—a psychiatrist."

"Clinical practice?" Sawyer asked, glancing my way.

"Yes."

I knew where he was going with this. "Is there a chance anyone here is one of his patients?" I asked. "Did he act like he recognized anyone, or did anyone greet him?"

Rachel shook her head slowly. "I don't know. He went down to the bonfire a good twenty minutes before we got there. Sadie and I were arguing. She didn't want to go, and I insisted. Everyone was already there when we arrived except for you two. He wouldn't have reacted to seeing a patient there though. Even greeting someone first is considered a breach of confidentiality."

Sawyer's face turned thoughtful. "Does he prescribe medications?"

Rachel nodded. "Yes. But he doesn't carry them with him, if that's what you're thinking."

"What about a prescription pad? Could someone have tried to get him to write a script out here?"

"I don't think so," she said slowly. "All of that's electronic now. He does everything on his tablet."

"Is his tablet here?" Sawyer asked.

"No," Rachel answered. "I made him leave it at home. No work on our trip. It was supposed to be family bonding time." Her voice broke again.

"One last question," Sawyer said. "Whose idea was the trip?"

She moved her head back and forth. "I guess mine. With everything that's been going on, I'm the one who wanted to get away and reconnect."

"So you picked the place?"

"No," she said, shaking her head. "I asked for the trip. But it was Ethan's idea to come here. I don't know why. It's not his kind of place at all. But the idea of a rustic getaway sounded like a good idea. Something where we'd all be together and really make some new memories." Fresh tears began to flow. "Instead, it's a nightmare."

Chapter Eighteen

Sawyer

We said goodbye to Rachel with promises to check on her again soon. Then I opened the door to my SUV for Olivia, motioning for her to get in. We could have easily walked down to our cabins, but I didn't want to leave my vehicle here. Part of me was still hoping for a miracle—that the road would open and we could get the hell out of here.

"What happened?" Olivia asked when I got inside and closed the door, throwing the shifter into drive.

"He wouldn't loan me his ATV. Said he'd take it himself to tell the sheriff."

"As in the same sheriff who investigated your friend's death?" she asked softly.

"That's the one."

"At least you'll get a chance to talk to him. Maybe he can give you more information about what happened to Grace."

"I've already talked to him. Before I came here. He was offended that I would even question his investigation and wouldn't tell me anything that wasn't in the official report."

"Oh." She sighed. "Well, what did you think of the owner? Could he have done this?"

"Maybe," I said. "He was pretty much exactly what I expected based on my research. Complete narcissist. Lies so well he probably half believes them. Said what happened was terrible, but there was no emotion behind it. No genuine empathy or concern for the family. No —" The sight in front of me made my jaw drop, and I completely lost my train of thought. "You've got to be kidding me."

Olivia followed my gaze to where Felix and Deb had emerged from the trailhead, hauling a sheet-covered Ethan. Felix carried one end, while Deb carried the other, walking solemnly toward the old pickup truck parked on the side of the road.

"Oh my," Olivia said, shaking her head. "They're really going to put him in a freezer, aren't they?"

"Looks like it." I slammed my hand down on my steering wheel, cursing. "The whole scene is contaminated now."

"Maybe that's the point," she murmured.

"You might be right," I admitted.

If the caretakers were involved, this was a great way to ensure there were no questions about their DNA being all over the body. I had to wonder how many of the other deaths involved situations where Felix and Deb had to move the deceased.

I watched as a cabin door opened and the teenager's dad—Joseph, if I remembered correctly—stepped out onto the porch with his fishing gear, dropping his pole when he saw Felix and Deb reach their truck and shove what was clearly a dead body into the back of it. He stood, his mouth agape, before opening his door and apparently calling for his family. His wife and his son joined him, looking equally astonished as Felix gave a little wave, slammed the tail bed shut, and climbed into the truck to drive away.

I turned to Olivia. "I'm going to go talk to them. Want to come?"

"Well, I don't want to stay here by myself."

"Come on, then." I climbed out of the SUV and headed over to their porch with Olivia by my side.

"Did you see that?" Joseph asked, shaking his head. "It looked like they were carrying a dead body! What do you suppose they were doing?"

"Well," I said, clearing my throat, "they were, in fact, loading up a dead body."

The woman—Meg, I thought—laughed, before realizing I wasn't joking.

"You can't be serious," she said. "It has to be some tools or something. An optical illusion."

I shook my head. "I'm afraid not. Last night, one of the other guests was killed on the waterfall trail."

Meg paled. "Oh no. Who was it? What happened?"

"It was Ethan. Sadie's dad. And it was murder." I watched Joey—the teenager—as I spoke.

He startled and crossed his arms defensively.

Meg turned white, her face falling in complete devastation. She looked at her husband and some sort of silent communication passed between them.

"It wasn't Joey," Joseph said, putting a protective arm around his son. "I know they got into it last night, but it couldn't have been him. After the bonfire, we came back to the cabin here and played card games until the storm died down. All of us. Joey was here all night."

Joey looked startled again, but he nodded in agreement. "Yeah. That's right."

I lifted my hands in defense. "Hey, man, I never thought it was him. Was just telling you guys what happened."

"You're sure... You're sure he was...murdered?" Meg trembled. "It couldn't have been an accident?"

I shook my head. "It was no accident."

She swallowed hard. "I think we need to pack up and leave. I don't want to be here anymore."

Joseph nodded in agreement. "Let's start loading up. We can hit the road in half an hour."

Olivia jumped in. "You can't. The road's closed. We're all stuck here for now."

Meg's eyes widened. "Stuck? Here?" Her hands began to shake.

"For now," Olivia said softly. "Hopefully they'll get the road opened soon. I want to leave too."

Joseph frowned. "If the road's closed, does that mean the police can't get in to investigate?"

"The owner of the place is heading to get the sheriff via ATV," I explained. "So hopefully we'll get somewhere soon. In the meantime, stick together. There's safety in numbers. I'd avoid the trails, just in case."

"Maybe it was the ghost," Joey said, a glimmer of excitement in his eyes. "The one they told us about last night."

"Maybe," his dad agreed, flicking his eyes to his wife.

"Can I go check on Sadie?" Joey asked, looking to his parents for permission. "I mean, it was her dad and all."

Joseph and Meg exchanged glances.

"I don't think that's a good idea," Meg said.

Joseph's hand tightened on Joey's shoulder. "Better stay with us."

Joey slumped. "Aw man, you are so boring. This bites." He turned around and walked back into the cabin, slamming the door behind him.

Meg attempted to apologize. "Teenagers," she said, trying to laugh it off. But her hands were still trembling, and there were tears in her eyes.

"It's a rough age," Olivia agreed.

"Absolutely," I said, nodding. "Listen, we're heading in. Let us know if you need anything, okay? We've all gotta stick together until we can get out of here."

"Thanks." Joseph reached out and gave me a firm handshake. "You guys be safe."

"You too."

When we were out of earshot, Olivia murmured, "You spoke to them differently than you did anyone else. Why?"

"Because they both think Joey did it." I kept my voice low. "And I don't want them to know I see that."

"I noticed that," she agreed. "They stepped in and gave him an alibi."

"Exactly. What do you want to bet they have no idea where he was last night?"

She shook her head. "It's crazy. Do you really think a teenager could do something like that?"

"Hell yeah I do." I walked up to my cabin and unlocked it, letting Olivia in first without even asking if she wanted to come in. It seemed we'd reached an unspoken agreement that we were together in this. It was an arrangement I liked. A lot.

Way more than I should, considering she was still Judge Mitchell's daughter.

"We're talking about murder," she argued. "I know he's got an attitude problem, but—"

"The attitude is the least of his problems. He's also got raging testosterone and a brain that hasn't fully developed yet. That's a terrible combination."

"I suppose you're right," she said, though her tone suggested she didn't fully agree.

"Of course I'm right," I said, snorting. "I was a teenage boy myself once. Not my finest years."

"Hmmm..." She mused for a moment. "Ethan was a psychiatrist. Do you think there's any chance Joey was one of his patients? That might explain why he was so adamant about Sadie not hanging out with him."

"That's an interesting thought," I said, feeling oddly proud of her for thinking of it. She was sharp and insightful, both qualities I appreciated. "I was wondering about something like that myself when Rachel mentioned it. Say Joey's got an anger problem, started getting into trouble. Parents get scared and make him go see someone. Ethan's not going to say anything about it or even act like he knows him because that would violate his confidentiality. Parents aren't going to say anything, either—especially when Ethan turns up dead."

"It's all speculation," she said. "But I'd rather it be Joey than Rachel."

"You like her and Sadie, don't you?"

"I do." She sighed. "I feel connected to them. It's hard for me to believe that Rachel could have done this. If she did, I can't imagine what will happen to Sadie. She's still so young, and if Rachel goes to prison, she'll have lost both parents all at once."

A flicker of unease hit. "You're not suggesting it'd be better for her to live with a murderer than to turn Rachel in, are you?"

She avoided my eyes. "Not exactly. But...maybe. I mean, we don't really know what was going on in their home life, do we? What if Ethan was abusive to Rachel and she killed him out of desperation?"

"Murder is murder. And guilt is guilt," I said.

"Is it always that simple?"

I paused before answering. Because the truth was no. It wasn't always that simple. I knew that things weren't always black and white. My career choices meant that I'd spent a whole lot of time living in the gray. But I wanted it to be simple. Needed it to be, especially if she ever found out who I was and what I'd done.

"I don't know," I finally said. I swallowed back everything else I wanted to say—the conversations we'd eventually have to have if whatever this was between us was going to continue.

She gave me a long look. It made me uncomfortable, knowing how perceptive she was.

"Bourbon?" I asked, feeling like a coward.

She raised an eyebrow. "It's a little early for that, isn't it?"

"Liv, our day started with a dead body. It's never too early for bourbon on a day like that."

She gave a little smile. "'Liv?'"

"It's a cute nickname. I won't call you that if you don't like it though."

"I do like it, actually." Her smile turned shy. "And point taken about the bourbon and the dead body thing. So sure. Pour me one."

I grabbed two glasses and poured a generous shot for each of us. "So tell me how it went with Rachel. What'd you find out?"

She swirled her glass, then took a tiny sip, closing her eyes in appreciation. "You really do have exceptional taste in bourbon."

"Thank you. But don't change the subject."

She put her glass down and gave me an amused look. "You told me not to interrogate her."

"And yet, I have a feeling you found out something anyway."

Her smile fell. "Sort of. But I don't really want to tell you, because... because I really don't want Rachel to be guilty."

"You telling me or not doesn't change her guilt."

She sighed again. "Sadie thinks Rachel did it."

"Really?" I had not expected that. "She told you that?"

Olivia nodded. "When Rachel wasn't around, Sadie asked me if I thought it could be her. Said her mom isn't a good person."

"Hmmm." I frowned, wondering what Sadie could have meant by that. "By all appearances, Rachel's a pretty typical upper-middle-class mom. Seems to love her kid, pays attention to her. Anxious, acts like she wants to do a good job. So that's an odd thing to say."

Olivia shrugged. "Maybe. Maybe not. *You* know what it's like to be a teenage boy. *I* know what it's like to be a teenage girl." She gave me a wry smile. "Hating your mother is pretty par for the course."

"Point taken. You spent some time with Rachel though. What do you think?" I was genuinely curious. Olivia might not have had my background, but she'd proven herself to be sharp and observant. And she saw people—really saw them. I'd known that the moment I saw the sketch she did of me. Maybe it was a skill she'd honed because of her art, or maybe it was just who she was. But I trusted what she saw in other people.

And hoped she didn't look too closely at me.

"Her grief is real," Olivia said simply. "I believe that. But she did say something that bothered me a little. She mentioned that Sadie has always been closer to Ethan. There was some strong resentment there. Then she said that now it would just be her and Sadie, so they'd have to work things out."

I took a swig of my drink, musing over it all. "Jealousy. Pretty common motive for murder, although this would be an odd example of it. But odd or not, that's motive just the same."

She leaned across the counter, gazing up at me with those wide eyes. "Come on. Spill. How do you know so much about all of this?"

A lie flew to my lips—an automatic evasion. But for the first time, I didn't actually say it. I sighed instead. I wasn't sure why, but I wanted to tell her the truth. Wanted her to know who I really was.

Wanted to see if she would still hang around if I did.

It was risky though. Too risky, considering the circumstances. If she pulled away, she'd be on her own out here. That was unacceptable for two reasons.

First, if she was an innocent woman who'd gotten dragged into all this, then she could be in danger. And I couldn't bear the thought of Olivia in danger.

But second, no matter how much I liked her, I knew I had to keep her on my suspect list. She had a gun that matched the shooting. She'd been the one to find the body and admitted to touching it in order to see if he had a pulse—a classic coverup for a killer.

Plus, I knew who her father was. So I knew she at least had the potential for being a skilled liar without a conscience.

No. I couldn't tell her the truth. Not yet. So a lie was all I could give her.

"I guess I watch too much television," I said, giving her a wink.

"Right." She gazed at me with narrowed eyes. "Who's keeping secrets now?"

I downed the rest of my bourbon in a single swallow, knowing we both had secrets we weren't sharing with the other.

CHAPTER NINETEEN

Olivia

Sawyer moved to the window, staring out of it seemingly deep in thought. I sipped my bourbon slowly, watching him.

He was a very interesting man.

He had a good soul. I could feel it. Could see it in the way he'd basically taken on the responsibility of keeping everyone here safe. He was easy to talk to. Smart. Interesting.

Yet, when it came to himself, he was a closed book.

I studied him. Broad shoulders. Ridiculously well-built. Strong.

He seemed to have investigative experience. Homicide detective? It would fit and explain his desire to find the killer.

Or former military perhaps? They didn't always like talking about what they'd seen or done. He seemed like the type to join the service. He was strong and cocky, and he had something of a hero complex. Yes, I could see him having served, maybe as a sniper or in the Special Forces.

On the other hand, his over-the-top secrecy suggested something more...clandestine. CIA perhaps? I could imagine that, too. Could almost picture him moving like James Bond, slipping into a party wearing an impeccably cut tuxedo only to steal some top-secret information or something equally thrilling.

I'd be so disappointed if I found out he was some bored pencil pusher who really was just acting out things he'd learned from binge-watching police procedurals.

"Incoming." Sawyer's voice—tinged with disgust—stirred me from my thoughts. Within seconds, there was a knock at the door.

He threw me an exasperated look before opening it. Adam and Eve were standing on his porch.

"There you are," Eve said, looking directly at me. "We've gone to your cabin three times this morning looking for you."

"Should have known she'd be here. Nice work, my man," Adam said, attempting to fist-bump Sawyer.

Sawyer ignored it yet again.

"Why are you looking for me?" I asked.

They both came in without being invited and plopped down on Sawyer's couch.

"We wanted to know how last night went in cabin thirteen," Adam said. "Though I guess you don't know if you slept here." He was clearly disappointed by the thought.

"She didn't sleep here," Sawyer corrected, his voice gruff. He closed the door and took a seat across from them with a pained expression on his face.

"My mistake," Adam said, raising his eyebrows. "Good for us though. Tell us—what happened? Did you have any paranormal experiences?"

"Well," I said, glancing at Sawyer. I could tell he disapproved of the whole ghost hunting thing, and I found myself not wanting to disappoint him. But the truth was that I'd had some paranormal experiences. Or what had felt like them anyway. Sawyer had offered some reasonable alternatives. But I really wasn't sure what to think about what had happened the night before.

"Oh, tell us!" Eve said, bouncing up and down. "It's obvious from your face that something happened!"

I took the last empty chair and began to tell them about the scent of lavender, the ghostly man outside my window, and the photographs being moved.

"Oh man," Adam said, his eyes wide. "That's huge! Way better than our experiences. Can we interview you for our channel? We'll set up the cameras in your cabin and you can tell us the same story, exactly like that. We'll shoot some B-roll of you making tea, get a good shot of the obituaries. It will be epic!"

"I don't know." The thought of telling my story publicly made me want to panic.

"It will be great," Eve coaxed. "You're gorgeous and will look so good on video. It will go viral for sure."

"I don't think that makes me feel any better. It's strange enough to talk about this with you guys. I don't want to do it publicly." Not to mention the fact that my father would kill me. He'd warned us all not to do any interviews. This was something completely different than what he'd imagined, but I knew better than to cross that line anyway.

"Come on," Adam said. "It will be your fifteen minutes of fame. We'll get everything ready and meet you at your cabin in, say, an hour?"

"She said she doesn't want to do it," Sawyer interjected, his voice commanding an authority that said it was final.

Adam's eyes went wide and he raised his hands in surrender. "Okay, man. I got it. But before you decide for sure, do you at least want to see the evidence we got last night?"

Sawyer rolled his eyes, moved back to the window, and ignored them.

I was curious though. "What evidence?"

"We caught some great EVPs!" Eve exclaimed, her face lighting up.

"What are EVPs?"

"Electronic Voice Phenomena," Adam explained. "We use recording devices and ask questions. Sometimes the ghosts will say something that we can't actually hear audibly, but it shows up on the audio later."

"Pseudoscience," Sawyer muttered under his breath.

"So you caught a ghost...speaking? To your device?" I asked, trying to understand. I'd heard of ghost hunters before, of course, but had never bothered to watch any of the shows or learn anything about it.

"Yeah!" Adam exclaimed. "Want to hear?"

"I do," I said, feeling a bit guilty as I glanced at Sawyer. He was leaned up against the window with the last of his bourbon in hand, staring at me with a look of utter disappointment.

I didn't want to disappoint him. Disappointing anyone felt terrible, but his approval really meant something to me. This was interesting though, and I was genuinely curious about what they'd heard.

Adam whipped an audio device out of his pocket and pushed some buttons on it, cueing up what he wanted me to hear. "Put that next to your ear," he said. "It's faint, so pay attention."

I nodded and did as he'd said. At first, I just heard him and Eve talking, asking questions like "Is anyone here with us tonight?" and "Can you tell me your name?"

But then Eve asked, "Who killed you?"

It was faint, but I heard an odd sound in the background that sounded a lot like the word "Ethel." I almost dropped the recorder.

"Oh my goodness," I said, my eyes wide. "Did she say 'Ethel'?"

"That's what we heard!" Eve squealed. Her eyes were bright with excitement. "I think Grace spoke to us! Everyone's always believed Ethel did it, but can you imagine if we just proved it? We'll be famous!"

"This could be our big break," Adam added. "Help us move to a real network! We could get a bigger crew, upgrade our equipment, and go to private locations. It might be a game changer!"

"That's fascinating," I said, handing the recorder back to him. "Have you caught anything else?"

"Not sure yet," he said. "We haven't been able to go through everything. It will take days to sort through everything we recorded."

Sawyer straightened suddenly. "So you were recording all night?"

"Until about three," Adam confirmed.

"Just audio or video too?"

"Both," Adam confirmed, grinning. "Why? Have you decided to stop being so skeptical now that you've heard our EVP?"

"Not exactly. Where were you recording?"

"Mostly our cabin," Eve said. "But when the rain stopped, we went down to the lake with our thermal camera."

"You have thermal cameras?" Suddenly, Sawyer was very interested.

"Yeah, of course. The theory is that, if a ghost is present, we'll pick up some sort of heat signature," Adam explained.

"I thought ghosts were cold," I said, frowning. "In movies, people always feel chilled when a ghost goes by."

Adam shook his head. "The cold spots—theoretically, anyway—are from where a ghost is pulling energy from the environment to try to manifest. The heat signature would be the actual energy of the manifestation. So, either way, a cold spot or a heat signature can mean that a ghost is present."

"That's convenient," Sawyer muttered.

I shot him a look.

"Anyway," Sawyer said, bringing the topic back to his own interest. "Were you outside filming at all around midnight? Say from eleven to one?

"No," Eve said, shaking her head. "It was still storming then. We didn't head out until after two."

"So no outside video until then? What about the inside cameras? Did you have any facing your windows, where you might have a view of the outside?"

"Not really." Adam shot him a curious look. "We may have caught windows as we were walking around, but nothing would have been focused on them. Why are you asking?"

Sawyer leaned forward. "Because there was a murder here last night, and I'm wondering if there's any chance you caught the killer."

"A murder?" Adam's jaw dropped. He looked over at me. "Holy cow. I told you someone might die. Honestly, I'm surprised it wasn't you. No offense. But if Ethel was going to kill someone last night, I'd think it would be the one who looked the most like her sister."

"Thanks," I said, rolling my eyes.

"So, who was it?" Eve asked. She appeared concerned, unlike Adam.

"Ethan," I said, answering for Sawyer. "Sadie's dad. He was killed on the trail that goes to the waterfall."

"Oh man." Adam's eyes went wide. "I did not see that coming. He doesn't fit the pattern at all. Ethel must be expanding her killings. But hey, there could be a new ghost here tonight!" He brightened, turning to Eve. "Make a note. When we investigate, let's try to contact Ethan. His spirit is probably still stuck here on the property."

Sawyer spoke, his voice cold. "We're stuck here, too. The road is closed, so the owner of the property is going to take an ATV to get the authorities. I'm sure, when they arrive, they will be fascinated to hear how eager you are to have people die here."

Adam raised his hands. "Hey, man. Not eager. But look, people know the danger. Do any research at all on this place and you know there's been deaths. You book a stay here at your own risk."

"I didn't know," I said quietly.

"Really?" He looked at me like I was stupid. "Why on earth did you come here, then?"

"For the lake." I shrugged. "The pictures were beautiful. Obviously, I've learned an important lesson to do my research before booking a place to stay."

"Yeah," he snorted. "Man. Bad luck."

"Apparently."

"Maybe it wasn't luck at all," he said, his face turning serious. "Maybe Ethel's spirit drew you here. We don't know everything about how the spirit world works. But what are the odds of you randomly picking *this* place, of all the lakeside cabins available? What were the odds of a blonde named Grace picking it last year? You better watch your back. If Ethel likes murdering people who look like her sister, you could still be next on the list."

A chill crept down my spine. He was right. What were the odds? Astronomical, probably. Maybe Ethan had been a mistake and I was the real target.

"Come on, Eve," Adam said, standing and grabbing her hand. "Let's go shoot some updates on what happened. Maybe we can get some footage of the crime scene."

Sawyer practically growled from the corner. "Stay away from that trail. It's already been contaminated enough. Unless you want your DNA out there, along with all of our testimonies about how you hoped a murder would happen this weekend."

Adam gulped, his face turning white. "Oh. I didn't think about that. You're right. We'll stay away, then. You said it was the waterfall trail?"

"That's right. And when you go through your video evidence, I want you to pay attention to your windows. We think Ethan was killed sometime around midnight. If you happen to have footage of anyone walking by or leaving their cabins, it could be crucial evidence in the investigation."

Adam brightened. "Hey, if we caught something, it could make the news! Let's go take a look, Eve."

"Also," Sawyer said, "you might not want to tell anyone else you were recording all night. If the killer thinks you may have caught him—or her—on camera, that could put you in danger."

Eve's eyes grew wide. "Let's go, Adam, and see if we found anything."

"You two"—Adam stopped in the doorway and pointed at us—"need to seriously consider doing that interview after all. Between her experiences and your brooding vibe, it will be major. This is a chance for all of us to make a mark." Then he saw Sawyer's face and fled the cabin.

THE MOMENT THEY LEFT, THE SPELL BROKE, AND THE FEARS Adam had stirred up within me dissipated. The ghost stories seemed less real somehow when it was just me and Sawyer. His skepticism felt like an anchor in the storm. But his attitude toward Adam and Eve was a mystery to me.

I tossed a pillow toward him. "Why do you get so worked up around them?"

He groaned and rubbed a hand over his face. "I don't know. "

"They're just kids looking for thrills," I chided him.

"No, they aren't. They're adults looking for fame. There's a difference." He stood up and paced. "Does it matter if they embellish the truth for their videos? Probably not in the grand scheme of things. But I take the truth seriously. I take *investigations* seriously."

"They're investigating ghosts. It's not the same thing. Honestly, I think it's really interesting."

"I like facts. Things that can be proven." He studied me for a minute, like he was about to say something personal for once, but he decided not to. "What they're doing is looking for anything at all that will back up their personal theories."

"How is that any different than what we're doing?" It was a genuine question. We'd been coming up with theories about what had happened to Ethan and looking for evidence that would support one of them. Was that really so different from what Adam and Eve were doing with their ghost hunting?

"It's totally different," Sawyer argued. "They've got a story in their heads about what happened and they're only looking for evidence to support it. I guarantee they'll ignore anything that doesn't fit their preconceived idea of a 'haunting.' I don't have an agenda here. I look for the truth—no matter what the fallout is."

I knew he was talking about more than just our current situation. "Are you ever going to tell me what you really do?"

He gave me a look that was unreadable. "Yes. You have my word. I'll tell you. But not today. Not until we get out of here."

I hid a small smile. If he wasn't going to tell me until we'd gotten out of here, that meant he intended to see me again even after this was over.

And I liked that. A lot.

He clapped his hands on his knees. "I've got to jot down some things. Then I need a shower. Helps me think. You good hanging out here, or would you rather join me?" He gave me a wink.

I laughed out loud. "I think I'll be okay out here."

"Back in twenty." He threw the pillow I'd tossed earlier back to me, then got up and headed out.

When Sawyer left, I picked up my phone again, hoping something had changed and I'd have reception. But the signal was still down. I felt restless, and without his calming presence, the anxiety of the situation started getting to me. I found myself wishing for my sketchbook or for something—anything—to keep me busy and distracted.

Sitting on the couch, thinking about being stuck on this haunted property with a murderer, was going to make me crazy.

I got up and went to the kitchen, automatically tidying up. Then I decided to take a look at the rest of Sawyer's cabin. I didn't think of it as snooping. After all, it wasn't as if this was his private home. Besides, he'd taken a look through mine just the day before. I was simply curious about the place, wondering what his setup looked like.

His living room was decorated similarly to mine, minus the obituaries. Those had been missing from Rachel's cabin too, making me think mine was the only one to have that particular touch. The antlers were also missing from the windowsills. There were still way too many animal mounts, but here, it came across more like an upscale hunting lodge and less like...well, like the death cabin, as I'd started thinking of it.

I walked down the hallway, studying the pictures on the walls. They were watercolor paintings. Originals, by the looks of them. The colors had faded some and the paper had yellowed a bit, suggesting both that they'd aged and that they hadn't been created using professional quality supplies. A hobby artist perhaps? Maybe someone in the family?

They were all of the lake and had been done at different times of the year. One in particular, a winter snow scene with a pink-and-purple sky, was quite good. I stared at the signature in the corner, startling when I realized the smudged cursive said *Ethel MacLaine*.

Had Ethel really painted these images of the lake where her sister had drowned? If Adam's stories were true, Abel had barely been able to look at the lake, choosing to build his new home where he wouldn't even catch a glimpse of it through the windows. But Ethel had repeatedly painted it, creating beautiful images of her sister's final resting place.

It was incredibly strange.

I wandered down the hallway, poking my head into the second bedroom. It was a tiny room with bunk beds, perfect for travelers with kids. Then I went past the bathroom, where I could hear Sawyer humming to himself in the shower. I paused at the door, my heart picking up speed as I imagined him in there. Had he been serious when he'd asked if I wanted to join him? Probably not. He was cocky and liked to tease.

Regardless, I wasn't the kind of woman who jumped into bed with a man she barely knew. No matter how tempting the idea was.

I forced myself to keep walking and poked my head into the room Sawyer was using to sleep in. I grinned when I saw it. Despite the fact that I'd woken him earlier, he'd somehow found time since to make his bed with military precision. It felt like confirmation of my earlier theory. I'd bet money that he had a background in the armed forces.

There was a leather-bound notebook open on his desk. It caught my eye because I had a similar sketchbook that I liked to carry when I traveled. Did he sketch? I hesitated, but only for a moment. After all, he'd already seen my work. Fair was fair.

I walked over to the desk, expecting to see some rough sketches or maybe even some nature journaling.

Nothing could have prepared me for what was actually on that page.

Chapter Twenty

Sawyer

"What are you doing?" I froze as I walked into my room and saw Olivia. She was as white as a ghost, and her lip quivered like she was about to break into tears.

She held up my notebook, her hand shaking. "You lied to me," she whispered. The sting of betrayal was written all over her face.

"I never once lied to you." My voice came out about ten times harder than I meant it to.

"You're not here investigating a friend's death." She tossed my notebook onto the ground and stood up, her voice strengthening. "What are you, a reporter? Did you follow me here, looking for a story?"

I held up my hands. "Liv—"

"Don't call me that." Her voice broke.

"Olivia," I said, feeling the sting of her rejection. "I didn't follow you here. I didn't even realize it was you until last night."

"I don't believe you," she said, shaking her head.

"I give you my word." I moved toward her, trying to make her understand. "I didn't know."

"Sure is a lucky coincidence for you, isn't it?" Bitterness rang through her voice. "Do you really expect me to believe that you just randomly picked the same resort as I did and pulled in right after me? And that you had no idea who I was when you jumped in to befriend me? When you made me feel like you were here to protect me?"

"It's not what you think."

"Then what the hell is it?"

"I'm not a reporter," I said. "I'm not after a story. Truth be told, I probably shouldn't be talking to you at all. It's a conflict of interest that's been killing me ever since I figured out who you are. Every word I told you was true. I really am here to investigate Grace's death. I'm a private investigator. My license is in my wallet." I pulled it out of my pocket, opened it up and tossed it to her.

She studied it. I could tell she wanted to believe me—but didn't.

"Look at the date on those notes," I said, motioning to the notebook, its pages splayed out on the floor. "The most recent ones I have about your dad are from over a month ago. If you kept reading—which you shouldn't, because it's private information—you'd see there's an entire section after that about my investigation into Grace's death. I wasn't lying to you."

She picked the notebook back up and flipped through it. It was clear from her face that she was starting to see I was telling the truth.

"So you're a private investigator," she said like she was trying the words on for size.

"Yes."

"And you were investigating my father?"

I let out a breath, tensing my jaw. "Yes."

"Who hired you?"

"No one."

Her face jerked back in shock. "What do you mean?"

I stared at her for a beat, then decided to hell with it. I was going to tell her the whole truth, consequences be damned. "Liv, your dad is the reason I became a PI to begin with."

"What are you talking about?" She looked like she was going to boil over with rage.

"I became a PI in order to run an investigation into what your father was up to. See, I had a buddy I'd served with overseas."

"So you were military," she murmured. "I knew it."

I nodded. "I was a SEAL. That was a long time ago. But the buddy I served with had a kid who wasn't handling the military family life well. He missed his dad and felt angry and lost. Got into some trouble hanging out with the wrong crowd. Super minor stuff—nothing violent. The kid needed counseling, maybe some community service. Instead, he got sent to juvie on his very first charge. And he never came home."

She paled. "Please tell me you're not talking about Rusty Barnes."

"I am."

"I've seen the story on the news," she said, her voice shaking. "My dad's harsh—I'll admit that. He was always hard on me and my sister, and it wouldn't surprise me at all if he was overly tough with his sentencing. But that doesn't make Rusty's death his fault."

"Harsh? This is a hell of a lot worse than harsh." I scoffed. "Rusty had no business being sent to a place like that. The only reason it happened was because your dad accepted over a million dollars in bribes from that juvenile detention center. They paid him to keep that shithole full of kids so they could keep the money flowing. That absolutely makes Rusty's death his fault."

"No," she whispered.

"And it wasn't just Rusty," I continued, my voice growing louder. "He was 'too harsh' with countless kids, all to line his own pockets. It went on for years. And I can prove it."

She shook her head. "You're wrong. He couldn't have done it. He wouldn't have. Yes, he tends to go for harsh sentencing, but he respects the law. It's all a lie!"

"It's not a lie!" I couldn't stop my voice from rising. "He's the only one lying to you!"

"Do you even know what this has put my family through?" She began pacing, ignoring what I'd said. "There are reporters camped out across our house day and night. We can't even go out to eat without someone confronting us. My father had to get extra security, but it wasn't enough. Someone actually broke into our home, Sawyer." She stopped pacing, looking at me again with that betrayal written all over her face and unshed tears welling up in her eyes.

"Are you even hearing yourself?" I was flat-out yelling now. "I'm sorry someone broke into your house, and I'm sorry you got caught in the crossfires with this. But, Olivia, you cannot honestly be complaining that you lost the ability to eat out when these kids lost their entire lives. Rusty? Every time he was supposed to get out, your dad found another reason to extend his sentence, until that poor kid gave up hope and slit his own wrists. What about that, Olivia? How is that fair?"

She blinked away the tears, stiffening. "What happened to innocent until proven guilty? My father hasn't even gone to trial yet. He's being framed or-or something."

"No." I grabbed her by the shoulders and forced her to look me in the eye. I lowered my voice, speaking deliberately. "Olivia, I am very good at what I do. I promise you he's guilty. And he's going to pay for it. I'll make sure of it."

She froze, her mouth agape. When she could finally speak, her voice was tiny, broken. "You're going to destroy my family."

I dropped her arms like they were hot coals. I couldn't believe it. Even after everything I'd said, she was still only thinking about her family and not the kids her dad had harmed.

I'd thought she was different than the rest of them. Hoped for it. And it crushed me to the very core to see she wasn't different at all.

"I cannot believe how selfish you are," I said. My tone was low and deadly, and I knew I should stop talking. But I didn't. "When I saw your sketches and how perceptive you are about the world around you, I thought you were different. Even when I realized who you were, I thought you were this one bright light in your wretched family... That you were here to get away from them. But no. You're only here for yourself. Only worried about *your* peace. You're a child. A selfish, spoiled child. You probably don't want the money to stop, do you? Probably need it to bankroll your life as an artist. I bet you've never done a real day's work in your life."

Her eyes went wide with shock. I'd wounded her. And I'd done it deliberately.

Wordlessly, she stepped around me, walking down the hallway. I followed her and watched her pick up her purse and head for the door.

"Stop," I said.

She turned around. I could see both hurt and hope on her face—hurt from the things I'd said and a glimmer of hope that I'd take the dagger out of her back and apologize.

But I wasn't about to say I was sorry.

I was going to push the dagger in deeper.

"Now that the truth is out on the table about who your family is, I'm going to point this out. Ethan was shot with a nine mil Glock—like the one you've been unsuccessfully concealing this whole time."

"You cannot be serious," she said. Her expression changed to disgust.

"I am serious. Like I said, I'm very good at my job. And right now, my job is figuring out who killed Ethan. You had the means. I have to consider that."

Her face turned red with rage. "I wouldn't even own a weapon if it wasn't for you. Sawyer, I was there when that man broke into our house. Alone." She started shaking as her voice lowered and broke. "I locked myself in a bathroom and called nine-one-one. Whispered so he wouldn't hear me. But he did. He found me. Broke down the door and told me he was going to kill me so my father would know what it was like to lose a child, too. Did you somehow miss *that* story in your investigation?"

She didn't wait for me to answer. "Thank God the police got there before he hurt me. But it was a nightmare. Do you have any idea what it's like to know you might be about to die?"

Guilt stabbed me, but I walled up my heart and refused to let it in. "Of course I do. I told you I was a SEAL. You think we sat around playing video games and having tea parties? Look, I'm sorry for what you went through. Really. But that wasn't my fault. It was your father's. He's the one you should be angry at. If he hadn't done what he did, that never would have happened to you."

"You don't know my father. Or me."

"I think I do. I know exactly who your father is and what he's pulled in his career. I'm not saying you killed Ethan. But if you did, I'll find that out too. Apples usually don't fall far from the tree. "

She shook her head. "You can say and think all sorts of terrible things about me, but if you think I would ever shoot someone in cold blood, then it's clear you're a jaded, angry, miserable man who sees nothing but the worst in everyone. And I feel sorry for you."

She'd attempted a stab with her words—and it landed. Though I'd never let her see it.

"I didn't say it was in cold blood," I said, keeping my voice level. "Could have been self-defense. Could have just gotten scared out there, fired without thinking. There's all sorts of ways it could have gone down. I'm just saying, if you did it, you might as well confess now, because you won't get away with it."

"I can't believe I ever trusted you," she said softly. With one last look, she opened the door and walked out.

CHAPTER TWENTY-ONE

Olivia

I WAS SHAKING WITH ANGER AND GRIEF AS I WALKED TO MY cabin. I should have known that Sawyer was too good to be true. He'd waltzed into my life looking like a knight in shining armor, flashing that killer smile of his, and claiming he wanted to protect me.

Part of me had longed for that. Had needed it after everything that had happened.

But it was him I'd needed protection from all the time.

The nightmare of the charges against my father and everything that had happened after—it was all Sawyer's fault. My father had mentioned that these allegations had come from some wannabe hero with a vendetta, looking for someone to blame.

And when I'd run away to this place, trying to escape from all of it, I'd somehow walked right into that wannabe hero's arms.

As I opened the door to my cabin, my mind raced, going over every detail of the conversations I'd had with Sawyer. Had I given him anything he could use against my family? Any detail an eager reporter would happily pay him for?

I'd told him my father was harsh. And he'd heard me talking to Sadie about how my parents fought, too. About how I'd often wished they would divorce.

I closed my eyes, falling back against the door as I imagined my father's reaction to seeing *that* splashed across a headline. There would be hell to pay.

I hated Sawyer. Hated that he'd continued stringing me along, spending time with me even after he knew who I was. Even after he knew he was my father's number-one enemy—and therefore mine as well.

Yet part of me—the part I'd tried so hard to keep locked away since the day the news had broken—had a sinking feeling Sawyer was right.

Questioning my father had never been allowed. But if I was being honest, I'd always had an inkling that he wasn't always entirely...ethical. There had always been signs that things weren't quite right. And when the news had broken about the allegations against him, I'd felt sick, fearing they were true. I'd simply known better than to ever voice it.

My father was harsh. Powerful. He wanted respect and demanded loyalty. My mother didn't give him the first, but even she wouldn't dare go against him.

He'd always lacked compassion. Never once had I seen him have a drop of empathy for a single person he'd sent away. Not even when he'd heard the news about Rusty's death. *Good riddance,* he'd said. *Another criminal off the streets for good.*

Even then, I'd winced, feeling the unfairness of it all. Rusty had just been a kid. A troubled one perhaps, but a child nonetheless.

A kid like Sadie. Or Joey.

Or, if I was being honest, like my brother. He'd been a troubled kid, too. He'd made countless mistakes, defying my father at every turn and embarrassing the family name. And the truth was that, if he had been anyone else's child, he probably would have ended up somewhere like that horrid juvenile detention center. But he was Judge Mitchell's only son.

That came with a kind of privilege most people didn't have.

He'd paid the price for his defiance in other ways—my father had made sure of that—but never through the legal system. Never in a way that would have taken him out of my father's reach or caused any public embarrassment.

I let out a breath and walked to the sofa, collapsing onto it.

Sawyer wasn't wrong about my father. Deep in my heart, I knew that. Had known it since the moment the news had dropped.

I just hoped he was wrong about me. Maybe I was selfish. Maybe I *had* been too willing to turn a blind eye to the truth in order to keep my life as peaceful as possible.

He didn't know what it was like though, living with someone like that. Someone who had the power to move heaven and earth in order to make things go his way.

Was I wrong to hate Sawyer? No. He'd still been dishonest with me, and that was something I couldn't forgive. But if I separated myself from the situation and pretended this whole story was about some other family instead of the one I'd been trained to be fiercely loyal to, I had to admit that I might have a little respect and admiration for him. He'd chosen a battle that wasn't his to fight, chosen to stand up for kids who couldn't stand up for themselves. He was braver than I was. Willing to sacrifice and fight for justice.

It was ironic, really. If I didn't hate him so much, he was exactly the kind of man I could fall in love with.

It didn't matter though. The chemistry between us and everything we'd shared since I came here... None of it had been real. He'd lied. Besides that, we'd been forced into this false intimacy because of the intensity of the situation. In any other world, it simply would have been a mild flirtation. Nothing more. Nothing less.

Whatever it was, it was over. The road would surely open soon, and when it did, I'd get out of here as quickly as possible. With any luck, I'd never have to see Sawyer Reed again.

And I'd try to pretend I was fine with that.

THE AFTERNOON DRAGGED BY MORE SLOWLY THAN I EVER would have believed possible. I couldn't even paint. I pulled out all the supplies and set up at the kitchen table, attempting a few scenes from my sketches the day before, but my focus was gone.

I tried to blame it on the fact that I was in a haunted cabin, at a resort with an active murder investigation, and not on the fact that I felt an annoying sense of guilt about my reaction to Sawyer.

The cabin *was* distracting. More than once, I thought I caught the scent of lavender in the air. My hair stood on end every time.

I decided to pass the time by taking a nap. Unwilling to sleep in the living room with the obituaries, I headed to the bedroom—locked the door, just in case—and curled up underneath the blankets. Exhaustion set in and I dozed off quickly, finally relaxing.

But I was woken by the faint sound of a woman's voice. I sat up, unable to even breathe.

The voice was haunting, and unnatural somehow. It sounded like she was crying and whispering all at once, a tangle of words and emotion I couldn't unravel.

The bedroom was perfumed with the undeniable scent of lavender, and the air felt ice cold.

Fear paralyzed me. I was afraid to move, afraid to even look around the room for fear of what I might see. My heart thudded against my rib cage as I took shallow breaths, gripping the sheets in my hands. I squeezed my eyes shut, wishing I could block out the sounds.

Then her voice slowly faded away. The temperature returned to normal and the lavender disappeared. I let out a shaky breath, finally daring to look around the room. I was alone. It was as if nothing had even happened.

I wanted to leave. But I had nowhere to go. My choices were to grovel and apologize to Sawyer, asking if I could stay with him, or take my chances with someone else here—someone who might be a murderer. As much as I hated Sawyer, I knew he hadn't killed Ethan. His sense of justice was too strong for that. He was the only person here I felt I could trust completely as far as that went.

I couldn't bring myself to face him though. So I moved to the living room, pacing and constantly watching out the window, hoping to see the welcome sight of police vehicles or work crews or even the crazy care-takers here to let us know the road had opened.

But nobody came.

WHEN DINNER TIME ROLLED AROUND AND THE SUN BEGAN TO fade, I couldn't stand it anymore. I didn't know where I was going, but I knew I didn't want to be in this cabin when darkness fell. Of everyone here, the obvious choice for company was Sadie and Rachel. My heart told me Rachel hadn't killed her husband. Even if she had, I didn't think she'd hurt me.

So I pulled out the pasta I'd packed and decided to make enough to share, planning to walk over and offer to have dinner together. It was a simple meal for a glamping getaway—pasta tossed in olive oil with minced garlic and herbs, topped with freshly grated cheese. But having made it a thousand times, I knew it was tasty and filling. Comfort food for a difficult situation.

I dished it up into a bowl I'd found in the cabinets, stacked paper plates and forks on top of it, and headed out the door, locking it behind me. When I started walking, I saw Sawyer sitting on his front porch. My heart betrayed me, leaping at the sight of him. Despite my anger, everything else was still there too—the attraction, the chemistry, the draw I didn't completely understand. The sense of safety when he was around.

My steps slowed automatically. I wondered if I should stop and say anything or keep my eyes on the road, ignoring him completely.

But I couldn't keep my eyes off him. My gaze met his as he studied me, never moving. When I got close to his walkway, his cold voice stopped me in my tracks.

"Is that a peace offering?"

It was exactly the wrong thing for him to say. All thought of apologizing to him fled.

I scoffed. "Hardly. I'm taking dinner to Rachel and Sadie. Not that it's any of your business."

His hand tightened on the arm of his porch rocker like he wanted to break something but was holding himself back. "Stay safe," he said, finally, before turning his eyes away from me.

Two little words that immediately began melting the ice in my heart.

But I was too damn stubborn to let him know it.

. . .

NEITHER RACHEL NOR SADIE ANSWERED THE DOOR. I knocked three separate times before giving up, deflated. It was understandable that they'd want privacy right now. But I was a little worried about the tension between them and wanted to make sure Sadie was okay.

I also didn't want to go back home.

I turned away from their cabin, walking slowly back toward mine, warring internally over what to do. Thankfully, I didn't have to battle long. Adam and Eve stepped out of their cabin, stopping me.

"Hey, girl!" Eve called, waving at me. "We're headed to the bonfire pit. Want to come?"

"You're having another bonfire tonight?" The idea shocked me. After all, someone had been killed here the night before. This no longer felt anything like a vacation.

"Totally," Adam said as they caught up to me. He lowered his voice. "And look, if you want some weed, just say the word, okay? We don't mind sharing."

"Oh. Thanks, but I'm good." I attempted to hide the shock on my face. With a judge for a father, I'd lived an incredibly sheltered life and had never once tried marijuana, even though it was now legal in most states. It wasn't in Wisconsin though, and I wasn't about to break that law, even as a twenty-three-year-old woman who no longer answered to her dad.

Although, since I still lived at home and he paid my bills, I supposed I technically did still answer to him.

"If you change your mind, just let us know," Eve said, smiling brightly. "It can open up the senses. Help you experience more on a hunt."

"I'm not sure I want to experience more paranormal activity out here," I said, falling in step beside them as they walked toward the fire pit. It felt a bit wrong considering the circumstances, but I was grateful for an excuse not to go home. And despite how Sawyer felt, I kind of liked them. They were silly, sure, but they were sweet.

I caught a glimpse of Sawyer out of the corner of my eye. He was still sitting on his porch, watching us. I couldn't help it—I turned and looked right at him just in time to catch what looked like hurt on his face before his mask came back up. A stab of guilt hit, but I waved it away. Maybe he was a good guy. Maybe he was even a hero. It didn't change the fact that he'd lied to me.

"I'm sorry," I said, forcing my attention back to Adam and Eve. "What were you saying?" I'd completely missed the conversation, distracted by my thoughts of Sawyer.

"Just wondering if you had more activity today," Eve said, giving me a strange look, then looking past me at Sawyer. "But I can see why you didn't hear me. You guys have a fight or something?"

"Something like that. I don't want to talk about it. As far as activity, yeah. I smelled lavender again. Then, when I was napping, I thought I heard a woman crying. My room got really cold and the lavender became overwhelming."

They exchanged looks. Adam was practically shaking with excitement. "Man, how about we all investigate at your place tonight? It sounds like that's the epicenter. I'm so mad they didn't let us stay at that one."

"Did you request it?" I asked, curious.

Eve nodded. "Of course. That's where we wanted to be."

"That's so weird," I said, mulling it over. "Sawyer requested it too, but they didn't give it to him, either. I'd actually asked for a different cabin, but they moved me to thirteen. Isn't that odd?"

Adam snorted. "It's odd to me that Sawyer asked for that one when he acts like he's so high and mighty and that what we do is stupid. Why do you think he wanted it?"

Despite feeling betrayed by Sawyer, there was no way I was going to return the favor and tell them why he was here. "Privacy, probably," I lied. "He seems like the type who'd rather be deep in the woods, alone in a tent, instead of at a resort full of guests."

Adam and Eve both cracked up.

"You've got that right," Eve agreed. "Still, he is kind of dreamy."

"Hey," Adam interjected, offended. "That hurts, baby."

"Oh, babe," Eve immediately cooed. "You know he's not my type at all. You're the kind of guy I go crazy for." She threw her arms around his neck and kissed him hard enough to make his head spin.

I bit my lip, trying not to laugh. Adam and Sawyer couldn't have been further apart in looks. Sawyer's biceps were nearly as big as Adam's scrawny waist. Sawyer was at least six foot one, where Adam couldn't be more than five foot five. Sawyer walked with his head held high, while Adam hunched over and shuffled a bit like he was protecting himself from a punch to the gut.

I had a feeling he'd been teased quite a bit in high school and was glad he'd found Eve—beautiful, sweet Eve, who loved him dearly. They were an interesting match, but they clearly adored each other. And they shared the same passion, which was great. It was important to have something in common.

What did Sawyer and I have in common? Exactly nothing.

Worse, why did I care so much? I'd known him for barely more than twenty-four hours. It was pathetic that I was still thinking about him.

I needed a distraction, and I was feeling rebellious, ready to do something—anything—to prove I was more than what Sawyer seemed to think I was. A dangerous thought floated through my mind, tempting me to cross a line I'd never crossed.

I cleared my throat, attempting to sound casual. "Hey, maybe I will take you guys up on that pot," I said, shrugging.

"Really?" Eve squealed. "Here you go." She pulled a joint out of her pocket, lit it, and passed it to me.

I took it in my fingers the way I'd seen others do in the movies and took a drag from it, immediately coughing it back up. This was awful. And it smelled terrible. Who on earth would want to do this?

Then I remembered Sawyer. Determined to make myself forget, I wrapped my lips around the joint and tried again.

Chapter Twenty-Two

Sawyer

Daylight faded as heavy clouds moved in from the west. I stared out at the dark waters of the lake, brooding. Olivia and I were done. She was so angry that she actually preferred the company of Adam and Eve over me. That pretty much said it all.

I tried to forget how natural it had felt to talk to her. How right it had felt when I'd held her. The way she saw right through me, even when no one else could.

It didn't matter anymore. It was over. She'd learned the truth of who I was and hated me for it. Worse, I'd been so disappointed in her response, in her selfishness, that I'd deliberately hurt her with my words, erasing any chance of us getting past it.

Although, based on her reaction, I didn't think there had been a chance of that even before I'd opened my big fat mouth. Her loyalty was to her no-good, corrupt father. Or his money. Either way, I'd lost a hell of a lot of respect for her today. Respect that I'd given too quickly.

Still, even if the friendship between us was lost, I wanted her to be safe. Nothing had changed in that regard. I was still worried about her out here. And now, she was making reckless decisions like trying to take dinner to a woman who might be a killer. I had to wonder why. Was it misguided trust? Fear of being in cabin thirteen alone?

Or maybe it was the deep sweetness that I suspected was still in there, despite her allegiance to her father.

I put my hands behind my head, mulling it over. I knew a thing or two about loyalty. It had been deeply instilled in us SEALs during our training, to the point where I'd lost my own judgment about one of the men I'd worked with, initially defending him when he'd been accused of sexual harassment. My loyalty to him, to our team, had clouded my vision, making me unable to see the truth of who he was until a second woman had come forward. It was one of my biggest regrets.

I could see it being the same for Olivia. Her dad was a force to be reckoned with. He was the type to demand allegiance to the family. And if he'd told her these claims against him were false, maybe she legitimately believed him.

Problem was I didn't know if her reaction was based on training or selfishness. And I wouldn't know unless we had another conversation, which she clearly had no interest in doing. She was too busy hanging out with potential murderers, with no thought of the danger in which she might be placing herself.

My fist clenched at the thought.

I caught a familiar scent on the wind and groaned. Great. Someone was smoking weed out here. And I had a good idea of who.

I stood and headed toward the fire pit.

ADAM AND EVE WERE BOTH STONED AND GIGGLING WHEN I came around the corner and caught sight of the group at the bonfire. Olivia was sitting quietly, holding that big bowl of something she'd tried taking to Rachel in one hand and a lit joint in the other. She was startled when she saw me and immediately looked away.

I walked straight to where she was and squatted down beside her. "What the hell are you doing?"

"Just trying to relax," she mumbled.

"Have you ever smoked weed before?"

"Sure. Countless times."

I shook my head. "You're lying."

"Fine." She rolled her eyes. "This is my first time."

"Get up," I said, plucking the joint from her hand and grinding it out on the ground beneath my boot.

"What?" She finally looked up at me.

"I said get up. You're coming with me."

She shook her head. "I don't want to."

"And I don't really care what you want right now." I was too tired to keep the irritation out of my voice. "You're putting yourself in a dangerous situation, and I'm not going to stand by and watch it. Get up and follow me or I'm going to throw you over my shoulder and carry you."

"You wouldn't." She turned her eyes away from me,

"One thing you need to learn about me," I said before standing up from my squat.

"What's that?"

"When I say I'm going to do something, I mean it." I grabbed her, threw her over my shoulder, and started marching back toward my cabin.

"Put me down," she protested, kicking against me.

I wrapped my arm around her legs to stop her, trying not to enjoy the feeling of those firm thighs underneath my palm. "No. You're making bad choices, Liv. Weed? Seriously?" I couldn't keep the disgust out of my voice. "At a time when you need to keep your damn wits about you?"

She stopped fighting. "I was trying to forget you." Her voice was muffled against my back, but I heard her just the same.

My heart almost stopped.

"Well, too bad. I'm not that easily forgotten."

WHEN WE REACHED MY CABIN, I PUT HER DOWN IN ONE OF the porch rockers, then took the one next to her. I felt stormy inside and wanted to keep lecturing her. But something about the look on her face stopped me. She looked broken, dejected, and sad.

I knew at least part of that was my fault, and I hated it.

So when I got control of my temper, I sighed and asked, "How do you feel?"

"Fine," she said, pulling her jacket tighter and rewrapping the scarf around her neck like it was armor.

"I'm asking how high you are," I said, unable to keep the tension out of my voice.

She immediately glanced up toward the camera I'd pointed out the day before.

"Don't worry about that," I said, shaking my head. "I dismantled it earlier."

"What? Why?"

I shrugged. "Richard said it was for the protection of the guests. I don't need his protection, and I value my privacy. Now, back to my question—how high are you?"

"I'm not," she replied in a small voice.

"What do you mean?"

She sighed. "It was too gross. I coughed it all up. Didn't really get any. I don't feel anything at all."

That was a relief, at least. I wouldn't have minded her sleeping it off at my place, but it wouldn't have been ideal. "Good. I'm not trying to be uptight, but, Liv, please be careful." I turned toward her, placing a hand on her knee so she'd look at me. "We're at a place where a lot of people have died, and you know what happened to Grace. You shouldn't be taking chances. Not here. Not now."

"I know." She held my gaze, and something passed between us. It felt like a truce. Maybe even more.

I pried the bowl out of her hands. Somehow, she'd managed to hang on to it even when I was carrying her. "Let's see what we've got in here."

She gave a small laugh. "Just pasta. I thought Rachel and Sadie could use a good meal. I guess we could eat dinner together. If you want."

I opened it up. It looked—and smelled—heavenly. Just like Olivia. "I'd like that."

"Help yourself."

I studied her for a moment. "Olivia," I said before clearing my throat, "I said some things earlier I'd like to take back. I called you selfish and accused you of potentially being involved in Ethan's death. I'm sorry for that. We may see the world differently, but I know you have a good heart."

The last of the anger on her face melted away. "I'm sorry, too." Tears welled up, but she blinked them away. "You weren't wrong. About me *or* my father. I don't want to think of him as being a monster. I've been trying to deny it. But he's not a kind person, and he's always had a lack of empathy for those kids. I just don't want to believe he could really do something like that. It's so wrong."

"It's hard to learn that someone we love—someone we're loyal to—isn't who we think they are," I said, choosing my words carefully. "I know that better than anyone."

"I still hope this is a mistake. That somehow you're wrong," she said.

"I'm not."

She looked at me, searching my eyes. "You really have proof?"

"A mountain of it. Trust me, they wouldn't have filed charges without it. No one wanted to go against Judge Mitchell unless it was airtight."

The last of her hopes seemed to crumble. "He promised us all that this would go away. That everything would be fine, because no one would find a shred of evidence against him. I tried so hard to believe that was because he was innocent. "

"I'm sorry," I said. I really was. Not for having caught him—he deserved everything that was coming. But sorry that she was going to suffer because of his mistakes.

She looked up at me. "He was so confident. But you found the proof."

"He was good, I'll give him that. But my team and I are better."

"What do you think will happen to him?"

I shrugged, scrubbing a hand through my hair. "That's above my pay grade. At best, he'll be disbarred. Probably pay some serious fines. If they want to make an example out of him—and they should—he'll get a few years in a federal prison."

"I can't even imagine that." Her voice wobbled.

"No offense, but the punishment should fit the crime. Don't you think?"

"Is the world always so black and white for you?"

"When it comes to something like this, it is," I muttered.

She pulled her knees up to her chest, silent for a moment. "You're right. As hard as it is for me to accept it all, if he really did what you say, then...then you need to make sure he never does anything like that again."

"I'm still sorry you got caught in the crossfire. I never intended for anyone else to get hurt." I needed her to know that—that what had happened to her mattered to me.

She looked over at me, holding my gaze. "I wanted to be angry at you for that, but it wasn't your fault. Not really. My father is the one who put us all in danger by making the choices he did. You were just trying to get justice."

"I appreciate that. I'm still sorry it happened."

She swallowed hard, turning her gaze back to the water. "I guess all this means my life is about to change in some big ways. I know you'll think that's a selfish thought. But I don't mean to be selfish. Just practical. Everything's going to be different now. My life—my family—will never be the same."

"Yeah, things will change. But change isn't always a bad thing."

She sighed. "I've never been good with it. But I guess I'll just have to learn, huh?"

"I guess you will." I watched her, feeling a pang of empathy. "Listen, how about I dish up some of this dinner? You need to eat."

"Okay." She gave me a small smile. "Thanks, Sawyer."

"No problem." I got up, taking the bowl with me. I was glad we'd come to a truce. Not just because I liked her, but because at the end of the day we were still trapped on this property with a killer. I felt responsible for her, and it was easier to make sure she was safe if we stuck together.

Because I had a bad feeling that more trouble was coming—and my gut was rarely wrong.

Chapter Twenty-Three

Olivia

Sawyer disappeared inside the cabin. A few minutes later, he returned with two plates of pasta. He handed me mine and put his on the table beside his chair, then disappeared again, returning with a bottle of wine and two glasses.

"I thought we needed to keep our wits about us?" I teased.

His mouth turned up in a playful smile. "I've seen your father's wine cellar. I have a feeling you're a lot more experienced with this than with what you were trying earlier tonight. I'm sure you can enjoy a glass with dinner without losing your senses."

"You're right about that," I said, laughing. I accepted the glass, taking a small sip and savoring the notes. He had good taste. "That's lovely. Malbec?"

"You got it. Maybe not the right choice for a light pasta, but it's all I brought."

"It works anyway," I said, distracted. He had been in my father's wine cellar? I had to wonder how deep his investigation had gone. It was an uncomfortable feeling, knowing he'd dug into my family like that.

"Good." He gave me a thoughtful look, watching me trace the rim of the glass with my finger. "What's wrong?"

"It's just odd that you know so much more about me than I do about you. I mean, you've been in my house. Were you searching it?"

"No." His voice was firm. "Your father invited a group of people over for drinks and I scored an invitation. That's the only time I was there. Being in his circle was part of my cover. People open up to you more when they think you're one of them."

"It still feels strange."

He looked out toward the lake. "Ask me a question. Anything that isn't related to my work or time in service. Ask me something personal and I promise to tell you the truth."

"Hmmm..." I thought it over. "Where's your favorite place in the world?"

"Italy," he said without a moment's hesitation. "It's different there. Time moves so slowly. The sunshine, the food, the wine—there's nothing like it."

"I've never been, but it's on my wishlist."

"What's your favorite place?"

I took a deep breath, smiling as I thought back to some of my favorite memories. "The ocean."

"Oh yeah?" He looked at me with interest. "I thought you said you weren't much of a swimmer?"

"I'm not," I confessed. "But I love it anyway. It almost doesn't matter where, either. I love the rocky coastline in Maine and the sandy beaches in Mexico. Put me beside the water and I'm happy."

"I'm a big fan myself. The energy of the water is something else. The ocean is this whole other universe, one where we're just visitors." He took a giant bite of my pasta. "Oh man. This is amazing."

"Thank you." I couldn't help but smile.

"You're a great cook."

"You should see what I can do with a full pantry," I said, laughing.

"Maybe when we get out of here, you can show me."

He said it casually, but I could hear the question in it. When all this was over, would I follow my father blindly and treat Sawyer like an enemy? Or would we still be friends?

I picked at my pasta, feeling a surge of fear. Defying my father was unthinkable.

But so was defending him if the allegations were true. And in my soul, I knew they were. I think I had known since the day the news broke. I'd just been too afraid to face the truth.

"Maybe I will," I finally said, looking up at him. Three little words that felt like a sword, severing the ties between me and my family. Even contemplating a continued friendship with Sawyer was betrayal. And part of me wasn't at all sure I could do that.

But despite my reticence, our eyes locked, and heat built between us. All the anger from before had shifted into something else—something much more interesting and begging to be explored.

He leaned forward like he was ready to start some of that exploration, but he stopped when we heard the sound of a vehicle headed our way down the gravel drive.

"Not a guest," he said, his eyes darting down to the other cabins. "All our vehicles are still parked."

"Think the road is open?" I asked, feeling hope and disappointment at the same time.

He let out a groan as the old pickup truck rattled into sight. "It's the caretakers."

He stood and flagged them to pull over, jogging down the steps to meet them. I followed behind, not wanting to be left out of the conversation.

"Hello, Mr. Reed," Felix said, hopping out of the cab and shaking Sawyer's hand firmly. "Got some good news for you folks."

"What's that?"

"Flooding subsided and the creek's passable. Crew came by and said they'll get to work on the tree first thing in the morning. If all goes well, you'll be outta here by noon."

"That is good news," Sawyer agreed. "Any word from Sheriff Patterson yet?"

Felix shook his head. "Nah. Phones are still down. Mr. Moore stopped by earlier and told me he was going to take an ATV into town to let the sheriff know about our situation here, but he hasn't made it back yet."

Sawyer frowned. "Does it normally take that long to make a round trip?"

Felix shrugged. "No, but I figure this isn't the only tree down in these parts. Could have had trouble getting through, maybe had to take a different route. Or maybe he decided to stay in town for the night. The sheriff probably won't come out here until the road's open anyway."

"That's a pretty sorry way to handle a murder investigation," Sawyer muttered.

"It's not like whoever did it is getting away now, are they?" Felix asked, shrugging again. "We're all stuck here. For now, anyway."

"Doesn't that worry you?" I asked, butting into the conversation.

"Does what worry me?" Felix looked like he'd just noticed I was there.

"That we're stuck here with a murderer."

He snorted. "Only person who puts the fear into me is my dear wife, and I've slept next to her for over forty years. All this petty nonsense between guests don't get to me. Besides, it's obvious his wife's the one who killed him, and she ain't got nothing against the rest of us."

"Why do you say it's obvious she killed him?" Sawyer asked.

He threw his head back and laughed. "Because I'm married, son. You'll understand one of these days. Now, it's been nice chatting with you, but I'm going to let the other folks know about the road now so everyone can get packed up tonight. Unless you want to tell them all for me."

Sawyer and I exchanged glances. "We'll spread the word," he said.

"I thank you for it," Felix said, nodding solemnly. "Some of these folks out here are downright crazy. Those ghost hunters?" He shook his head. "Crazy, I tell you."

Sawyer grinned. "I couldn't agree more."

We watched as Felix climbed back into his truck and turned around, heading back toward his home.

"I don't like this," Sawyer said. There was an edge to his voice that made me anxious.

"About Richard not being back yet?"

He nodded. "Don't get me wrong. I'm ready to get out of here. But if the road opens before Richard gets back with the sheriff, whoever killed Ethan can just disappear."

"Unless Richard is the one who killed Ethan," I pointed out.

"True."

"So are we going to tell everyone about the road?"

"Not yet," he said, shaking his head slowly. "I think for now we're going to keep that detail to ourselves.

Chapter Twenty-Four

Sawyer

As Olivia and I headed back to my porch, we saw Sadie and Joey coming down from one of the other trailheads on the far end of the lake. Olivia frowned but waved Sadie over. At first, it looked like Sadie was going to ignore her, but after a minute, she reluctantly changed course, grabbing Joey's hand and dragging him toward where we were.

I leaned over, whispering in Olivia's ear. "Looks like they're an item now."

"Speaking of things we don't like. He's too old for her, and I don't like his attitude," she muttered under her breath. But she plastered a smile on her face and spoke warmly when Sadie approached. "What are you guys up to tonight?"

"Just went for a walk," Sadie said, crossing her arms and avoiding Olivia's gaze.

"Have you eaten? I tried to take dinner to you and your mom, but nobody answered."

"No. She didn't make anything. She was sleeping when I snuck out." Sadie rolled her eyes. "She wanted us to just stay cooped up in that cabin with the lights off all day like it would bring Dad back. But it won't." Her tough bravado faded as her voice caught.

Joey surprised me by putting an arm around her in comfort. He was currently at the top of my suspect list, but he did seem to have empathy for Sadie, which was a vote in his favor.

Didn't mean he hadn't killed her dad just to get him out of the way though.

"No, it won't," Olivia said softly. "Do you guys want some food? I cooked enough to feed an army."

Sadie and Joey exchanged glances and he shrugged.

"Sure," Joey said. "Food sounds good."

"I'll make plates for you." Olivia gave me a look before she slipped into the house. I could read her like a book. She felt invested in Sadie, and she wanted me to find out if Joey was a safe person for her to be around.

"Did you guys have a nice hike?" I asked, shoving my hands into my pockets and rocking back onto my heels, mimicking the laidback stance my father always took when he was interrogating me.

Not that I'd ever fallen for it.

"Yeah," Sadie said, relaxing a bit once she realized we weren't going to lecture her. "It's really pretty out here. And it felt good to just...move."

"I know what you mean," I said, nodding. "Exercise is the best therapy."

"Exactly." She shot me a small smile.

Olivia returned with two plates loaded with pasta. "Here you go," she said, handing them to the kids. "We can grab camping chairs for you."

"Nah," Joey said before shoving a giant bite into his mouth. "We were up on the ridge, looked down and saw they're having another bonfire tonight. Thought we'd head over there."

Olivia shot me a worried look. Again, I could see what she was thinking as clearly as if it were written all over her face.

"Perfect," I said smoothly. "That's where we were headed too."

. . .

ADAM AND EVE HAD FINISHED THEIR SMOKES BY THE TIME WE got there, thank goodness. The thick odor of marijuana still hung heavy over the area, and I saw Joey and Sadie grin at each other. They clearly knew exactly what they were smelling.

"You guys came back!" Eve called out, smiling radiantly. "I figured you'd be busy all night." She shot Olivia a wink.

Olivia turned a deep shade of red. "We were just eating dinner."

"Hey, this pasta is really good," Sadie said, plopping down into one of the camping chairs I'd just set up.

"Thanks." Olivia sat beside her, and I parked myself right by Olivia.

With Adam and Eve both very relaxed, to put it mildly, the group was quiet. Despite everything, I started to feel a sense of peace. The skies were clear and the stars above us were gorgeous. The flames were hypnotic, and as the smell of woodsmoke began to overtake the lingering pot odors, I started actually enjoying myself. Without thinking much about it, I reached out and put an arm around Olivia, caressing her shoulder with my thumb.

Wasn't even sure why I did it, really, other than the fact that I wanted to. But she looked up and gave me a sweet smile, then timidly put a hand on my knee. I felt like I'd won some sort of prize.

If only the guys could see me now. Falling all over myself for a girl I barely knew. It wasn't like me at all.

But then again, Olivia wasn't like anyone I'd ever met.

I leaned over, whispering in her ear. "If you forget where we are and everything that's happened, this is kind of nice."

She turned her face toward me so that her nose nuzzled my cheek. "I think that's how my whole future is going to have to be. Forget everything that's happened and just try to find the joy in the moment. But... maybe that's okay."

"Maybe it is."

I gently gripped her chin in my hand, lowering my lips to hers. This time, I kissed her softly and slowly, savoring every last taste, even though we were surrounded by other people.

For the first time in my life, I didn't care.

"Liv," I began, but I was cut off.

"There you are!" Rachel cried out in a panicked voice as she ran toward the fire. "I woke up and you were gone! What were you thinking?" She rushed to Sadie and grabbed her by the shoulders, shaking her.

"Stop it," Joey said, shoving her hands away. "Leave her alone."

Rachel stared at him in shock. "She's my daughter."

"Yeah, but I hate you!" Sadie pushed her plate off her lap, onto the ground, and launched out of her chair, taking off toward the lake.

Rachel just stood there. "I don't... I don't understand."

"Let me talk to her," Olivia suggested, standing.

Rachel nodded.

"I'll come too," I said.

But Olivia held out a hand. "Just give me a minute with her, okay?"

Anxiety gripped me. I stood, putting a hand on Liv's hip. Her gaze caught mine. "I don't want you alone out there," I admitted, my voice low.

Her eyes softened. "I'll be fine. Look, you can see her from here. We'll stay in sight, okay?"

I wrapped my arms around her waist. "See that you do," I murmured into her ear. "I like looking at you."

She gave me a knowing grin. "I'll be right back."

I sat down and watched, feeling helpless as she walked away.

Chapter Twenty-Five

Olivia

I crossed my arms, trying to stay warm as I walked away from the heat of the fire. The storm from the night before had dropped the evening temperature by at least fifteen degrees, and the night was so cold that I could see my own breath, like miniature ghosts floating through the air with every exhale. I wrapped my scarf up higher, trying to capture some of that warmth. Sadie was only wearing a sweat-shirt. She had to be freezing.

She was crying when I reached her. I didn't know what to say, so I put a hand on her back and stayed silent until she was ready to talk.

"I hate her," she finally said as she wiped snot from her nose.

"You don't," I said. I knew she couldn't. Even with what I knew about my father, I didn't hate him. Family bonds ran deep.

"I do." She shook her head. "I know she killed him."

"Sadie, why do you keep saying that?"

"Because." She blew out a heavy breath. "She probably wanted him out of the way so she could be with her boyfriend."

My stomach dropped. "Boyfriend? Your mom was having an affair?"

She nodded. "Yep. I told you she's not a good person."

My mind raced. If Rachel was having an affair, that did not look good for her. Between that and her jealousy over Ethan's relationship with Sadie, the motives for wanting him dead were stacking up.

"How do you know?" I asked. "And does she know you're aware of it?"

She shook her head. "No. I haven't confronted her about it. Dad told me a few weeks ago."

"Ethan knew?" This was looking worse and worse.

She nodded miserably. "One day, I came home from school earlier than normal. My volleyball coach was sick, so our practice got canceled. Anyway, Dad was home, working in his office. I was going to let him know I was there but stopped when I heard him talking on the phone to someone. He was telling her that he wished they could be together and that he thought about her all the time. I confronted him and that's when he told me the truth."

"Wait." I was confused. "It sounds like your dad was the one having an affair."

She shook her head. "He wanted to. But he hadn't actually gone through with it. He was just tempted, and I'd caught him in a moment of weakness. He explained how Mom had been cheating on him for over a year and how she'd shut him out and, well, you know. He was so lonely. But he was glad I'd caught him before he made a mistake. He loved her so much, despite everything." Her voice broke.

"Whoa. That's heavy." And a very inappropriate conversation for him to have with his teenage daughter.

"Tell me about it."

"Sadie, you and your mom only have each other now. You have to talk about this."

She turned to me. "No. She has *him*, whoever he is. I'm on my own."

. . .

SADIE DIDN'T WANT TO COME BACK TO THE BONFIRE, SAYING she needed some space. I didn't feel good about leaving her alone, but she was adamant that she didn't want me around. I finally walked away, trudging slowly back to the group, trying to figure out what to say.

Rachel was having an affair.

It looked more and more like Rachel had killed Ethan, and my heart broke for Sadie. Losing her dad was bad enough. But if Rachel was guilty, Sadie was about to lose her mom, too. She really would be on her own. What would happen to her? I hoped she had grandparents or an aunt and uncle to take her in. It was just awful.

I was so caught up in my own thoughts that I almost didn't notice it, but a muffled cry caught my attention. I froze, listening, remembering the sounds in my cabin earlier.

It happened again. I strained my ears, realizing it was coming from my left. Without even thinking, I slowly walked in the direction of the noise.

The whimpering grew louder, and I realized it wasn't ghostly. It sounded like a puppy. My heart caught in my chest as he howled, then whined again.

"Here, puppy," I called, stopping to whistle.

He howled again as if in answer, but didn't come any closer.

Sawyer jogged down to where I was. "What's going on?" he asked.

"Do you hear that?" I called the dog again.

The dog's cry grew louder in response.

Sawyer frowned. "Yeah. I do."

"Do you think it's trapped somewhere?"

"Maybe. Hang on. I'll grab a flashlight." He jogged off and returned quickly, shining a light toward the boathouse. "I think the sound is coming from in there."

We walked toward the rundown building, swinging the light from right to left in case the dog was caught on something outside.

"He sounds hurt," I murmured. "Poor baby."

We got to the door and Sawyer frowned, eyeing the padlock. It hung loose, and the door to the shed was cracked open.

"Wait here," he said. "Just in case."

"Just in case what?"

He gave me an unreadable look. "Just in case," he repeated.

"Okay." Nervous butterflies fluttered in my stomach.

He pulled his pistol, opened the door, and disappeared inside the building. I bit my lip, shivering while I waited for him to return. Something about this place felt so spooky, so...deadly. Sawyer kept telling me that I shouldn't get so worked up over the stories connected to this land, but on a night like tonight, with the sky black and the wind moaning through the trees, it was hard not to think of ghosts.

I breathed a sigh of relief when Sawyer returned, carrying a very wiggly puppy.

"Oh, poor thing," I said, reaching for the dog and pulling his warm body into my arms. He scrambled his way up my chest, eager for attention. His puppy breath was hot on my face, and I laughed, trying to avoid his frantic kisses. "He must have gotten trapped in there. He seems okay physically though. Was he just scared?"

"Sad, I think," Sawyer said. "We've got a problem."

"What is it?"

"Richard Moore, the owner of this place."

"What about him?" My stomach sank before he even answered, somehow knowing—or fearing—what he was about to say.

Sawyer's face went hard. "He's dead."

Chapter Twenty-Six

Sawyer

OLIVIA'S FACE WENT WHITE WITH SHOCK. I PUT ONE HAND on her shoulder to steady her and held a finger to my lips, warning her to be quiet.

"I don't understand," she said, clutching the puppy like her life depended on it. "How... Is he... I don't—"

"Shhh. I don't want the others to hear. Not until I can tell them and watch their reactions myself. His body is inside the boathouse."

"Was he shot like Ethan?"

I shook my head. "No. He was bludgeoned with an oar."

She went from white to green. "I think I'm going to be sick."

"Hold it together. I need you to stay focused. You understand why this is so bad, right?"

She nodded slowly. "It means the police aren't coming."

"That's part of it," I confirmed. "This had to have happened hours ago. Probably late this morning, shortly after I spoke to him. It must have been while you and I were at Rachel's or in my cabin, because after you left, I headed out to my porch and stayed there the rest of the day."

Confusion clouded her eyes. "I was at my place for hours. Why did you sit on your porch that whole time?"

"Because I needed to keep a watch out for you. I needed to know you were okay." The words came out strained. I still didn't understand why I cared so damn much about a woman I'd just met. But I did.

"Even after the horrible things we said to each other?"

I nodded. "Yeah. If something had happened to you, I wouldn't have been able to stand it."

She gave me a tiny smile. "I still can't believe any of this. Thank God the road is opening tomorrow and we can get to the police."

"Yes," I said slowly. "But, Olivia, here's the other thing you need to think about. When it was just Ethan, there was a good chance it was personal. Now…"

"Now, we have no idea why someone is killing people," she said slowly, realizing what I was getting at.

"Exactly. And we're stuck here with whoever is doing this for at least one more night."

I LEFT OLIVIA OUTSIDE WITH THE DOG WHILE I WENT BACK inside to take pictures of the crime scene. Felix and Deb would probably trample all over this one too, moving Richard's body the minute they heard. It was enough to make me consider keeping the discovery to ourselves so that the police would actually have a chance of figuring out who did this.

But unless these murders were completely unrelated and committed by different people—possible, but unlikely—we were dealing with someone who'd murdered twice in a span of twenty-four hours.

Meanwhile, Adam and Eve were getting high and shooting videos for their channel like nothing had even happened. Sadie and Joey were slipping off alone. Rachel didn't seem to be able to stop Sadie, and Joey's parents didn't even seem to care. Everyone needed to seclude themselves in their own cabins and stop acting like this was still a vacation. Maybe telling them about Richard would finally get them to realize they were in actual danger out here.

I scanned the room with my flashlight, putting together a picture of what had happened. There was a row of boat oars hanging high on the wall, with one missing. That one was on the floor, close to Richard. The end of it was bloody—just like his head.

I wasn't going to get close enough to get blood on my shoes. Just being in here was bad enough. I was very aware that my DNA would now exist at two crime scenes, and I'd have some explaining to do when authorities finally arrived. But even from a distance, I could tell he'd been hit multiple times. If the first blow had taken him to the ground, either it hadn't killed him or the killer hadn't been confident it had.

Multiple blows to Richard. Multiple shots in Ethan. Either the killer was emotional and angry or wasn't particularly effective. Or both.

I squatted to the ground, taking it all in. There were boot prints in the dust. Some likely belonged to Richard, but the others? They probably belonged to the killer. Of course, nearly everyone out here wore boots—after all, we were in the woods. But the size could narrow down my suspect list.

There were at least two different sizes. A larger one, and an average-sized one. I looked at Richard's feet—large. So the average-sized prints belonged to whoever had been in here with him. That ruled me out, at least, I thought with a smirk. It ruled Liv out, too, for that matter. She had tiny feet that matched her petite body. Plus, she wore old-fashioned boots with a little heel on the bottom. So she wasn't a match.

But I'd sure as hell be on the lookout for whoever was.

Something caught my eye on the other side of the body. I stood up and slowly walked the perimeter of the room, placing myself where I could see it without getting close. It was something scrawled in the dust. I cocked my head, trying to read it, then took a photo with my cell phone camera and flipped it around.

Ethel.

My eyes narrowed as I studied the word written in the dirt. The killer had clearly intended for whoever investigated this murder to connect it to the ghost stories surrounding this place.

But I stood by what I'd said before about Ethan's death. Ghosts didn't bludgeon people with boat paddles. Living, breathing humans did.

The real question was why someone would kill Richard. The most obvious answer was to stop him from going to the police. If that was the case, then his death was on me, I realized with a stab of guilt. I was the one who'd asked him to go, and I was the one who'd told everyone he was doing it. But I had to wonder if there was more to the story.

I scanned the boathouse, realizing there wasn't an ATV here, and there didn't appear to be room to store one. So, if he hadn't come here to get his ATV, what was he doing in the boathouse?

And who would have known he was here?

Chapter Twenty-Seven

Olivia

Sawyer went back inside to take pictures of the body with his cell phone, knowing that Felix and Deb were likely to disturb this crime scene too. I waited outside with the puppy, grateful I had something warm and snuggly to hold on to. Ethan's murder was bad enough. A second murder made things a thousand times worse.

I needed to tell Sawyer the things Sadie had told me about Rachel. But part of me wondered if it really mattered anymore. Rachel killing her husband was hard enough to imagine. Killing the owner of the property? Why? It didn't make any sense.

Sadie was convinced it was her mom, and the affair story certainly made things look bad. But I just couldn't see Rachel randomly killing Richard.

Unless it wasn't random. Was there any chance Rachel's affair was with Richard? If so, maybe he freaked out when she killed Ethan. He could have told her he was going to the police and she panicked. Or maybe *he* killed Ethan to be with her, and when she found out, she lost it because she never really planned on leaving Ethan at all.

That was all crazy speculation though. And Rachel had said that Ethan picked the vacation spot. Out of the thousands of lake cabin rentals in the area, would he really have randomly picked the one Rachel's lover owned?

Unless he knew exactly who she was having an affair with and chose it because of that. Maybe he came here planning to confront them both. Maybe he confronted Richard, and Richard shot him... Then Rachel flipped out and killed Richard.

My mind raced, trying to figure out the puzzle. Sawyer was right; it felt even more crucial now. The stakes were even higher. If this wasn't about Rachel's affair, and it was totally random...

I was terrified we might not all make it through the night.

Sawyer came back a few minutes later, grim-faced and looking emotionally exhausted. But I apparently didn't look much better, because as soon as he saw me, he asked if I was okay.

I opened my mouth to answer but couldn't come up with a single intelligent thing to say. Okay? Of course I wasn't okay. Yet how could I say that? I was alive and healthy. Two other people had lost their lives in the last twenty-four hours. I was more okay than they were—that was for sure. I just shrugged and let out a little laugh of disbelief. This entire trip was like something out of a horror movie.

"I get it," he said. "More than you know. When things like this happen, your brain goes into a different mode."

"Yeah." I nodded. "That sounds about right."

"Come on." He shut up the boathouse, then put his hand on my elbow and led me away from it. "You're freezing out here. Let's get back to the fire."

I buried my face in the puppy's warm fur, grateful for this wiggly little symbol of life. With all the death we'd faced, I wanted to somehow soak up all of this vitality and pure puppy love. "Are you going to tell everyone about Richard?"

"Yeah," he said slowly. "On one hand, I don't want to. Might be better if the killer thinks he—or she—got away with this one. But I'm sure someone at the fire saw us down here. Besides, there are innocent people here too. And they deserve to know what's going on."

I shivered. "Unless knowing makes them go crazy and start doing awful things to each other."

He slipped an arm around me, pulling me close. "You're not wrong. Human beings can be unpredictable. But right now, I'm more worried about how everyone's blown off Ethan's murder and started treating this like a vacation again. False sense of security."

"I need to tell you something," I said, keeping my voice low. "So let's walk slowly."

"What is it?"

I quickly told him what Sadie had told me about Rachel's affair.

"Hmmm..." He trudged up the hill, rubbing his beard with his free hand. "That's very interesting, actually."

"I know. But I still hope it wasn't her."

"I hope so, too."

"Why do you think someone killed Richard?"

He looked at me. "Probably to stop him from going to the police before they can get away."

SADIE WAS BACK AT THE FIRE PIT WHEN WE GOT THERE, sitting as far away from her mom as possible. Rachel stared at her with an expression of hurt and shock. Joey sat by Sadie, staring Rachel down like he dared her to approach. The tension was so thick you could cut it with a knife, but Adam and Eve didn't seem to notice. They were curled up together, giggling and making out like no one was even around.

Joey's parents, Joseph and Meg, had joined the group. Of everyone, Meg appeared to be the most shaken by what had happened. She kept watching Joey with something that almost looked like fear. Her hands were shaky, and her foot twitched. Unlike the night before, her head wasn't buried in her cell phone. She was as tense as a lion about to pounce.

Joseph, on the other hand, seemed to be trying hard to make things as normal as possible. When Sawyer and I arrived, he jumped up to shake Sawyer's hand and asked if there were any updates.

Sawyer glanced at me, then cleared his throat. "Actually," he said in a voice loud enough to get everyone's attention, "since we're all here, I do have some news."

I took a seat. The puppy scrambled out of my arms and dove for the ground, then took off running toward the road. I felt a little ache in his absence. He'd felt like a talisman against the horrors of this place, and the world seemed to grow instantly colder without his warmth. But I couldn't go after him. Not when Sawyer was about to break the news about Richard.

Everyone turned toward him. Rachel's face was blank, numb. Meg looked fearful. Joseph sat down by his wife, put an arm around her, and looked up at Sawyer expectantly. Adam and Eve were both grinning like Sawyer was about to put on a show. Joey had a smirk on his face. Sadie crossed her arms and let out a little huff.

And Sawyer watched it all. I saw his eyes move from person to person, calculating and making note of their responses. Circumstances aside, I loved watching him do this. He was such an interesting person—so observant and thoughtful. If we had met under almost any other circumstances... And if he hadn't been the one to bring my father down...

But I shook off that thought, focusing instead on what Sawyer was beginning to say.

"I spoke with the caretakers just a bit ago. They said the flooding has gone down and progress on the tree will start tomorrow. If all goes well, we'll be able to get out of here tomorrow afternoon."

Visible relief washed over Rachel's, Joseph's, and Meg's faces. Sadie's face went stony, like she didn't want to leave with her mom. Joey put his arm around her and whispered something into her ear that made her smile.

Adam frowned as Eve booed.

"Think they'll let us stay anyway?" Adam asked. "We booked for the entire week. I hope the police don't shoo everyone out of here."

This time, Sawyer's face was the one to turn stony. "Yes, we wouldn't want to interfere with *your* investigation."

Adam lifted his hands in defense. "Look, man, I won't get in their way. But we spent a good chunk of dough coming out here, and I'm just saying we still need to get our money's worth for the channel."

"Glad your priorities are straight," Sawyer muttered before turning back to the rest of the group. "There's something else."

Joseph leaned forward, looking concerned. Meg's cheek twitched, but she said nothing. Adam and Eve ignored Sawyer completely, whispering to each other frantically about their own plans. Joey tensed, and Sadie bit her lip. Rachel's relief vanished, replaced by the numbness she'd worn before.

Sawyer watched them all before speaking. "There's been another murder," he said. "Richard Moore, the owner of Hidden Gem Lake, was killed today."

"What?" Rachel was the first one to speak, looking truly shocked. "Are you serious?"

"I'm afraid so."

Rachel looked from him, to me, to Sadie. Then she sat back in her seat, looking defeated again.

Meg was shaking even harder. "I can't believe this," she cried out. "And nobody can get a cell signal? We're all just...sitting ducks? Trapped here, waiting to get murdered one by one?"

Joey glared at her. She saw it and clamped her mouth shut. Joseph put an arm around her and squeezed.

"What would you suggest we all do?" Joseph asked, deferring to Sawyer.

"Well, there are two possible approaches," Sawyer said. "Either we agree there's safety in numbers and all stay together tonight. Or we all seclude ourselves in our own cabins. But I really don't think anyone needs to be going off alone hiking or anything like that." He shot a pointed look toward Sadie.

"I vote for safety in numbers," Meg said, her voice quivering. "Let's pick a cabin and all stay together."

"No," Rachel said, staring at Joey and Sadie. "I think we should seclude ourselves."

Adam popped up. "No offense, but we won't be staying locked up with you guys. We have work to do, regardless of what the rest of you choose."

"I really advise you to stop your hunting tonight," Sawyer said.

"Look, mate," Adam said, grinning. "You do you. But work doesn't stop as a business owner. If we aren't filming, we aren't making money." He stood and grabbed Eve's hand, pulling her up. "Peace out, folks. Hope we all make it through the night. But if you don't, feel free to tell your story to us. We'll have our equipment out and ready."

They scampered off, with Sawyer shaking his head.

CHAPTER TWENTY-EIGHT

Sawyer

WHEN ADAM AND EVE LEFT THE GROUP, I CAUGHT OLIVIA'S eye and jerked my head toward my cabin. She nodded and stood to leave.

Meg jumped up. "You guys are leaving, too? What happened to safety in numbers?" She shot Rachel a disgusted look. "If they want to go off on their own, fine. But the rest of us could stay together."

Joseph stood beside her, putting a protective arm around her shoulders. "I'm not so sure staying together is the best idea," he said, giving her a meaningful look. "Joey, why don't we all head back to our cabin? We can start getting packed up and be ready to hit the road as soon as it opens tomorrow."

Joey rolled his eyes. "I don't know why everyone's getting so worked up over two old dudes kicking the bucket anyway. I mean, sorry," he said when Sadie jerked back, clearly shocked that he'd referred to her dad that way.

"Sadie, we need to go," Rachel said firmly. She stood and crossed her arms, finally showing some authority.

Sadie looked crushed. She hung her head and followed her mom, casting one last sorrowful look at Olivia.

Olivia watched them go, then fell into step beside me as we walked toward my cabin.

"So, what are you thinking?" she asked as soon as we were out of earshot from the others.

"I have a couple of possible theories," I said carefully.

"Alright. Who do you think it is?"

I shook my head. "I'm not going to tell you."

"Why not?" She stopped suddenly. "Wait. You don't still suspect me, do you?"

"No," I said, grabbing her arm and getting her to walk again. "I know it wasn't you. Your feet are all wrong."

She looked down. "My feet? What are you talking about?"

"Doesn't matter. Listen, the reason I'm not telling you is because that would contaminate things."

"Contaminate? Sawyer, you aren't making any sense."

I stopped and turned, facing her. "What do you do when you have a hypothesis?"

She looked confused. "Test it?"

"Exactly. A theory isn't good enough. Not for a murder investigation. Right now, I've got ideas but no evidence. I can rule a few people out, but that still leaves too many possibilities."

She frowned. "Will you at least tell me who you've ruled out?"

I debated, then decided to bring her into the loop. "Alright. I've ruled out me and you, obviously. Beyond that, if we assume that we're dealing with just one killer, then we can also rule out Rachel, Eve, and Sadie."

Hope sparked in Liv's eyes. "You can rule out Rachel?"

"If," I said, cautioning her again, "we're only dealing with one killer. I can't rule her out completely when it comes to Ethan, but I don't think she killed Richard."

"How do you know?"

I grinned. "Same reason I know it wasn't you. Her feet are all wrong."

She let out an exasperated sigh. "Will you please stop talking in riddles and just explain what you mean by that?"

"Fine," I said, ushering her into my cabin. "There were two sets of footprints in the boathouse. One belonged to Richard. The other, presumably, belonged to his killer."

"Ah," she said, her eyes lighting up. "I understand now. You looked at our shoes. Everyone else is in hiking boots. Eve, Rachel, and I aren't."

"You're sharp," I said, grinning again. "You're wearing fashion boots with a heel. Stupid choice for the woods, if you ask me, but it will do you some favors this time. Rachel came to the bonfire wearing the same slippers she was wearing at her cabin this morning. And Eve's black combat boots have a distinctive tread on the bottom. They don't match."

"Rachel could have put on different shoes to kill Richard though," Liv pointed out.

"Only if she thought far enough in advance to put on shoes that were too big. Her feet are at least two sizes smaller than the ones in the boathouse."

Olivia smiled, taking a deep sigh of relief. "I'm so glad. I didn't want it to be her. Sadie was wearing hiking boots though."

I nodded. "She was. But she's also the shortest person out there, and the boat oars were hung high. Plus, my gut says she loved her father and never would have killed him. So I'd say it's safe to eliminate her—*if* we're looking for one killer."

Olivia frowned. "Adam's on the shorter side, too. And he and Eve have an alibi. They were ghost hunting during the time Ethan was killed."

"We can't eliminate him based on that. We think Ethan was killed sometime around midnight, but that's not certain. We're basing that on the man you saw, but it's possible that was unrelated. It's also possible you saw Ethan heading toward the waterfall trail but that he wasn't killed until sometime after. We have to consider that he could have been killed anytime between him leaving his cabin around eleven and, based on rigor, I'd guess two or three at the latest. Adam and Eve were outside ghost hunting during that window, and Adam could have slipped away at any point. He also has a motive. He wanted someone to die here."

"I guess he didn't seem totally surprised," she said, though she was clearly skeptical.

"There's more. The word 'Ethel' was scrawled in the dust beside Richard."

Her jaw dropped. "Seriously?"

I nodded. "So you can see why that would point me back toward Adam. I'd almost written him off, but he probably has more motive than anyone to make this look like a ghostly event."

"You're right," she said. "So we've eliminated Rachel, Sadie, and Eve. But Adam's a suspect, and that still leaves"—she counted up on her fingers—"four possibilities, counting him."

"Seven," I corrected.

"Seven?" Confusion clouded her face until she realized what I was getting at. "You're still considering the caretakers to be suspects?"

"I am," I said, nodding in confirmation.

"So Adam, Joey, Joseph, Meg, Felix, Deb... That's just six."

"You're forgetting about Penny, your housekeeper," I pointed out.

Her face turned white. "You're right. I'd forgotten about her. But I haven't seen her since yesterday. She probably left before the storm. I didn't get housekeeping service today. Did you?"

"No. But someone lives in the first cabin and I'm guessing it's her. If we hadn't had our blowup this afternoon, I'd have gone knocking on that door for information. But we did and I stayed put, so..." I shrugged.

Her shoulders sank. "You didn't have to sit on your porch, keeping guard over my cabin."

"Yeah. I did. I'd already made a commitment to keeping you safe while you're here, and our fight didn't change that."

Regret filled her eyes. "You're a very decent guy, Sawyer Reed," she said softly. "And I don't know how to reconcile that with the fact that my family will expect me to hate you."

"You're a fascinating woman, Olivia Mitchell. You're someone I'd really like to spend more time with. And I don't know how to reconcile that with the fact that you may never speak to me again once this is over."

She held my gaze a long minute before speaking. "At least we'll always have the death cabin," she finally said, forcing a smile.

"The death cabin?" My eyebrows shot up.

"That's how I think of it now," she said, giving a small laugh. "Between the obituaries, the poor animals on the wall, and the antlers everywhere... It's a cabin literally filled with mementos of death."

I shook my head. "You're not wrong. And that's creepy as hell."

"Tell me about it." She sighed, then brought the conversation back to where we'd been. "So, seven potential suspects. And Adam's at the front of the list. So, what's the plan? Confront them one by one?"

"Unlike on TV, confrontation rarely works. Not in this kind of situation, anyway. Befriending someone tends to work better. You earn their confidence, get them to relax... Then they slip up."

Her lips pursed. "But you promise you aren't doing that with me?"

"Scout's honor."

"Okay. So, how are we going to do it?"

I grinned. "How do you feel about going on a ghost hunt?"

"I CAN'T BELIEVE YOU GUYS CHANGED YOUR MIND," EVE squealed as Olivia let them into cabin thirteen. "Can't you just feel the difference in energy here? This place is *so* haunted."

"Totally," Adam agreed, his eyes glued to the equipment in front of him. "I can already tell this is going to be the epicenter for activity. You sure you won't do an interview?"

"No interview," Olivia answered weakly. "Just the investigation. And neither I nor Sawyer can be filmed. You promised."

He shook his head. "Yes, I promised. I don't know what the big deal is though. Most people like getting their fifteen minutes of fame!"

"Not us," I said, giving him a warning look. "So, what's first?" I was trying my hardest to act interested. Keeping my eyes from rolling was a true test of my strength, but I'd hung in there so far. I'd told them—quietly—that I had reason to believe Ethel might have been involved in Richard's death and I was trying to keep an open mind about the whole thing. That I was ready to face the truth about this place.

I was after the truth, alright. Just not their version of it.

"We do most of our stuff handheld," Adam explained. "But we'll set up a few cameras in the other rooms. That way, we get full coverage. We'll have to go through all that footage later."

Olivia frowned. "That must take a ton of time."

"Oh, sure." He nodded. "But it's important. Some of our best evidence has been caught that way. Sometimes spirits don't want to interact with people, so they'll stay away from us when we're investigating. But you might catch them on camera or audio in one of the empty rooms."

Olivia's head tilted. "Like...an actual image of them?"

"Well...no, not usually," he admitted. "Full-body apparitions are rare, and I've never caught one personally. But you might see an orb or a shadow. Or a voice on the audio, like that one we played for you earlier. One time, we caught a door closing by itself. Another time, we caught a book getting shoved off a table. Awesome stuff!"

"Interesting," Olivia murmured.

"So we'll just get these cameras set up. Then we'll meet in here and see if we can get something to interact!"

I had to fight even harder to keep a straight face, but I did it. I grabbed a camera and offered to set it up in Olivia's bedroom. The thought of Adam in there made me want to punch something.

He gave me a doubtful look. "Do you know how to work these?"

"I've had some experience," I said, almost succeeding at keeping the sarcasm out of my voice.

"Okay, then." He shrugged. "Olivia, why don't you help Eve set up in the kitchen? She can show you the ropes."

Olivia threw me a look that said she didn't like getting roped into this at all. I grinned—at least I wasn't the only one who was miserable.

I took the camera to Olivia's room, giving it a quick look over. They were small, portable cameras—easy to tuck into small spaces—with memory cards for storage. I quickly sped through some of the footage from the night before, curious. One camera wasn't the whole picture, but based on my quick glance, it appeared that their night had gone pretty much as they'd said—investigating in their cabin until after the storm was over. The time stamp showed them leaving through the front door at 2:03. That was pushing the window for Adam having murdered

Ethan, but it was possible. However, from the time they went outside until they went back in shortly after three, the camera had rolled nonstop. It wasn't a perfect alibi, but it cast a lot of doubt on my theory.

I knew they'd come looking for me soon, so I got busy figuring out where to put the camera. The corner nightstand looked like a decent place, with a view of the whole room, so I put it there and started to turn it on. But a tiny flash of red caught my eye. It was coming from the vent up by the ceiling.

My stomach turned when I realized what it was.

I pulled out my pocket knife to unscrew the vent cover. Yep. Exactly what I'd been afraid of.

A video camera. Pointed directly at Olivia's bed.

Chapter Twenty-Nine

Olivia

I was nodding politely, listening to Eve chattering about ghosts, when Sawyer called my name.

"Just a sec," I said, excusing myself. "Let me see what he needs."

I walked down the hallway, slipped inside my bedroom, and found him standing in front of an open vent with visceral rage on his face. The veins on his neck bulged and every muscle in his body appeared tense, as if he were ready to pounce.

"What in the world happened?" I asked, my jaw dropping.

"This. A camera—pointed at your bed. Either Richard or the caretakers, I'm guessing. One of them has been watching you—videotaping you—while you're in here." He spat out the words with anger so sharp they felt like daggers being thrown into the room.

I sank down on the corner of the bed, stunned. It was a violation I couldn't even begin to comprehend.

"That's...that's horrible," I said, feeling my face turn crimson. It was worse than horrible. It was unthinkable.

"I wonder if that's why they moved you to this cabin. You and Grace both." Sawyer's rage slowed to a mild simmer as his mind began to work the puzzle.

"Maybe you're right," I said. "But why just this cabin? Why not have cameras in all of them? Then you wouldn't have to shuffle guests around."

"It's possible there are cameras in the rest," he pointed out. "We don't know yet. But if this is the only one, it would give us the reason why they routinely move single women into this cabin."

I shuddered. "That's disgusting."

"It sure is." His face turned thoughtful. "Grace was engaged to a SEAL. He'd taught her some situational awareness skills. I have to wonder if she discovered this and confronted either Richard or Felix. If so..."

"They might have killed her to keep it quiet," I said, finishing for him.

"Exactly." With a pained look, he placed the camera back in the vent and closed it.

"What are you doing?" I asked, stunned. "Why are you putting it back?"

"If the camera belongs to Richard, he won't be watching it tonight anyway. And I want it right where I found it when I tell the police tomorrow."

"Got it," I said, letting out an exhale. "But it's going to be hard to sleep in there, knowing I'm potentially being watched by that creepy old man."

"I turned it off. But you can always sleep at my place. We both know it's going to happen eventually anyway." He winked at me, making my heart quicken, before he headed toward the living room to rejoin Adam and Eve.

Sawyer Reed always knew how to stun me into silence.

As we walked down the hallway, everything suddenly went dark. Sawer paused. I put my hands on his back, just to reassure myself he was there, and could feel the tension in his tight muscles. He moved forward slowly, then relaxed.

"They're doing their thing," he whispered.

I held on to him as my eyes slowly adjusted to a room lit only by the faint glow of moonlight shining through the window. After a moment, I could make out Adam and Eve, both standing in the center of the room, holding up various pieces of equipment. I wasn't sure why they needed to turn off the lights to investigate, but it certainly added to the spookiness. I could feel every hair on the back of my neck standing straight up as I glanced around at the shadows, just waiting for something to appear.

"We think Grace is here," Adam said excitedly, motioning for us to draw closer. "She hasn't spoken to us yet, but the EMF detectors have been going crazy. And can you smell the lavender?"

I took in a long breath and realized he was right—once again, the air was perfumed with the sweet scent. I reached out and grabbed Sawyer's hand, feeling shaky. Could Grace hurt us? It was hard to imagine that a spirit who smelled so lovely could possibly be dangerous, but ghosts were uncharted territory for me. And while Sawyer was one hundred percent convinced we were dealing with a human murderer, I had to wonder if he was wrong.

"Are you here with us, Grace?" Adam asked, holding out what I assumed was an audio recorder. "And if you are, can you touch this machine that's sitting on this table? If you touch it, it will light up and let us know that you're here."

Nothing happened.

"We want to help you, Grace," Eve said. "Just touch the machine and let us know you're with us."

The machine flashed.

"Woohoo!" Adam said, pumping his fist in the air. "That's great, Grace. Thank you. Can you do it again?"

Nothing.

Sawyer spoke up. "Is that the EMF detector you mentioned?"

"Yes," Adam explained. "It detects spikes in electromagnetic frequencies."

"Gotcha." Sawyer nodded. "I'm actually familiar with EMF. So when you say it detects electromagnetic frequencies, you understand that means it detects general power usage. Right? Cell phones. Wi-Fi signals. Bad wiring. Faulty spark plugs in a car driving down the road. All things that are completely normal."

Adam appeared to be genuinely hurt. "Yes, but spirits can also manipulate the electromagnetic fields to communicate. Obviously, you just saw her do it."

"Or we saw a random spike that wasn't related to your question at all."

As if to prove his point, the detector lit up again.

Eve laughed. "I don't think Grace likes you, Sawyer. Do it again, Grace! Prove that you're real."

Nothing.

"Let's try something else," Sawyer suggested. He walked over and flicked on the living room lights.

"What are you doing?" Adam wailed as we all covered our eyes. The bright lights felt blinding after having been in the darkness.

"Investigating," Sawyer said. He started moving furniture around as easily as if he were moving canned goods. "Aha!" he said after moving the big arm chair in the corner.

"What?" Adam asked, exasperated.

Sawyer leaned behind it and grabbed something, pulling it out to show us. "What does that smell like?"

I moved toward him and took the wall plug-in, sniffing it. "Lavender." I passed it to Adam and Eve. I suddenly felt very foolish.

Eve sniffed it and frowned. "Why would someone put a lavender-scented plug-in in a place known to smell like lavender when Grace is here?"

Sawyer looked at her like she was stupid, but thankfully, he kept his voice measured and polite. "Probably to add to the illusion that the place is haunted."

"Illusion?" Adam blinked furiously. "You're kidding, man. This place *is* haunted."

At that very moment, I heard the same cries I'd heard earlier in the day. I grabbed Sawyer's arm. "There it is!" I exclaimed. "The woman I heard crying."

"Grace!" Eve said, grabbing the EMF detector.

"Everyone be quiet," Sawyer said, frowning. He listened closely to the muffled noises, then walked slowly toward the hallway, stopping under a ceiling vent. He paused, listening, then pulled out his pocket knife. "Someone grab me a chair."

Adam ran to the kitchen and grabbed one of the dining chairs, bringing it to Sawyer. By that point, Sawyer had already loosened the vent cover.

"Give me your flashlight," he said.

Adam handed it to him, and Sawyer stepped onto the chair, shining the flashlight into the ceiling space. He leaned forward and stuck a hand in, emerging with a portable speaker.

"No," I gasped. "That's fake, too?"

The speaker emitted the sounds of the lady crying again. The noise was much louder this time, now that it wasn't hidden in the ceiling.

Adam and Eve looked at each other, both clearly shocked.

"That's not cool," Eve said, shaking her head. "Fake evidence really destroys the credibility of what we do."

"I don't understand," Adam said. His face fell. "Why fake anything? This place is legit haunted. There's no need to pull crap like this."

"That's a really good question," Sawyer said slowly. "And I intend to find the answer."

CHAPTER THIRTY

Sawyer

ADAM AND EVE PACKED UP THEIR EQUIPMENT SHORTLY after the audio discovery. The find had zapped their enthusiasm for the hunt. They said they were going to look over their evidence from the night before and see if anything had been faked in their cabin as well. Before they left, I told them not to tell anyone else what had happened.

"Why not?" Adam asked.

"Information is power," I said simply. "We now have information that the other guests don't. I think it's best if we keep it to ourselves for the time being. And if you guys are up for it, we might do a different kind of hunt together later."

"What do you mean?"

I shook my head, unwilling to answer. "We'll talk later."

He nodded and shook my hand, disappointed. I found I preferred him that way. A dose of reality made him a much more palatable person.

"So," Olivia said, moving to my side after they left. "What now?"

"Grab your stuff," I said. "We're saying goodbye to cabin thirteen."

. . .

A FEW MINUTES LATER, WE WALKED TOWARD MY PLACE WITH all of her things.

"Now that we're out of the house and away from the cameras," I said, keeping my voice low, "I'll tell you what's next. My focus has moved away from Adam. Someone like him could have scrawled a name in the dust, but he hasn't had access to cabin thirteen. There's too much going on here that's connected to the people who live and work here full time."

"Agreed." She shuddered, likely remembering that camera that had watched her in moments when she had assumed she was alone.

Still pissed me off.

"I'm going to go take a look around Richard's house. You don't have to come. In fact, you probably shouldn't. But after everything, I figure you don't want to be at your place alone. So you can stay at mine or hang out in my car with the doors locked if you don't feel safe in the cabin."

She frowned. "Why should I not come with you?"

"Breaking and entering is illegal," I said, raising my eyebrows. "No need to get you into any trouble."

She shot me a look. "For someone who seems bound and determined to hold everyone else to the law, you don't seem to have a problem breaking it yourself."

"Taking a look around a dead guy's house is a far cry from murder," I pointed out. "The police will go through it all tomorrow anyway—at least, they should. Once you're dead, privacy no longer exists. I'd never cross that boundary with a living suspect. I'd find a better way to get the information I needed. But Richard is dead and we've got a fast-approaching deadline."

"Not so black and white, is it?" she asked, her lips twisting in a little smile.

"Maybe not this time," I admitted. "If Richard never made it to the authorities, then odds are, our murderer is going to disappear the moment the road opens. And I have a problem with that. Especially since good old Sheriff Patterson might make me his prime suspect."

"Good point."

"I was also hired to find out what happened to Grace. And I suspect the answers I'm looking for are in that house." I hoped they were, anyway. Otherwise, the mystery of Grace's death might have died with Richard.

Olivia stopped in the road, leveled a gaze at me, and braced herself like she was getting ready for a fight. "Okay. You need to look in Richard's house. But I'm going with you."

"Okay."

She opened her mouth to argue, then realized what I had said. "Wait. Okay?" She took a step back. "No lecture about how I shouldn't put myself in danger or how I'm not prepared to do something like that?"

I shrugged. "If you're with me, I know I can keep you safe. I wasn't going to force you to come, but I'm not going to stop you if you want to."

Her shoulders relaxed. "Fair enough. Let's get my stuff inside. Then we'll head up there."

AN HOUR LATER, WE WERE HUDDLED TOGETHER ON THE EDGE of the woods, staring at Richard's house. I'd insisted on walking, as I didn't want to draw any attention to what we were doing by taking the car. To stay hidden, we'd taken a route through the woods instead of his driveway.

I wanted to avoid getting caught on video, if possible, and Richard sure seemed to have a thing for cameras. The police would be looking at all of that, and it would absolutely look suspicious that I'd broken into his house after he was found dead.

I'd already been the one to find two dead bodies though, so who was I kidding? I would be the number-one suspect no matter what—unless I could prove who the real killer was.

I surveyed the place with my night-vision scope.

"What are you doing?" Olivia asked in a whisper.

"Checking for cameras. This scope will pick up anything using IR."

I swung it back and forth, looking for the telltale glow of an infrared camera.

Bingo.

"There," I said, pointing. "He's got two cameras up front. If I had to guess, one is facing the door and one is facing the driveway."

"So, what now?"

"Now, we check out back."

I motioned for her to follow me as we skirted around the house, staying in the tree line where we wouldn't be seen. When we spotted the back door, I stopped, using my scope to check again.

Nothing.

Richard was obviously someone who cared about his security. What were the odds he'd neglected to put up a camera back here? Slim to none.

"I'm not seeing anything back here," I said slowly. "Maybe we got lucky and the storm knocked out one of his cameras last night."

"So, is it safe?" she prodded.

"Safe is relative," I muttered. It was possible the one back here was better hidden. Or that he'd used more expensive technology that I couldn't pick up with this scope. But it was a chance I'd have to take if I wanted to get a look inside. That, or I'd have to go through a window. But door locks were easier to pick, and I didn't want to leave any damage behind.

"That doesn't make me feel better."

"It's not supposed to. Come on." I motioned for Liv to follow me.

We walked a little farther along the edge of the trees, ducking out on the opposite side from where the dogs were kept. The puppy had been sweet, but I was still iffy about the full-grown ones, and I hoped to avoid getting them riled up and noisy.

"Stay close," I said, keeping my voice low.

"What if the door is locked?"

"Oh, I'm certain it will be." I flashed her a quick grin. "Takes more than a door lock to stop me."

Her eyebrows shot up. "Where'd you learn to pick locks?"

"Lock-picking school." I chuckled softly.

She made a face to show she didn't believe me, even though I was telling the truth.

But the skill wasn't necessary anyway. When we reached the door, the handle twisted in my hand. I frowned, glancing back at Olivia.

"He lives out in the middle of nowhere," she whispered, shrugging. "Maybe he doesn't worry about locks."

I shook my head. "That's not the impression I got of him. Maybe he left in a hurry though."

Something felt off. Intuition, training, whatever you wanted to credit it to—my senses were sharp, and they were all screaming that something wasn't right. With Olivia here, I contemplated walking away. But I couldn't.

The hunt was on, and I smelled blood.

"Stay close," I said for the second time in a matter of minutes. "And keep quiet."

"What's wrong?"

"I'm not sure." I slowly pushed open the door and walked inside, one careful step after another. Everything within me said we weren't alone.

And I'd experienced far too much to ignore my senses.

We moved across the kitchen, taking a quick look into the dining room, then the living room where Richard and I had spoken, freezing when I heard a noise coming from upstairs. I put a finger to my lips, then began climbing the stairs with Olivia close behind

At the end of the upstairs hallway, light spilled out from a door left ajar. I heard rustling noises like someone was shuffling through paper. I motioned for Olivia to hide in the hallway bathroom, then drew my weapon and made my way down to the occupied room.

I kicked the door open.

"Don't shoot!"

Penny, the housekeeper from Olivia's cabin, was standing wide-eyed behind a desk. She dropped the papers she'd been holding, and threw both hands into the air, obviously terrified.

"What are you doing here?" I demanded even though she had the right to ask me the exact same thing.

She immediately started bawling. "I knew I wouldn't get away with it," she blubbered. "But I had to try."

"Get away with what?" I demanded. "Did you kill Ethan and Richard?"

She shook her head frantically. "No! No, I promise. That's not what I meant. Please don't hurt me."

I blew out a breath and holstered my weapon. "No one is going to hurt you. Sit down and tell me what all of this is about."

Penny sank into the desk chair and cast pleading eyes up toward me. "You're a cop, aren't you?"

"No, I'm not," I said, shaking my head.

A tiny bit of hope came into her eyes. "Can I... Is there anything I... I mean, what would it take for you to keep this between us?"

Her eyes drifted slowly down my body, letting me know exactly what she was offering for my silence.

I groaned in irritation. "Can you please just tell me what the hell is going on?"

Olivia slipped into the room and shot me a confused look. "Penny?" she asked. "Are you okay?"

Penny's eyes shifted from me to Olivia and back again before losing that hopeful look. She slumped backward. "I want a lawyer."

"I already told you I'm not a cop," I said between gritted teeth. "I can't get you a lawyer. But if you tell us what's going on, maybe we can help you. We're all on the same side here, right?"

She gave me a suspicious look. "What do you mean?"

I took a gamble. If there was one thing I'd learned during my brief stint as a PI, it was that sometimes you needed to play the cards you were dealt. Other times, you needed to play the person.

"You're here looking for something. Clearly, we are too." I gave her a charming smile. "Neither of us is supposed to be here, right? So maybe we can help each other out."

Some of that light came back into her eyes. "What are you looking for?"

I glanced at Olivia, hoping she'd play along. "Well, we have a problem. We found a hidden camera in Liv's bedroom tonight, and we need that footage. See, Liv's about to file for divorce, but if her sorry husband finds out about us, he'll use it to get out of paying her fair share in the settlement."

"Right," Olivia said, stepping forward and wrapping herself around me. "Sawyer and I have done a great job of keeping our relationship a secret, sneaking off to places like this to be together. But if that footage gets into the wrong hands..."

Relief flashed across Penny's face. "I understand. We really are on the same side, then. I was here looking for the same thing."

"Oh yeah?" I asked, trying not to let my excitement show. I stroked a hand up and down Liv's back, thoroughly enjoying our cover. "He caught some footage of you having an affair, too?"

She shook her head, then buried her face in her hands. "Worse."

She looked up and I could see it on her face—we'd gained her trust and she was about to confess. I'd seen this look before. Sometimes there was pure relief in finally unburdening yourself of a secret you'd carried for far too long. I kept my own face relaxed, even as I tightened my hand on Olivia's waist, wondering if she could see it too.

Penny sighed. "I used to have a problem with drugs. Had a hard time holding down a decent job. Felix got me a job working here for Mr. Moore. Said it wouldn't matter about my history, that with all the ghost activity they were having trouble keeping a housekeeper."

"Go on," I said, encouraging her.

"Anyway, it went pretty well at first." She flushed furiously. "But then, last year, a woman came to stay out here. A Grace something or another."

My heart began to pound furiously at the turn in her story. My senses had been correct. We were on a hunt, and it had led here, to this.

"Oh yeah?" I prodded, using every last reserve of my self-control to not react.

Penny turned an even darker shade of crimson. "This job don't pay much. So every now and then, I'd, you know, supplement it a little by taking something from a guest. A few dollars here or there from a wallet left in the room, or a couple of pills. Nothing much, just...a little. But then Grace came, and she had a bottle of oxy. Oxy was always my weakness."

I closed my eyes, fighting back the wave of sadness that came from remembering. Grace didn't do drugs. But Jim had struggled a bit with Oxy after being prescribed it post-surgery. It was the only thing that took away his pain, but he knew he liked it too much. He'd given his bottle to Grace for accountability. If his pain was severe, she'd give him a single pill. Together, they'd managed to keep him using it only when things got debilitating.

"Anyway," Penny continued, "I couldn't help myself. I took one right away, and then, well, I slipped a few more into my pocket. Too many. And then Grace had this gorgeous jewelry. Not expensive, just... pretty. Prettier than anything I'd ever had. And with the oxy in my system, they were so sparkly and shiny and I just couldn't resist. I took a couple of necklaces."

I gripped Olivia, holding on to her to keep myself quiet. Blood pounded in my ears. Grace had been a jewelry designer.

"The next day, Mr. Moore called me up here for a meeting. Told me he'd gotten some complaints about items being missing from the cabins, so he'd installed some cameras." She averted her eyes, clearly ashamed. "He showed me a video. Clear as day, there I was in Grace's room, taking her stuff. And see... Grace had drowned that night. He told me how it looked, how if he turned that video in, I was going to go to prison."

"I'm guessing you offered him the same arrangement you offered me?"

Out of the corner of my eye, I saw Olivia's eyebrows shoot to the roof over that remark.

Penny blushed. "He suggested it. Offered to keep quiet about things as long as I, well, you know."

"Yeah, I know."

"Oh, Penny," Olivia said, shaking her head. "That's horrible. I'm so sorry."

"It's better than prison," Penny said as if it were that simple. "But when I heard Richard was dead, I knew the police would go through his things and find that recording." Her eyes filled with tears. "It's so unfair. Everything I did, everything I went through... It was all for nothing."

I gritted my teeth. She'd stolen from Grace. Had been in her room the day she died. But nothing in her statement indicated any involvement in her death.

She might know something though. And if we helped each other, I'd continue earning her trust. It also benefited me to be able to keep searching his house. Because who knew what else he had on video?

I was fighting back anger though, for Grace and the casual manner Penny had spoken of her death. I knew I needed to take a step back, get my head on straight, so I could continue this. So I was counting on Olivia to step in for me.

I pasted a relaxed smile on my face. "So we all need to find his video footage. You help us and we'll help you. Deal?"

"Deal," Penny said, her body sagging with relief.

Chapter Thirty-One

Olivia

"Any ideas where he's keeping it?" Sawyer asked. He was attempting to keep his voice casual, but I could hear the tension in it —and I could feel it in the way he gripped me like he was hanging on for dear life.

Penny shook her head. "I mean, this is his office, so I'm guessing it's in here. I had just started looking though."

"Perfect," Sawyer said. "How about you ladies keep going through everything in here, see what you can find. And I'll check some of the other rooms?"

I shot him a questioning glance. He smiled at me, but it wasn't real. Something was wrong, and I could only assume that it was because we'd been talking about the death of his friend and he'd had to pretend not to even know her. I was starting to realize that Sawyer was someone whose feelings ran deeper than they initially appeared.

I gave him a reassuring smile. "That's a great idea. We'll cover this room and catch up with you in a bit."

He nodded and left.

"So, what have you already checked?" I asked, turning back to Penny.

"Just the filing cabinets so far," she said. "And I tried to get on his computer, but I can't guess the password."

"Well, there are plenty of other places to check," I said, turning slowly to take in the whole office. Richard had been the opposite of a minimalist. "Why don't we tackle these bookshelves? Maybe one of the books has a false compartment or something."

She brightened. "Hey, that's a good idea." She came out from behind the desk and started on one end, while I searched the other. After a minute, she glanced my way. "Your boyfriend sure is a dreamboat."

I opened my mouth to automatically reply that he wasn't my boyfriend but stopped, remembering our cover. "He is," I agreed with a smile.

"Odd place for a lover's getaway though." She frowned. "Not where I'd pick. Most of our guests out here are ghost hunters or people looking for a thrill."

A prickle of unease went up my spine. Did she suspect we were lying? "My fault," I explained. "It was my turn to choose a spot, and I was just looking for something with a lake. The pictures were pretty online. I didn't know about the ghost stuff."

"Gotcha."

"You said Richard had trouble keeping housekeepers because of ghost activity. Did you ever experience anything like that here?" I was genuinely curious. Sawyer had debunked my experiences, but the legends remained. Surely Richard hadn't faked *everything*. If Adam was to be believed, the stories went back a hundred years.

Penny's face became guarded. "Yes..." she said with a bit of hesitation.

"But it didn't scare you?"

She shook her head.

"Hmmm." I studied her face, wondering if she'd had any real experiences or if she was just part of Richard's scam. "We know Richard was faking things in cabin thirteen," I said, keeping my tone casual. "When we found the camera, we also found his lavender spray and the recording of the woman's voice."

Her face flashed with relief. "I wasn't supposed to tell anyone about that."

"So you knew?"

"Of course I knew. I clean that place." She snorted. "He couldn't hide it from me."

"Do the caretakers know, too?"

She shook her head. "No. I had to help him hide it from them. If Felix had to repair anything in the cabin, I had to go take down the plug-in and turn off the audio. They would be furious if they knew."

"Why would they be furious?"

She rolled her eyes. "They miss the days when hardly anyone stayed here. Mr. Moore's parents never tried to make a full-time income off of this place. They had other jobs and only cared about booking enough to pay for maintenance and upkeep here. That's how Felix and Deb liked it. But Mr. Moore has big ideas. He knew the ghost angle was a big draw and said it could put this place on the map, maybe even make it onto one of those big-time cable investigation shows. Then it would be booked solid every weekend."

"I see." I mulled it over, checking a few more books. "Sounds like the caretakers didn't get along with Mr. Moore."

"Oh, they hated him," she said, laughing. "They'll be so glad he's gone. He doesn't have a wife or kids, so the property will go to them now. I figure they'll close the tourist side down completely." She sobered. "I guess that means I'll be out of a job."

"At least you'll be free of him though," I said.

"That's true." She cheered up. "And if we find that recording and I don't end up in prison, I guess things will work out okay for me after all."

"Sounds like it," I agreed even though I wasn't at all sure Sawyer wouldn't turn the evidence into the police. We hadn't had a chance to talk privately and I didn't know what he was thinking.

But I knew he'd be very interested to hear about the tension between the caretakers and Richard. Between that and their inheritance, that made for quite a motive.

It didn't explain Ethan's death though. Unless we were looking for two different killers—maybe even three, counting Grace.

"Penny, do you know anything about the guest who died here yesterday?" Asking her was at least worth a shot.

She shook her head. "No, I sure don't. I stayed up here with Mr. Moore last night—part of our arrangement"—she blushed—"and I didn't hear about it until after your boyfriend came up here and told him."

"How did he react? When Sawyer was gone, I mean."

"Honestly?"

"Of course."

"He was happy," she admitted. "Said it just added to the reputation of the place, would draw in more investigators and make for better TV when he landed one of the bigger deals."

"He sounds like a cruel man," I said quietly.

"He was," she said with a sadness washing over her face that made her look ten years older.

It was clear he hadn't been kind to her, and knowing how he rejoiced over the deaths of his innocent guests, I found it hard to mourn his.

Another thought hit. "Hey, Penny?"

"Yeah?" She looked up, her eyes still cloudy.

"One more question. Did either of you go into my cabin this morning and put the obituaries back in place?"

A guilty expression flashed over her face. "Yes. I'm sorry. That was me. Mr. Moore made me."

"How did he know I'd moved them?"

She bit her lip and averted her eyes again. "He has cameras everywhere."

WHEN WE'D SEARCHED EVERY CORNER OF RICHARD'S OFFICE, I plopped down onto his chair, exhausted. "It's not in here," I said. "Maybe we should go look for Sawyer."

"Yeah, maybe he's had better luck," Penny agreed. "By the way... Thank you for not turning me in. Yesterday or today."

I sighed. Honestly, when it came to Penny, I had no idea what the right thing to do was. She'd stolen drugs and jewelry from a guest who'd later died. That didn't look good. But she seemed like someone who'd had a hard life and rarely got a break, and that made me want to help her.

"We all make mistakes," I said.

"Exactly."

We left the office and went in search of Sawyer. He wasn't in any of the upstairs rooms. We headed downstairs but didn't see him there, either.

Penny frowned. "Where did he go?"

"I'm not sure." I began poking my head into each room again, softly calling out his name, hoping we'd missed him somehow. The dark house felt so eerie without him. It was starting to realize how quickly he'd become a symbol of safety in my mind.

He made me feel safe. He made me feel protected.

And I still had no idea what to do with that, considering the fact that he was my father's number-one enemy.

My anxiety continued creeping up as we went through the whole house again. After our second walk-through, we looked at each other, realizing the truth.

Sawyer was gone.

CHAPTER THIRTY-TWO

Sawyer

I left the girls to search Richard's office, knowing it would keep them busy for a while. But I doubted they'd actually find anything there.

Richard Moore was a conniving, dishonest narcissist. He wouldn't have kept evidence in his office. It would either be somewhere more difficult to find or out in plain sight—a cocky move to prove he was smarter than everyone else.

I popped my head into the upstairs rooms, appraising them and quickly deciding they weren't worth a search. Not yet anyway. My gut told me to keep going.

Downstairs felt warmer. The living room, with all its trophies, felt like his personal throne room. From a psychological perspective, I could see him wanting to keep his other trophies—the hidden ones only he knew about—here as well.

I walked around the space, letting my instinct guide me to a bookshelf in the corner. Like the one in Olivia's cabin, it was nothing but military history and thrillers.

I pulled a few books out at random before it hit me—this shelf was flush with the wall. I shook my head, realizing I'd been stupid to not see it from the beginning.

The bookcase was a Murphy door.

It only took a few seconds to figure out where the trigger was to open it. I walked inside the opening and it swung closed behind me, leaving me in total darkness. I turned my flashlight on, swinging it until I found a light switch.

When the lights came on, I realized I was in a narrow hallway. I followed it down until it turned the corner, opening up into a room. My jaw hit the floor when I saw what was in front of me.

The room was nothing less than a full security suite with multiple monitors and a killer computer system. Four different views were playing on the monitors—Richard's front porch, a cabin porch, a bedroom I immediately recognized as Olivia's, and the living room from another cabin. On that screen, Joseph walked into view, wheeling a packed suitcase to the front door before disappearing down the hallway again.

I wiggled the computer mouse, waking that screen, and realized Richard had eyes on the entire resort. Cameras monitored every porch, living room, hot tub, and bedroom in the place. Horror flooded me as I realized the implications. Richard had been spying on everyone who stayed here, illegally recording guests—including minors—in rooms where they had every expectation of privacy. Best-case scenario, he was doing it to try to catch paranormal activity.

Worst case... I didn't even want to imagine.

But if he had eyes on the whole compound, that meant he'd been able to come in here and check the cameras after I'd told him about Ethan's murder.

I sank back into the desk chair, mulling it over. Every front and back door had a video view—except his back door, which I assumed was the empty blue screen from a malfunctioning monitor. I really *had* gotten lucky with that one. But otherwise, there was full coverage. Richard would have been able to see who came and who went—and at what times. There was a very good chance he knew who the killer was.

I'd have bet money that's why he'd been killed.

I tried to rewind the footage to the night before, but I frowned when I realized everything started at eight in the morning. I could see Sadie heading over to Liv's, the two of them leaving for their hike, then later showing up at my place. But nothing before that.

Where was all the older footage?

This many cameras recording twenty-four-seven would take up a ton of storage space. Maybe he regularly reviewed the tapes and deleted everything, only permanently storing what he could use. Still, those had to be somewhere.

I clicked through the computer, trying to find any long-term stored files, but nothing was there. By all appearances, the only files on the system were footage that started a few hours earlier.

But Richard would never get rid of his leverage over Penny—or anything else he was using to blackmail someone. Somewhere, there had to be more.

And on them, I was certain we'd find the identity of Ethan's killer.

I glanced at my watch, realizing Liv was probably wondering where I was. I pushed back from the desk and headed down the hallway toward the false door, leaving the light so I could come back easily. The files had to be in here somewhere. It was the most logical place for him to keep them. Why risk moving them when you had a perfectly good secret room?

I just needed time to search.

I pushed the false door open and both women screamed.

"It's just me!" I said, fighting back a chuckle.

"Is that a hidden room?" Olivia's eyes grew wide with excitement.

"It sure is. Penny, did you know this was here?"

Her eyes were wide too, but the expression on her face was pure horror. "No. Richard never told me about it. Did you find the recording?"

"No," I said, shaking my head. "But I did find the system that recorded you. You guys come take a look." I held the door open, letting them go through it first.

Olivia gasped as she walked down the short hallway and saw the room. "It's like something you see on TV!"

"It really is. He's either making a fortune blackmailing people or selling videos or something."

Penny was silent, taking it all in with her jaw open. It was clear that, despite having spent so much time at Richard's, she'd never seen this room.

"Oh my word." Olivia walked closer to the monitors, holding a hand over her mouth when she saw the whole scope of images on the computer. "He's recording everything. There's Sadie, sleeping in her bed. That's unbelievably creepy. Can he do that? Legally?"

"No," I said, shaking my head. "Unless there's some vague, hidden line about it in that ridiculous rental agreement you have to sign when you book this place. Did you read it?"

She blushed. "No."

"I didn't, either. Still, even if it's mentioned somewhere in there, the law is against him on this one. Sadie—and all the other minors who stay here—aren't expecting cameras hidden in their rooms. If he's watching them undress..."

Olivia's face turned dark. "He's a monster."

"He really was," I agreed. "Hey, Penny, I was going to ask—"

I cut off when I realized she was gone.

"Where did she go?" Olivia asked, confused.

I looked around. "Do you think she found it while we were talking and snuck out with it?"

"I don't know," Olivia said, doubtful. "She was back behind us, and there's nothing there."

"Nothing that we noticed, anyway," I pointed out, sighing.

"She's scared. She's been through so much. I'm sure this was really overwhelming. Richard abused her. Then to come in and see all these cameras and know he's watching women and girls?" Olivia shook her head. "It may have just overwhelmed her. Do you want me to see if she's close by, try to talk to her?"

"No," I said. It was a gut reaction, my instincts kicking in again. "Stay with me. Please. We'll go find her together when we're done here."

"Okay." She swallowed hard. "Listen, while we were upstairs, I learned some interesting things."

"Oh yeah?"

"Yeah." She quickly filled me in on what Penny had told her about Richard faking evidence of the haunting and the caretakers inheriting the place.

"That's definitely motive," I agreed. "In good news, we have lots of footage from today. The files on the computer only go back to eight this morning, but that's enough for Richard's murder at least. I can look through the video and see if it gives us any clues about where people were."

"We don't have video from last night?"

"No." I grimaced. "Everything older has already been erased. I think he must have it stored somewhere else, on flash drives or an external hard drive or something."

She glanced around. "So we need to keep searching."

"Exactly."

"Is he monitoring the caretaker's cottage, too?"

I nodded. "Yep. Not inside their house. But front and back porch."

She shuddered. "Do you think they know?"

"Probably. The porch cameras are easily explained for security purposes." I shrugged. "They might not mind, considering how many strangers are on the property."

"You check the footage," she said. "I'm going to look around here for the old stuff. Maybe we'll find everything we need in one place."

"That would be nice," I agreed.

Though I had a feeling it wouldn't be that easy.

THIRTY MINUTES LATER, I'D FAST FORWARDED THROUGH A ton of footage, making notes on a pad of paper I'd found in Richard's desk. I was developing a theory about what had happened the night before. It made sense.

I just didn't have any actual evidence.

"Any luck?" Olivia called from where she was meticulously

searching the shelves at the back of Richard's secret room. The guy had this place set up like a bunker, with food, water, medicine, guns, ammo, and more. Olivia was determined to go through every nook and cranny.

"We can eliminate the caretakers," I said. "He checked in with them around one, presumably updating them on what he was about to do. So he was alive then. And he must have gone to the boathouse sometime before two, because that's when I headed to my porch. I would have seen him on the road if he hadn't already gone there. That entire hour, Felix and Deb were having a heated argument on their back porch about politics. Sounds like one leans red and one leans blue and they're both determined to convince the other one to change sides."

"Oh," she replied, sounding disappointed. "Is it bad I was hoping it would be them?"

I chuckled. "Nah. I get it."

"Have you been able to eliminate anyone else?" she asked.

"Actually, yeah. Adam and Eve were in their living room, recording interviews and reactions from what it looks like."

"Well, that eliminates several suspects. Why do you sound like there's bad news?"

I looked up from the computer, toward her. "You're awfully perceptive, you know that?"

She grinned. "Thanks. But you didn't answer my question."

I sighed. "Well, you and I were inside my cabin during that time, so the footage would have given me and you both fairly solid alibis had I not disabled the camera on my front porch. As it stands, the footage shows him alive at one, then us having a blow-up argument right before two and you storming out. I went out my front door, but I don't have proof that I was sitting there. Just my word."

She winced. "Ah. I see."

"You know how bad this all looks, right? You discovered Ethan's body. I discovered Richard's. We've both been at the crime scenes. Now we've broken into Richard's house and gotten caught doing it. We told Penny we were having an affair and needed to destroy the evidence—evidence Richard recorded. And I disabled the camera on my porch that would have given me an alibi for his death."

"When you put it that way, it does look pretty bad."

"You and I are both going to have a lot of explaining to do tomorrow. I'm sorry I dragged you into this."

She let out a long sigh. "I'm not. Yes, we're going to catch some heat. But we're innocent. That will come out in the end. I'm sure of it. In the meantime, it feels good to...to do something important. To try to get some justice." She looked down. "I don't get to feel that way very often."

I studied her. "So, assuming we get through this okay and neither of us ends up in some backwoods jail, convicted without due process... What's next for you?"

She shrugged. "I don't know. I've been thinking about that today, ever since, well, you know."

Yeah. I knew. Ever since she'd found out who I was and what her dad had done.

"And?"

She blew out a breath. "I still live at home. I'm still financially dependent on my parents, which is ridiculous for a twenty-three-year-old woman."

"Not in this economy, it's not. But you're a great book illustrator. Can you not make a living doing that?"

"That's the goal. But building a profitable, sustainable business takes time."

"I don't know if you'll have that. These court cases can drag out for months or even longer. But they could potentially freeze his assets in the meantime. Have you considered other jobs?"

"It looks like I may have to." She sighed. "Even if they don't freeze his assets, I'm struggling with the idea of going back home and living on my father's money now that I know where he got it. It feels tainted. Like everything I have was paid for with someone else's life. I hate that."

"That's fair, and I respect you for it. Listen—"

But she cut me off with a sharp gasp.

"What?" I jumped up, wondering what on earth had happened.

"I see it," she said, shaking her head and looking at me, shocked. "It's been right here in front of us the whole time."

"What has?"

She pressed something on the bottom of the shelf. A hidden drawer popped out. She grabbed a flash drive and stood up triumphantly. "This."

CHAPTER THIRTY-THREE

Sawyer pushed back his desk chair and flew up, running to grab the flash drive. His eyes were bright and excited—like he'd just felt a massive tug on a fishing line or had caught the football and was running to score the winning touchdown. He was in his element, and his excitement was magnetic.

As ready as I was to get out of this creepy place, I suspected I was going to miss him when it was all over.

"How did you find this?" he asked, his face lit up with delight.

I laughed, glad to finally be the one to surprise him. "When we were talking, I was looking at these." I pointed at the metal screw caps dotted across the length of the shelf. "I noticed they weren't spaced evenly. There's an extra one. See? It looks different too. Just a bit wider, and the paint is dull, like it's been touched a lot. I realized it was a button."

He smiled in admiration. "Damn. That was a nice catch. Not sure I would have even noticed that one."

"Thanks." I smiled up at him, my face flushing as our eyes caught.

There was such a natural connection between us. A magnetic energy pulling us together.

And I still had absolutely no idea what to do with it. Tomorrow morning, we would go our separate ways and might never see each other again...unless it was in a courtroom, where we'd technically be opponents and unable to even speak to each other.

That thought made me feel ill.

Sawyer's face softened, almost like he could read my mind. "Let's see what's on this," he said, his tone taking on a sense of finality.

"Okay."

He offered a hand to help me up from the floor. I followed him over to the computer, feeling a strange mix of excitement and disappointment. We were possibly about to find every answer we'd been looking for this whole time.

But that meant it would be over.

He stuck the flash drive in the computer. A list of files popped up, all with dates. The night before wasn't on there—the most recent file was from over a month ago. But Sawyer quickly honed in on one date in particular, clicking it as he glanced up at me.

"That was the night Grace died," he explained, a wave of emotion passing over his face.

I swallowed hard, putting a hand on his shoulder. He double-clicked the file folder, revealing three individual video files. He clicked the first one and a video player popped up on the screen.

The view was the bedroom of cabin thirteen. Anxiety fluttered in my chest. Even though this file was old, it still felt violating.

"That's Penny," Sawyer said, confused when the housekeeper peeked into the room, looking around like she was making sure it was empty.

"She told us she stole from Grace," I reminded him. "This is probably the video he used to blackmail her. The second one will probably show us what happened to Grace later that night. Do you want to move to it?"

"No," he said slowly, like the wheels were turning in his mind. "Let's let it play out."

On screen, Penny moved into the room, crouching beside Grace's suitcase to riffle through it. It didn't take her long to find the pill bottle. Even on the grainy camera, her joy was clear. She popped off the lid and quickly placed one under her tongue, closing her eyes and visibly relaxing as the drug began to hit her system. She started to put the bottle back into the suitcase, then hesitated and popped a second pill into her mouth. Then she shoved the bottle into her pocket and kept going, rifling through Grace's things.

Her eyes lit up when she opened the bag of jewelry. She picked what appeared to be the biggest, gaudiest necklace of them all and put it on herself before lying back on Grace's bed, staring at the ceiling as she stroked the pretty jewels.

"She's as high as a kite," I commented, oddly fascinated by the whole thing. I'd never actually seen someone on drugs like that before. It was so interesting to watch the way her face changed as the muscles around her mouth relaxed and her eyes became hazy and unfocused. Then her eyes closed as she appeared to drift off into a drug-induced sleep.

"Yes, she is," Sawyer said tightly.

"That's exactly the story she told us," I said, glancing at him. "Why is watching it making you so tense?"

"Gut feeling," he said simply, beginning to fast-forward the video.

And within seconds, it was clear his gut was right.

Penny was still asleep on the bed when Grace walked into the room. The timestamp showed that four hours had passed—and that Penny had been in Grace's room the entire time.

Grace appeared to be shocked. Penny jumped off the bed, holding her hands up as she tried to explain. But Grace was having none of it. She pointed at the necklace, then at the suitcase, and began yelling. Then realization dawned on her face. Grace dropped to the floor and started digging through her bag in search of something.

Penny's fists clenched, and her face turned to rage.

"The high is gone," Sawyer said, sounding defeated. "It hits fast and hard but wears off quickly. Withdrawal isn't pretty."

"You sound like you've had some experience," I said, glancing at him again.

He said nothing, but the look on his face confirmed it.

I gasped at the screen when Penny grabbed Grace by the hair. She pulled her out of the suitcase, then shoved her hard. Grace stumbled and fell, hitting her head on the sharp corner of the nightstand. Her eyes fluttered closed, and her body sank down.

Penny looked panicked. She stood frozen for a minute, then grabbed Grace by the feet and dragged her toward the bedroom door.

The video cut off.

Sawyer put his elbows on the desk, burying his face in his hands.

"I'm so sorry," I said, rubbing his back. "I can't imagine what it must be like to watch this happen to your friend."

He didn't respond. Just raised his head, looking drained in a way I'd never seen before. "Let's watch the next video."

"I can watch it if you want and tell you what happens," I offered gently. "If you can't handle seeing any more."

"No," he said. His voice was even harsher than when he'd told me about my father. "The least I can do is give her the honor of witnessing what happened to her. Of making sure the truth is known."

"Okay." I reached over him and started the next video.

It was still cabin thirteen, but this time, the shot was of the living room. Penny was dragging Grace by the ankles toward the back door. Halfway across the room, Grace's eyes opened and she held up a trembling hand.

Sawyer's body went tight as he leaned forward, watching.

Grace spoke. Even on the grainy video, I could read her lips. *Please.*

Penny dropped her ankles and started pacing, panicked. Grace tried to sit up but fell back down, holding her head.

Then Penny pulled out the pill bottle.

Grace's eyes went wide. She shook her head no. But Penny sat on top of her, forced her mouth open, and stuck two of the pills underneath her tongue. She held her hand over Grace's mouth and wouldn't let go, even as Grace fought it, clawing and shaking her head, trying to spit them out. But before long, Grace relaxed.

Like Sawyer said, the pills hit fast and hard.

When she stopped fighting, Penny got up. She grabbed Grace's feet again and pulled her toward the door.

The final video switched to the back porch, where Penny dropped

Grace, then opened the lid to the hot tub. My heart sank as I realized what she was about to do. Grace didn't even attempt to fight back as Penny struggled to lift her body into the tub. She pushed Grace down under the water, then closed the lid. Then she sank to the ground and popped another pill into her mouth, her hands shaking.

Sawyer cursed, his fists clenched so tight that his knuckles turned white.

"I'm so sorry," I repeated, not knowing what else in the world I could possibly say. What Penny had done was unthinkable. I felt like I might be sick, and I didn't even know Grace. I couldn't imagine what Sawyer was feeling.

He pulled the flash drive out of the computer. "We have to get this to the authorities. I'll lose my PI license for breaking and entering, but I don't even care. Grace is worth it."

"Sawyer, you can't. You love what you do."

"People matter more."

I took the drive out of his hand. "So *I'll* give it to them. I don't have a PI license. Or a criminal record of any kind. And I happen to have a lot of friends in the justice system who are likely to go easy on me, considering."

He stared at me, the wheels turning as he realized what I was offering him. "You would do that for me?"

I nodded. "For you. And for Grace."

His fingers came up and grazed my cheek. "You are a remarkable woman, you know that?"

I moved forward, into this...whatever this was between us. It was a total betrayal to my family. One my father would likely never forgive me for.

But I wanted it anyway.

Sawyer moved forward too, like he was as drawn to me as I was to him. His hands came to my waist, and I dipped my head down, leaning forward to brush my lips against his. But before I could, Penny's voice interrupted us.

"I hate to intrude on such a tender moment, but I'm going to need that flash drive," she said. Her voice trembled, a stark contrast to the practiced bravado of her words.

I jerked my head in her direction. She was standing at the entrance of the room, pointing a hunting rifle at us. Mascara streaked down her face from where she'd been crying.

Sawyer immediately stepped in front of me.

"Put the gun down," he said. That tired defeat had left his voice and he was all business. Pure authority. For a moment, I thought she might actually obey him.

"I can't," she said, sounding truly sorry for it. "I wish you wouldn't have come here. I was hoping if you found anything you'd just destroy it, protect us all. I don't want to hurt you. You need to know I'm sorry about that woman. Really. That was a mistake, and I've regretted it every day since. I was so scared of going back to jail that I freaked out and made the wrong choice, one that just put me in a different kind of prison with Mr. Moore."

"Then don't make a worse mistake," he said. "Put the gun down and we'll all walk out of here."

She shook her head. "If I put this down, we both know you're going to leave with that video and take it to the police. I already have a record, and the sheriff don't like me. He won't go easy."

"If he doesn't like you, why did he help you cover up Grace's murder?"

"He didn't know she was killed, much less that I had anything to do with it." Penny's eyes welled up with tears again. "Mr. Moore told him she'd gotten high on drugs, then got into the hot tub and drowned. There's a clear sign posted out there that you can't use it if you're intoxicated or under the influence. Wasn't his fault. Autopsy backed up his story."

"She had a cut on her head," I spoke up, incredulous. Was covering up a murder really that easy?

Penny took one hand off the gun to wipe her eyes before gripping it tight again. Her hands shook. "Mr. Moore showed him the drugs in her room—he made me put them back in her suitcase—and where she'd hit her head on the nightstand 'cause she got strung out and dizzy. Told him she probably fell while she was putting on her swimsuit. He had me undress her and put a bikini on her. We washed and dried her normal clothes."

Sawyer shook his head. "But the news report said she drowned in the lake. We were *told* she drowned in the lake."

Penny shrugged. "The news gets things wrong all the time. Mr. Moore said a death in the hot tub might look bad for the resort. He wanted ghostly tales, but he also wanted bookings. So he spread the story that it was in the lake, and Sheriff Patterson agreed it didn't make much of a difference and said he wouldn't contradict it."

Sawyer's voice turned tight again. "Well, you two certainly thought of everything."

"He was good like that. Good for one thing, at least."

"So why did you kill him?" I asked, stepping out from behind Sawyer. He tensed and moved in front of me again.

"I didn't." Penny shook her head. "I promise you. I didn't kill him or that guest last night. Just Grace, and that was an accident. I'm not a bad person."

"Yes, you accidentally stuffed her in the hot tub and drowned her," Sawyer said, his voice shaking just a bit.

"It was an accident," Penny repeated, her tone turning harsh. "I wasn't in my right mind. And I'm done talking about it. Give me that damn flash drive."

"What are you going to do with us if we do?" Sawyer asked.

Regret flashed across her face. "I'd lie to tell you and tell you I'd let you go, but I don't have the heart to do it. You know you both have to die. I haven't gone through all this just to go to jail now."

Sawyer shrugged. "I don't think letting us go would be a jail sentence. If you have the flash drive, we don't have any proof, and Sheriff Patterson doesn't like me any more than he likes you. He was annoyed when I started digging into Grace's death. Elections are coming up and it's clear he doesn't want an embarrassing mistake like that on his record."

She was wavering. I could see it when peeked out from behind Sawyer's broad back.

"Regardless," Sawyer continued, "you can't kill us here. Shoot us with a rifle like that and there's no way you can get rid of the evidence, no matter how good you are. The sheriff will know we died here, and that's going to lead straight back to you, Richard's mistress, the only other person with full access to this house."

"He might think Mr. Moore killed you," she said with less confidence than before. "After all, this is his rifle."

Sawyer shook his head. "Richard was killed hours ago. Rigor has already set in."

"But the police can't get here until tomorrow," she countered. "That's time for rigor to set in for you guys, too. Right?" Her voice was uncertain.

"Sure, but by then, Richard will already be decomposing. Penny, there's no way to hide the fact that he was killed first. Your only chance is to take us somewhere else, somewhere where they might not discover the bodies for a while. Then tomorrow, as soon as the road opens, you get out of here. You run and never look back."

She eyed him suspiciously. "Why are you trying to help me?"

"I suppose I shouldn't," he sighed. "Old habits. Tactical training. Can't seem to help myself. I like problem-solving."

"I think it's called 'mansplaining,'" I popped in, hoping to get a laugh from Penny—which I did.

It was clear to me that Sawyer wanted us out of this room, where he had a better chance of taking her down without one of us getting shot in the process. I hadn't known him long, but I knew him well enough to know one thing—he'd never in a million years help Penny get away with Grace's murder.

Penny stared him down before sighing. "I guess you're probably right. I don't have Mr. Moore here to help me cover up this one, so we better go out in the woods or something. Maybe you'll be eaten by animals and never be found at all. Sorry." She winced. "I guess that's not very kind of me to say."

Sawyer shrugged. "I get it."

"I'm walking out first. I'm not stupid, so don't try anything. Don't come close to me at all, got it? Or I'll shoot, no matter what happens after."

"Got it."

"Hands in the air," she said.

We both obeyed.

She slowly started backing out of the room, her gun still pointed straight at us.

"Stay back behind me," Sawyer said, his voice low.

Then he slowly started walking toward the door.

Chapter Thirty-Four

Sawyer

I kept my face placid as I followed Penny, making sure I kept enough distance between us for her to feel at ease. She didn't appear comfortable holding the rifle. All I needed was an edge—a moment when she let her guard down and there was enough room to maneuver.

I'd taken down far more skilled adversaries in the past. Penny would be a breeze.

Still, I knew better than to count my chickens before they hatched. It was a lesson we all learned. As a SEAL, you had to be cocky enough to believe you could do the job well and survive it. But you also had to be humble enough to know you shouldn't let your guard down. Complacency led to bad things.

I'd learned that lesson the hard way.

Penny moved through the false door into the living room, motioning for us to come through and step in front of her.

It was all the invitation I needed.

When she swung the gun away from us, using it to point to where she wanted us to go, I slammed into her with my full weight, like a linebacker taking an opponent to the ground. She was too stunned to fight back in any meaningful way. The rifle clattered to the floor, and I flipped her, pulling her to my chest with my forearm around her neck. When she went limp, I released her, breathing a sigh of relief.

Olivia looked stunned. "Is she dead?"

I shook my head. "No. Just unconscious. It was a sleeper hold. Here." I tossed her my flashlight. "Go look around and see if you can find something to tie her up with."

Olivia nodded wordlessly, then went to search. Within moments, she returned with a roll of kitchen twine.

"That will work." I secured Penny's wrists behind her back, then lowered her gently to the floor again. I pulled the flash drive out of her pocket and shoved it into my own. "I don't want to leave her here. But I also don't want to take responsibility for her all night."

"We could take her to the caretakers," she suggested.

"I was thinking about throwing her into the trunk of your car," I muttered.

Olivia shot me a look. "I think we're already in enough trouble as it is. Let's not make it even worse."

"You're right," I groaned. "And I don't want to be stuck watching her until the police get here. We need that time to prove who killed Ethan and Richard. I don't totally trust the caretakers though. I mean, they put a murder victim's body into a freezer. They're not exactly my first choice for a law enforcement substitute."

"I know. But unless we're going to watch her all night, do we really have a choice?"

"Fine. The caretakers it is." I stood and lifted Penny, throwing her over my shoulder—not missing the look of pure awe in Olivia's eyes.

A look that made me feel pretty damn great.

"HOLD YOUR HORSES," DEB HOLLERED WHEN OLIVIA BEAT on the door of their cottage.

"She sounds like she's in a mood," I said under my breath.

"I think she's always in a mood," Olivia replied smoothly.

"You've got a point."

The door flew open and Deb's eyes went wide. "Well, what in the world? What have you done to our Penny? And why are her hands tied up like that?"

Felix walked into the room, still pulling his pants on. His eyes sharpened, and he frowned as he came to stand beside his wife.

Olivia took the lead, a decision we'd made on the walk over.

"I found something," she said. "At Richard's house. You need to see this. Can we come in?"

"I guess you'd better," Felix said, eyeing Penny. She was awake but refused to speak or make eye contact with any of us.

Deb grumbled as she opened the door wider, gesturing for us to come inside. I followed her into their living room and motioned for Penny to sit on one of their hardback chairs, giving her a warning look that she better not try to run. She groaned, and I saw sadness flash on Deb's face. I hoped they weren't particularly close to her. If they were, I wasn't sure we could trust them to hold her there.

"This is what I came to show you," Olivia said, walking toward Deb. Felix closed their door and joined us where we stood clustered in the living room.

Olivia opened the laptop we'd grabbed on the way and showed them the footage from Grace's stay. I looked away—I couldn't bear to watch it again.

Deb gasped when she saw Penny shove Grace, then watched with tear-filled eyes as the incident played on. Felix's face hardened. He looked at Penny with disgust and crossed his arms.

When the video was over, Olivia closed the laptop and waited for them to speak.

"We didn't know," Deb said, her voice faltering. "We knew she'd had problems with drugs in the past, but she'd told us she'd changed. Everyone deserves a second chance. Almost everyone, that is. I guess we were wrong to get her a job here."

"Is she your daughter?" Olivia asked timidly.

Felix shook his head. "No. She's our niece. Takes after her ma, my no-good sister. We were hoping the work out here would do her some good. We knew she'd stolen from some guests. Had a couple of them report things missing to us, and they told us they'd caught her snooping around their cabins after check-in. We made her pay for what she took and told her under no circumstances could she go into the cabins once they were occupied. But honest to God, we had no idea she had anything to do with that poor girl's death. I wouldn't have believed she had it in her if you hadn't shown me that video."

Deb's eyes narrowed. "Hey, how did you get that anyway? What were you doing in Richard's house?"

Felix put a hand on her shoulder, squeezing. "I don't think that question matters much, does it now?" His voice was mild. He turned toward me. "This here girl on the video. She's a friend of yours?"

I nodded.

"I thought so," he said, his lips tight. "I could tell by the way you turned away, not watching it. This the reason you're here?"

"It is."

"You're former military, aren't you?"

"I am" I confirmed.

"Army?"

I shook my head. "SEAL."

He grinned. "I knew I liked you." He reached his hand out and shook mine firmly. "Sergeant Felix MacLaine, U.S. Army. Glad to have you here, brother."

I shook his hand and returned his grin.

"Richard was killed today," Felix said. "As the caretaker of this property, I'm going to have to head up there and check on his house. Feed his dogs. Go through his things and deal with them all. Might just be that I found this at his house tonight. And that's exactly what I plan to tell Sheriff Patterson. You got it?" He eyed his wife carefully.

She gave him the side-eye, then sighed and nodded in agreement.

"No need to complicate things," he continued. "We brought Penny here, and that's on us. She's got to face up to what she did and hopefully get the help she needs. Some people have to learn the hard way. Hate it, but that's how life goes."

I shook his hand again. "Thank you."

"What if Penny has a different story about how you got the video?" Olivia asked quietly.

"She won't," Deb said, wagging a finger. "Not if she knows what's good for her. We're the only family she's got left, and if she wants help getting a decent lawyer, she'll want to stay on our good side. You hear me?" She raised her voice at the end, directing the question to Penny.

Penny's body sagged in defeat. Any hope she'd had of Felix and Deb saving her was clearly gone. "I hear you."

Deb nodded, fresh tears pricking her eyes. "Good. Penny, how could you? After everything?"

Penny hung her head but didn't answer.

"Are you guys going to be okay with her tonight?" I asked in a low voice. Penny appeared defeated now, but desperate people did desperate things, and I didn't want her harming Felix and Deb.

Felix just grinned. "I may be an old soldier, but I can still handle myself, son. We'll be fine."

"Okay. Before we leave, I do have a question for you though."

"Go ahead."

"Why did you move both Olivia and Grace to cabin thirteen when they arrived?"

He snorted. "Well, that's easy. As a rule, I never let people who *request* cabin thirteen stay in it. You requested it. So did those two kids, the so-called ghost hunters. Number thirteen is the most run-down, outdated cabin of them all, and Richard won't let us make any changes to it. The only people who ever ask for that one are people looking for a scare."

"I see."

"I tell you," he said, shaking his head, "this whole ghost nonsense has about made this place unbearable. So I always put someone who *didn't* request it in that cabin, or I leave it empty altogether. We're down a few cabins right now—remodeling some of them, and then the heat went out in another one yesterday. Leaving it empty wasn't an option. Olivia here didn't seem like the crazy ghost type, so I figured she was a safe bet."

"Well, that explains that," I said, satisfied. "Are you aware that Richard has been faking paranormal activity in cabin thirteen?"

Felix's jaw dropped. "You've got to be kidding me."

"I'm afraid not. But in good news, your paranormal activity might be about to die down."

"Well, that's a blessing anyway," Deb said, relieved. "At least one positive might come out of this awful weekend."

But Felix's face turned serious. "I take it you're looking into the other two deaths, too?"

"We are," I said.

Olivia's head jerked like she was surprised I'd included her in it. But I hadn't even considered doing otherwise. We were starting to feel like a unit. And while I normally investigated alone, I was finding I really enjoyed having a team again. Especially one that included her.

In fact, it was something I couldn't stop thinking about.

Felix motioned toward Penny. "Is she responsible for those, too?"

I glanced over at her. "I don't think so."

He chuckled and pointed at himself and Deb. "Apparently, we had even more motive than I knew about. Have you ruled *us* out?"

I grinned. "Yeah. When you go through Richard's house, you'll find all his recording equipment in a hidden room behind the bookshelf in his living room. During the time he was killed, you and Deb were here at the house having an argument about politics."

Deb slapped his arm. "Oh, lordy, that's downright embarrassing. I can't believe people heard that."

"Woman, you wouldn't have to be embarrassed if you'd vote my way," Felix thundered.

"Don't you even—" Deb started, but I cut her off.

"You guys will have to work that out on your own. But if you need an alibi, it's there." I looked at Olivia. "You ready?"

She nodded.

Felix grabbed my arm. "How are you going to figure out who did it?"

I grinned. "I already know who did it. Now, I just have to prove it."

"How are you going to do that?"

"Simple. I'm going to set a trap."

Chapter Thirty-Five

Olivia

We left Penny with Felix and Deb, trusting that they would keep her in custody until someone could go for the sheriff. Meanwhile, we loaded back into Sawyer's SUV and headed toward the cabins.

"So we're setting a trap?" The idea thrilled me—as long as I didn't think about the potential danger involved. It was strange, really, how safe I felt with Sawyer around. Penny had pointed a rifle at me, but I hadn't felt nearly as afraid as I had the night I'd been home alone during the break-in. When Sawyer had moved in front of me, I'd known he would do whatever it took to protect me from her. And I knew he'd do the same during whatever trap we set.

"Correct. I'm pretty sure I've put together a clear idea of what happened using logic, my gut, and the elimination of other suspects. But I'm not sure how far logic is going to go with Sheriff Patterson. If we can get a confession on video, I'd feel a whole lot better about things."

"That would go a long way toward getting him off your back," I agreed. "So, are you going to tell me who did it, or are you going to keep it from me so I don't 'contaminate' your trap?"

He looked over at me and grinned, taking a hand off the steering wheel to squeeze my knee. "I'd say you've earned the right to be read in."

"Okay." I smiled back, biting my bottom lip. "Read me in, then. But I'm going to guess first."

He chuckled. "Alright. Who do you guess?"

"Joey. He's one of the only ones we haven't eliminated yet, and we've suspected him from the beginning. He probably got pissed off when Ethan didn't want him and Sadie hanging out and thought he was doing Sadie a favor by getting rid of her overly controlling father. And like you said, he's got that raging testosterone and an underdeveloped frontal lobe."

Sawyer parked in front of his cabin and turned to face me. He was wearing that cocky grin of his, and I knew immediately I'd guessed wrong.

"So, not Joey, then?" My eyebrows shot up and I tried to give him an annoyed look, but I couldn't completely fight back my smile. That arrogance that had irritated me so much when I'd first met him had grown on me. After all, if anyone had earned it, he had.

"Not Joey," he said. "*Joseph.*"

My jaw dropped. "Joseph? But he's the nicest guy out here!"

Sawyer nodded. "Yeah, he is. Nice guys kill too."

"What makes you think it's him?"

"It all fits. Think about it. We assumed when he jumped in with an alibi that he was covering for Joey, because that's what he wanted us to think. But it gave him an alibi, too. Meg and Joey both immediately backed up his story about all being together. We didn't buy it then. We just didn't realize why he wanted us to."

"Okay." I was trying to follow him. "But what about motive? He doesn't seem like the type to snap over someone insulting his son."

Sawyer shook his head. "Motive is where I was hung up, too. For the longest, I just didn't see any. But then Sadie told you that story about her father saying Rachel was having an affair."

"You think Rachel and Joseph were having an affair? They never gave any indication at all that they knew each other."

"Not Rachel and Joseph. Ethan and Meg."

My jaw dropped again. "Ethan and Meg? What? Are you serious?"

"I can't prove it," he cautioned. "But even you heard that story and thought it sounded like Ethan was really the one cheating. I think you were right and that he lied about Rachel to smooth things over with Sadie. Joseph, Meg, and Joey all raised their hands the night of the bonfire, saying they knew about the ghost stories. Joseph mentioned that they'd been here before. And remember how Rachel said Ethan picked the place and that it was totally unlike him?"

"Yes," I said, nodding slowly. "You're right. She did. You think he came here on purpose to be with Meg?"

"I do. I don't think either of them actually wanted to be with their families on this getaway and that they planned on rendezvousing together. Probably on the waterfall trail, though why they would try to meet on a trail during a storm, I have no idea."

My eyes lit up. "There's a covered gazebo at the end of it. Maybe they had plans to meet there."

He grinned. "That would make sense. The night of the storm, I saw two people—a man and a woman, by the looks of it—underneath the cover of the boat shed. I couldn't see who it was, but if it was them, they probably would have been unable to get in, like us. So maybe they made plans to meet at the gazebo later."

"Or Joseph had figured out Meg's lover was here," I pointed out.

He nodded. "Yeah, that's another possibility. Rachel didn't see what happened when Ethan arrived at the bonfire. Could have been some signs of recognition or surprise. Some looks between them that clued Joseph in. Maybe he knew she was having an affair but didn't know with who until that night. We don't know. But that's my theory. That Ethan and Meg were having an affair, and Joseph killed him because of it."

I sat back, trying to take it all in. "That's crazy. But you're right. It fits. It also makes sense with Meg's reaction. She wasn't just afraid. She was absolutely devastated. And tonight, at the bonfire, she was one who wanted us to all stick together. Maybe she knows and is afraid to be alone with him."

"I noticed that, too. She may suspect Joey—Joseph may have even told her it was him. She keeps looking at him with a ton of raw emotion. But regardless, she's grieving, and I don't think it's just over her son."

My mind raced, filling in the blanks. "So then, with Richard... You're thinking Joseph found out he had footage that proved it was him and killed him over it?"

"Exactly. On Richard's setup, he was able to watch four cameras at once. One of them was still directed at Joseph's cabin. I think, after I tipped him off about the murder, he went straight to his security room and tried to figure out who did it. It would have been fairly easy with eyes on every door in the place. All he needed to do was see who left their cabin at the same time as Ethan."

"So he saw that Joseph left and, what, confronted him?"

Sawyer shook his head. "I bet he tried to blackmail him. Richard loves having power over people and clearly has no regard for the law after the way he let Penny get away with murder and keep working here. He also never bothered confronting her about the petty thefts, though he would have seen those too. I'm guessing he wanted to see how much money he could squeak out of Joseph."

I let out a breath. "But he underestimated him."

"Yeah. Joseph is tall enough to grab the oar, and he was desperate enough to use it. Then he tried to throw off suspicion by making it look like it was connected to the ghost stories here instead of directly tied to Ethan's death."

"It all fits."

"Yep. Now, we just have to prove it."

"So what kind of trap are we setting?"

He grinned again. "We're going on another ghost hunt. Only this time, I plan to catch a killer."

Chapter Thirty-Six

Sawyer

I shoved what happened to Grace down deep and snapped into mission mode. There was nothing I could do to bring her back, but I'd made sure her killer was going to pay—and now, I needed to do the same thing to the man who'd killed Ethan and Richard.

The stage was set and everything was in place. Now, all I needed to do was one of the things I did best: lie.

"You ready?" I murmured into Liv's ear as we climbed the steps to Joseph's cabin.

"Ready," she answered under her breath.

I wrapped one arm around her waist, pulling her tight against me, then knocked on his door.

Joseph opened it, looking like he hadn't slept yet. Still, he appeared confused that we were there so late. "Hey, you guys," he said. "What's going on?" His eyes darted back and forth between us, calculating.

"Got some great news," I said, grinning. "Thought I'd pass it on. I know how worried your wife is."

"Oh yeah?" His eyes brightened. "Hopefully good news about getting out of here? We're already packed up and ready to hit the road as soon as it opens."

"Same," Olivia said with wide eyes. She shivered and snuggled into me, playing the part of the scared girlfriend to perfection.

"No more news on the road," I said, shaking my head. "But we were at the caretaker's trying to get some extra blankets and a neighbor came by on his ATV. Felix told him what was going on out here. He said he was going to get the sheriff right away and would be back within the hour. So at least we'll have the law out here tonight."

Joseph's fingers tightened on the doorframe. "Yeah," he said, nodding. "That's great news." He smiled, but his voice was hollow.

I leaned forward. "Between you and me, I'm pretty sure it was that weird ghost hunter dude who did it, and I can't wait to see the sheriff put the cuffs on him."

He cocked his head. "Oh yeah? You really think it was him?"

Olivia shivered again, blinking those wide eyes. "You heard him that first night saying someone might die out here! And after Ethan's death, all he could talk about was how this was going to help his channel out and finally put him on the map."

Joseph nodded slowly. "Now that you mention it, he is pretty weird. I bet you're right."

"Plus," I added, "how fishy is it that the person who's been video-taping everything hasn't offered any of it up? I mean, they admit they were outside 'ghost hunting' all during that storm when Ethan died. Multiple video recorders, thermal heat cameras, and audio recorders everywhere, and you're telling me they haven't found *one* piece of evidence about who did this?" I scoffed. "Only way that's possible is if they're protecting themselves."

Joseph played it cool, but he couldn't hide his micro expression. His eyes widened, just briefly. "Yeah, you're right," he said, chuckling nervously. "Did you ask them to see it?"

Olivia jumped in. "*I* did. I was actually interested in the ghost aspect because some super creepy things happened in my cabin. I'd smelled lavender, just like they said I would, and heard a woman's voice. Plus, I saw a ghostly figure of a man outside my cabin that night. So I wanted to see what they'd found. But they said no, that it takes too much time to go through everything and they didn't want to waste any time that could be spent ghost hunting. Said they wouldn't bother until they get back home."

I rolled my eyes. "Likely story, huh? That's when I started figuring it was him. And as soon as the sheriff gets here, I'm going to tell him."

Joseph gripped the doorframe even tighter. "Smart," he said, attempting a grin. "Adam will never know what hit him."

"Exactly." I gave him an easy smile. "But until the sheriff gets here, I think we'll stay put in my cabin, and you guys should probably do the same. Adam's already killed twice. We don't want to risk him killing again."

"Good point. We'll stay locked in." He looked as if he wanted to say something else but changed his mind. "Just let me know if there's anything I can do to help."

I gave him a firm handshake. "Just take care of your family and stay safe."

"Will do."

He stood watching as Liv and I walked away. I waved to him from the front porch of my cabin before we headed inside and locked the door.

"Do you think he bought it?" Olivia asked.

I moved to the window and pulled my scope out, watching. "Oh yeah. He bought it. He just went inside. He's probably pacing right now, deciding what he's going to do. He can't take a chance on the sheriff getting video evidence against him. Not with everything he's already gone through."

"I hope this works."

"Me too." I put my night scope down and grabbed my black hat, pulling it over my head. "I've got to go now."

"I'm coming with you," she said.

"You're safer here," I said firmly.

"I feel safer with you."

"Last time you were with me, a woman pointed a gun at you," I pointed out.

Liv crossed her arms. "I'm not staying here alone. Haven't you ever seen any scary movies? That's exactly how the woman always dies. So if we're doing this, we're doing it together." She looked adorable standing her ground like that. Her hair was a mess and her eyes showed the strain of everything we'd been through this weekend. But I couldn't help thinking that she'd never looked more beautiful.

"Fine," I relented, pretending to be way more annoyed than I actually was. "Let's go."

Liv and I went out my back door, moving quietly with our eyes on Joseph's place the whole time. I'd kept the deck lights off on purpose. We kept ourselves low, trying to remain covered, until we slipped off the porch and into the trees. We stayed in the tree line, cutting behind his cabin and the empty one next to it, until we got to Adam and Eve's place. I used my scope to keep an eye out for Joseph and sent Liv up first.

She moved stealthily across the open area, onto their porch, and through their back door. They'd kept it unlocked for us, knowing the plan. When Liv was inside, I followed, never letting Joseph's cabin out of my sight.

When I entered, Eve silently clapped her hands. "This is so exciting!" she whispered.

"Glad you think so," I said, fighting an eye roll. "Adam, keep watch on the front of their cabin. I've got the back."

"Got it," he said.

We both moved to the windows, him with his thermal camera and me with my night scope. At least he was good for something. I might not have had much respect for his ghost hunting, but I liked his gear and his investigative experience gave me something to work with.

We waited thirty minutes before Joseph finally made a move. "He just went out his back door," I said softly. "He's got his gun. Everyone take cover."

I hadn't wanted them here at all. But since they'd all insisted, I'd made them at least agree to stay hidden in one of the bedrooms.

I'd deal with Joseph alone.

Liv came over and gave me a soft kiss on the cheek. "Be careful," she said.

I grinned. "Don't worry. I've got this."

I STAYED HIDDEN IN THE DARK AS JOSEPH APPROACHED THE cabin. He came up to the front door and knocked—quietly, like he was giving himself cover but hoped nobody actually heard. When nobody answered, he jiggled the doorknob, which we had conveniently left unlocked for him.

My pulse skyrocketed with the thrill of the hunt. *Come on in, Joseph. The water's fine.*

The doorknob turned, and the door slowly creaked open. He poked his head in and spoke quietly enough to not wake anyone who was sleeping. "Hello? Adam? Eve?"

He stood waiting, watching. A long minute passed before he seemed convinced he'd been unheard. Even in the low light, I could see his shoulders relax as he took a deep breath.

That's right, Joseph. You've got this.

He pulled the door shut behind himself and clicked on a small flashlight, scanning it around the living room. I tensed and pulled my body back behind the half-wall that hid me. I wasn't ready to be seen. Not yet.

His light landed on the kitchen table, where we'd left Adam's equipment out on display. Two laptops and half a dozen different video recorders, all right there for the taking. It was almost too easy. But considering Joseph's apparent insecurity while murdering, I wanted to give him an easy win.

I also wanted to keep him laser focused on this end of the house so he wouldn't go searching in the back rooms where Liv was hidden.

Joseph stepped forward, then hesitated. I tensed again. Did he sense that this was a trap?

He stood half frozen, like he was contemplating what to do. Finally, he took a step forward. Then a second. One slow step after another, until he was standing over the kitchen table. He put his gun down and reached for the first camera, popping the side open and removing the memory card.

I flipped the lights on.

He whirled around, finally seeing me where I stood with my arms crossed, leaning against the dining room wall.

"Hello, Joseph," I said.

He blinked twice before changing his facial expression. "Sawyer! I'm so glad you're here. I got to thinking about what you said about Adam and decided someone needed to get this evidence before he could dump it. Come help me."

"Nice try. I know everything, Joseph. Why do you think I came to your cabin and told you about the recordings? I'd already been through all of this evidence and know exactly what you did. I just needed to get you here."

He shook his head. "You don't understand."

"I think I do," I said, moving forward calmly. I expected him to go for his gun and was ready to disarm him when he did.

But instead, he backed up, clearly more afraid of me than I was of him. So I took his gun from the table and stuck it into my pocket. It was another win. I was wearing gloves, but he wasn't—his fingerprints would be all over it, and I'd bet my life that this was the same gun that had shot Ethan the night before.

"The proof is here," I said, gesturing at the recorders in front of me. "I already told you—Adam and Eve have recorded every minute of this vacation. They record *everything*, man. But I'm not a cop, and I've made some mistakes of my own, so"—I shrugged—"maybe I don't care. Seems like you might have been justified. Your wife was having an affair with Ethan, wasn't she?"

His jaw dropped. "How do you know that?"

"It was obvious she didn't want to be here with you. When you guys got here, all she could do was look around for something better. She was looking for *him*, wasn't she?"

Anger flashed on his face. I had him. "Every year, we've come here as a family. Sure, it's creepy and weird, but it's become a tradition. Something we laugh about all year long. But this year, she had to tell *him*. Couldn't bear to be away from him for even a weekend. I came out here hoping to save my family, man. But she had to ruin everything."

"Did you know she was having an affair before you got here?"

He nodded. "Yeah, I knew. It was obvious. She'd started going to him for so-called 'therapy.' Wouldn't stop talking about him. Then one day, she said she'd stopped therapy, and she just shut up about him. I thought maybe it was over. Maybe he'd even cut her off as a patient for ethical reasons. But a buddy of mine saw them together at a hotel a few weeks ago." He shook his head. "I tried. I tried to win her back."

"That must have been horrible, showing up here and realizing she'd invited her affair partner," I said, building rapport. It was a tactic that worked more often than not. Make a connection, show some empathy. People couldn't wait to spill their guts.

"Like a knife to the heart," he said. "And when she snuck out of bed that night, I knew she was going to see him."

"What did you do?"

"I followed her. I never meant to kill him. I only took the gun because you've got to carry some protection in the woods." His face twisted into something dark and ugly. "But when I got there and saw him with his hands on her, I was so angry."

"I get it, man," I said. "He'd taken what was yours."

"Exactly." Relief washed over his face.

"Did she see you kill him?"

He shook his head again. "No. I waited for her to leave, then followed him. Confronted him on the trail. I was just going to tell him to back off, to leave our family alone. But he was so arrogant and said she loved him in a way she'd never loved me. The things he said... I couldn't take it. I punched him in the face. He *laughed*. Said I punched like a girl. So I pulled out my gun and..." His voice trailed off like he couldn't bring himself to say it.

"And you shot him," I said, filling in the blanks.

"Yeah." His body sagged with the weight of his confession. "Yeah. I shot him. He had it coming."

"Then, when Richard tried to blackmail you, you killed him, too."

He hung his head. "The kind of money he wanted would have sunk us. I'd have lost her for sure."

"You loved your wife," I said, feeling a surprising amount of sympathy for him.

"I do." He looked up. "You get it. You aren't going to tell anyone, are you?"

"I don't have to," I said.

"What do you mean?"

I almost felt bad about the hope on his face. "I told you. Adam and Eve record everything."

CHAPTER THIRTY-SEVEN

Olivia

A COOL WIND SWEPT OVER THE LAKE THE NEXT MORNING. I
stood beside it, gazing out at the beautiful water. This place was truly
stunning. And now, in the hands of the caretakers, it might finally be
able to be what it always should have been: a refuge from the world
instead of a place where a con artist had faked a haunting and destroyed
lives.

Hopefully now, the land would have a chance to heal.

I wrapped my scarf around myself, taking in a deep breath. Footsteps approached. My lips turned up in a small smile. I recognized the
cadence of Sawyer's walk without even looking. It was still startling to
think how quickly we had fallen into rhythm with each other—especially considering how much I'd disliked him that first day.

"Hey," I said, turning to greet him with a warm smile. "How did it
go?" Sawyer and Felix had kept watch over Joseph and Penny all night.
As soon as the work crew had arrived, they'd sent for the sheriff.

He gave me a thumbs-up. "Sheriff Patterson took Penny and Joseph both into custody. They're both in handcuffs in the back of his truck right now. Felix showed him the footage of Penny, and Adam showed him Joseph's confession. I turned over the murder weapon. The sheriff still wants to talk to everyone, but it's a pretty open-and-shut case at this point."

"Until some criminal defense lawyer gets it all thrown out on a technicality," I said, rolling my eyes.

"Jaded much?" He laughed.

"Yes." I nodded, turning back to the lake. "I think it's safe to say I'm officially jaded."

He was quiet for a moment, sticking his hands into his pockets. "So, Liv, have you decided what's next for you?"

"I don't know." Except I did. I just didn't like it. "I guess I just have to take things one step at a time. I'll go home, because that's the only place I have to go right now. Try to find a job to help tide me over until I can build my business. Start looking for a place to live. I have some savings, but they're from him, and I don't know if I feel right about using them."

He cleared his throat. "Would you... Would you be interested in a job offer that didn't have anything to do with art?"

I gave him a funny look. "Like what?"

"My PI agency is looking to expand." He grinned. "I'd give you a hell of a reference."

I stepped back, stunned. "Me? Be a private investigator?"

He shrugged. "Why not? You're smart. Observant. Kept your wits about you during a crazy weekend. And without you, I might not have solved Grace's murder. You're the one who found the flash drive."

I opened my mouth to immediately reject the idea but stopped. I'd never thought myself capable of anything like that, but...what if I was? As horrible as this weekend had been, I had to admit that I'd enjoyed working with Sawyer. It had felt really good to do something important. Something for justice.

A little thrill raced up my spine just thinking about it. Olivia Mitchell, PI. It could be amazing.

But just as quickly, reality set in. Join the agency that had investigated my father? It would burn every bridge in my family. I felt deflated, realizing that it was a ridiculous idea.

"My father would kill me," I said.

"He'd have to come through me first."

I looked up at Sawyer and realized he wasn't joking. I bit my lip. "Can I think about it?"

He held my gaze. "You can." He pulled his wallet from his pocket and fished out a card, handing it to me. "That's my info. Even if you decide you don't want the job, if you need me...you call me. Day or night."

I held his card in between my fingers, tracing his name with my thumb. Sawyer Reed.

I really didn't want to say goodbye to him.

Hours passed before we finally got the all clear to leave. Sheriff Patterson did his due diligence this time, interviewing every single person and taking careful notes. Rachel and Sadie were the first allowed to go. I punched my number into Sadie's phone, feeling sadness that I might never see either of them again. After going through everything we had gone through this weekend, it felt like we were bonded in some way—a way that someone who hadn't been here couldn't possibly understand.

"Hang in there," I told Sadie. "And text me anytime."

"I will." She hugged me tight. "Thanks for everything."

"Yes," Rachel added before throwing her arms around me. "You were my lifeline. Thank you."

"I'm so sorry about Ethan."

She blinked back tears. "I am, too. We hadn't been happy for a long time, but still. I had no idea about Meg, and I'm so angry that he would lie to Sadie like that and say I'd cheated on him. I'm furious at him. But I'm also very sad. I'd loved him for such a long time."

"I hope you and Sadie can heal now."

She glanced at her daughter. "I think we can. It's just going to take some time."

. . .

MEG AND JOEY DIDN'T SPEAK TO US BEFORE THEY LEFT. MEG couldn't stop crying, although I wasn't sure if it was for Ethan or Joseph. She and Rachel avoided each other completely, which was probably for the best. We didn't need any more violence.

Adam and Eve didn't want to leave at all, but Felix and Deb insisted. They were shutting down the rentals immediately, until all the video cameras and fake ghost activity could be taken care of. Part of me doubted they would ever reopen. They both seemed ten years younger with the weight of it all lifted off their shoulders. I hoped they'd live out the rest of their lives here in peace, without having to deal with any more crazy tourists.

Adam shook Sawyer's hand before they left.

"I appreciate your help last night," Sawyer said.

Adam grinned. "Not as much fun as ghost hunting, but I was glad we were able to do something. And hey, we still haven't gone through all the evidence. Maybe we caught something after all."

"Maybe," Sawyer agreed noncommittally.

I hid a smile. It was clear he didn't believe this place was haunted at all.

I wasn't so sure though. We'd found the plug-in hidden in my living room, but that didn't explain the scent of lavender in my bedroom when that door was closed. I'd searched, looking for something similar there, and couldn't find it. Nor did it explain why that room had become ice cold the day I smelled it. As far as we knew, Richard had no way of manipulating the temperature.

We also still weren't certain who I'd seen outside my window or who Sawyer had seen arguing by the boat shed. No one had admitted to being in either place. Plus, there was that EVP Adam and Eve had caught. I couldn't help but wonder if Adam was right, if the crazy energy of the storm had allowed something to manifest after all.

Part of me believed that Grace, Abel, and Ethel really were still here with us. It wasn't something I could explain. It was just a feeling, one that grew stronger when I sat alone beside the lake. There was a presence here. But it didn't feel threatening. It felt like deep sadness and regret.

· · ·

When it was just me and Sawyer left, the sheriff came over personally to speak to us again. He shook Sawyer's hand and said, "Well, I reckon I owe you an apology about your friend."

Sawyer's expression tensed. "I appreciate it."

"We should have looked closer. There just wasn't any reason to believe it didn't go down exactly like Richard said. To be honest with you, a small part of me wondered at first if he'd had something to do with it. But I did a little investigating. He had a solid alibi in town for the time of death. So I let it go."

"I understand," Sawyer said tightly, though it was clear he didn't. I knew that Sawyer would have kept digging.

The sheriff shook his hand again and clapped him on the shoulder. "I'll make sure it's taken care of this time."

"Thanks."

"You folks be safe getting home, now." He turned and walked away, heading back toward Felix and Deb.

"You okay?" I asked, moving toward Sawyer.

"Yeah. I'm dreading telling Jim what happened. But at least we have answers."

"Yes, thanks to you." I took a deep breath. "Sawyer?"

"Yeah?" He turned to look at me.

"I think I'll take you up on that job offer."

He grinned. "Really?"

"Really." I smiled, feeling lighter than I had in ages. Lighter, but also...excited. Alive. This could be a terrible decision, but one thing was for sure. It wouldn't be boring, and I'd finally be living life on my own terms.

"Liv, that's great. We'll get you started as an intern. It will take you some time to qualify for a PI license of your own, but there are a lot of ways you can work and get experience in the meantime." He seemed genuinely excited, which made me feel even happier.

"I need to take care of a few things at home first. It shouldn't take more than a week. After that, I'm free." I let out a breath, realizing this was real. I was making the decision and taking charge of my own life. "So, where are we going to investigate next?"

His grin widened. "Well...you're going to need a bigger suitcase."

THANK YOU FOR READING *THE DEATH CABIN*! I HOPE YOU enjoyed meeting Sawyer and Olivia and that the mystery kept you turning the pages!

Reviews are invaluable to authors—they, more than anything, sell books. If you enjoyed this story, I would so appreciate you taking the time to leave a review at your preferred vendor. It truly means the world.

Want to stay in touch? Connect with me on Facebook or Instagram. I love getting to know my readers! You can also sign up for my mailing list and receive Fiona's Hawthorn Tea recipe. If you don't know who Fiona is, you'll want to check out the Rosemary Mountain Mysteries!

Acknowledgments

Wanderlust is in my blood. Thankfully, I married a man with the same condition. We've been together for eighteen years and have traveled most of the United States, which is how we ended up staying at a little cabin resort that inspired the events of this book. On our first night there, I jokingly called it "the death cabin" and said I'd write a book about it someday.

Make no mistake, Hidden Gem Lake and the cast of characters there are both entirely fictional. But every great tale begins with a tiny grain of truth, and this story was born from a very real weekend getaway that we will never forget.

So, of course, my first thanks goes to my husband, Brandon. Thank you for being my adventure partner, and for all the crazy experiences we've had together. I love you and the memories we've made. I can't wait to see what the future holds!

Thanks also to my children, who remain a source of inspiration and joy. I love you and am so grateful to be your mom.

Thanks to my beta team for this book: Jessica, Candice, and Camille. You all provide different perspectives and your feedback is invaluable!

As always, a huge thank you to my editor, Mickey Reed, and my cover artist, Brooke Passmore. I appreciate you both so much!

In order to really get into Sawyer's mindset, I had conversations with as many people who have worked investigations as possible. Special thanks to Jacob, Tim, and Rooster for your willingness to chat and share your thoughts.

Finally, thank you to my readers. There really are no words to express how grateful I am that I get to create these worlds and share them with you. It's a dream come true. I hope this one gave you some thrills, some chills, and kept you turning the pages!

About the Author

Nicole Gardner lives in NE Arkansas with her husband, their two sons, and their two crazy dogs. If she's not at her desk, you'll likely find her either in the garden, or creating teas and tinctures in the kitchen.

Nicole's background is in psychology. This fascination with human behavior and relationship dynamics plays a significant role in her writing and the way she shapes her characters.

www.nicolegardnerbooks.com